T0265784

TENDRILS OF THE PAST

*Also by Anthea Fraser
from Severn House*

*The Rona Parish mysteries
(in order of appearance)*

BROUGHT TO BOOK
JIGSAW
PERSON OR PERSONS UNKNOWN
A FAMILY CONCERN
ROGUE IN PORCELAIN
NEXT DOOR TO MURDER
UNFINISHED PORTRAIT
A QUESTION OF IDENTITY
JUSTICE POSTPONED
RETRIBUTION

Other titles

BREATH OF BRIMSTONE
PRESENCE OF MIND
THE MACBETH PROPHECY
MOTIVE FOR MURDER
DANGEROUS DECEPTION
PAST SHADOWS
FATHERS AND DAUGHTERS
THICKER THAN WATER
SHIFTING SANDS
THE UNBURIED PAST
A TANGLED THREAD
SINS OF THE FATHERS
THE TIES THAT BIND

TENDRILS OF THE PAST

Anthea Fraser

**SEVERN
HOUSE**

First world edition published in Great Britain and the USA in 2023
by Severn House, an imprint of Canongate Books Ltd,
14 High Street, Edinburgh EH1 1TE.

Trade paperback edition first published in Great Britain and the USA in 2023
by Severn House, an imprint of Canongate Books Ltd.

severnhouse.com

British Library Cataloguing-in-Publication Data
A CIP catalogue record for this title is available from the British Library.

ISBN-13: 978-1-4483-0978-8 (cased)
ISBN-13: 978-1-4483-0991-7 (trade paper)
ISBN-13: 978-1-4483-0990-0 (e-book)

All Severn House titles are printed on acid-free paper.

MIX
Paper from
responsible sources
FSC
www.fsc.org   FSC® C013056

Typeset by Palimpsest Book Production Ltd.,
Falkirk, Stirlingshire, Scotland.
Printed and bound in Great Britain by
TJ Books, Padstow, Cornwall.

CHARACTER LIST

Cicely Fairfax
Theo, her son
Imogen, Theo's wife
Abby and Mia Fairfax, Cicely's granddaughters
Charles and Sarah Drummond, the girls' parents
Lily and Luke, their friends

Richard Coulson
Julia, his wife
Adam and Jamie, their sons

Nina Phillips, college nurse
Rob, her husband
Danny, their son

Rose Linscott
Fleur Tempest, her daughter
Owen Tempest, her son-in-law and deputy head of St Catherine's
        College
James Monroe, master at the college

Guy Burnside
Anya, his wife

Suzanne (Suzie) Maybury, bookshop owner
Terry, her partner

Madelaine Peel, a freelance journalist
Steve, her friend and fellow journalist

ONE

T he bodies were found by a mother on the school run. *'Abby usually comes running down the path as I draw up,' said Mrs Emily Barton, aged 34. 'I waited a moment or two and when she didn't appear I went up the path and rang the bell. There was no reply, which was strange; then I noticed a light on in the front room. So I looked through the window and – I saw them.'*

Dorset, February/March, fifteen years ago

'Sarah!'

Sarah Drummond loaded the last of the carrier bags into her boot and closed it before turning. And caught her breath. God, it was Luke! How was she supposed to greet him? Once it would have been an enthusiastic hug, but those days were long gone. Thanks to Lily.

'I thought it was you!' he said as he reached her and bent to kiss her cheek. 'How are you? How's the family?'

She smiled a little stiffly. 'Fine, thanks. And you?'

'Oh, same old, same old. Our lives are so hectic we hardly ever meet! Ships that pass in the night! How's old Charles? We see each other occasionally at the golf club, but only for the passing word.'

'He's fine,' Sarah said. Then, making an effort, 'He's been made a partner in the firm.'

'That's great! Do congratulate him for me!' He paused, eyeing the empty trolley. 'Suppose I park that for you and we go for a coffee and catch up?'

'Oh, I'm sorry,' she said quickly. 'I have to collect Mia from nursery.'

'Ah. Well, mustn't keep you, but I can at least relieve you of your trolley.' He gently removed it from her grasp. 'Good to have seen you, Sarah, and regards to Charles.'

Bloody Lily! she thought, as she climbed into the car. She knew Charles regretted losing Luke's friendship – or at least the manifestations of it – and it seemed Luke felt the same. As she drove to the nursery her mind drifted back over the years.

She and Lily had been room-mates at university, where they'd shared clothes and confidences and covered for each other over missed essays. And a year or two later it was to Lily she first confided that she was falling for Charles. Significantly, it seemed now, it was as they were discussing marriage that an unexpected divergence of opinion emerged, Lily stating categorically that she didn't intend to have children. Sarah, who'd always adored babies, was taken aback.

'Really?' she'd exclaimed. 'Why ever not?'

Lily had shrugged. 'Not part of my life plan,' she'd replied, and refused, then or later, to be drawn further. And Sarah, having told herself Lily would change her mind when she met the right man, soon forgot the comment.

Within the year Lily had met and married Luke and the couple became their closest friends, with whom they dined, went to the theatre and spent the occasional holiday. But as time passed Lily changed. Her career in advertising went from strength to strength and their interests no longer coincided, Lily's veering instead towards those of the high-powered executives she met in boardrooms around the globe. The inevitable result was that contact between the two families dwindled, breaking down completely soon after Abby was born.

Now, as Sarah drew up outside the nursery, she wondered for the first time whether Luke would have liked a family.

'You'll never guess who I bumped into today,' she remarked over supper.

'Then you'd better tell me!' Charles rejoined.

'Luke, in Waitrose car park of all places! I can't remember when I last saw him, which is amazing when we all live in the same town.'

'I see him sometimes at the golf club but they're both away a lot on business.'

'He asked me to congratulate you on the partnership.'

Charles nodded and Sarah was aware of a twinge of guilt, knowing she was chiefly to blame for the parting of the ways. But it was due to Lily's behaviour, and she still recalled her shock when she realized the width of the gulf now existing between them.

Abby had been about three months old at the time. She was teething, and Sarah and Charles had endured several sleepless nights when Lily arrived unannounced on the doorstep, looking as though she'd stepped from the pages of *Vogue*. Sarah was acutely conscious that her hair was a mess, her face bare of make-up, and that her patched jeans and old sweater were hardly *le dernier cri*. To add to her dismay Lily's cheerful greeting woke the baby, whom they'd just succeeded in putting down – and she did not appreciate being shushed.

'My goodness, Sarah, you really have turned into a brood mare!' she'd exclaimed, laughing to camouflage the barb.

It was like a slap in the face and Sarah was stunned. She'd held her emotions in check for the remainder of the visit, but on Lily's departure her temper flared.

'How dare she speak to me like that?' she stormed. 'If that's her opinion of me, I never want to see her again!' Charles had managed to calm her down and they had in fact met Luke and Lily on a couple more occasions. But the spiteful remarks kept coming, each masquerading as banter while hinting none too subtly that Sarah's interests were now confined to breast feeding and potty training, and finally she called a halt. Both husbands tried to heal the rift but Lily was uninterested and Sarah too hurt for them to succeed. The once-strong friendship unravelled, and until that morning Sarah had seen neither Lily nor Luke for the last four years.

Charles reached for her hand, bringing her back to the present. 'OK, sweetheart?' he asked.

She shook off her memories and nodded. 'OK,' she said.

'Hello, darling!'

It was her mother's voice and Sarah, struggling to hear her above the clamour of the children's teatime, moved into the hall.

'Hi, Mum.'

'I'm phoning to invite you and Charles to dinner a week on Thursday. I do hope you're free.'

Sarah smiled to herself. So this was how she was playing it! 'Er, yes, I think so. Thanks, we'd love to come.'

'And I thought I'd invite Theo and Imogen too, make it more of an occasion. Dinner rather than lunch this time,' she emphasized, 'so we can have a pleasant grown-up conversation without the distraction of the children.'

'Point taken.'

'I adore them, as you know, but now they're older they tend to dominate the conversation.'

'I said point taken, Mum.' Sarah gave a little laugh. 'You're not fooling me, you know! We're well aware that Thursday week just happens to be your birthday!'

'Well, yes, but that's immaterial.'

Anything less immaterial would have been hard to imagine. 'Speaking of which, we've still not decided what to give you. Is there anything you'd particularly like, or would you prefer a surprise?'

Cicely Fairfax paused. 'Well, there is something, since you ask. What I should really like is a photograph of you.'

'Oh, Mum!' Sarah protested, embarrassed.

'Really; you supply us with plenty of the children, which is lovely, but I haven't a recent one of you. And I mean a studio portrait, of course.'

'Oh Lord, do I have to?'

'No, dear, but I'd appreciate it.' Which, from her mother, meant she'd no option.

'Very well,' she said with a sigh. 'I'll book a sitting.'

'Thank you, darling. I look forward to it.'

Sarah had confidently expected that it would be at least another four years before she saw either Luke or Lily again, but, as sometimes happens, the couples were thrown together on two further occasions in quick succession, the first occurring barely ten days after the encounter in the car park.

The golf club dinner was traditionally held at the Grange Hotel in February in an attempt to brighten a cheerless month, and to add to the sense of occasion the dress code was black tie. Sarah had bought a new dress and was looking forward to the chance to dress up. The girl next door was babysitting and it was with an air of happy anticipation that they set out that evening. But as they paused in the foyer to check the seating plan the first doubts surfaced: they'd been seated at the same table as Lily and Luke, who, since they'd not attended the dinner for the last four years, they'd not expected to be present.

Sarah caught at Charles's arm, but he shook his head. 'No need to panic; there's another couple at the table, so Lily's bound to behave herself.'

'She'd better!' Sarah returned grimly. 'Or I shan't be liable for the consequences!'

They saw them as soon as they entered the bar, Luke distinguished-looking in his dinner jacket, Lily in ice-blue satin. Her short fair hair was expensively cut and her boyish figure showed off her designer dress to perfection. There was no option but to join them.

'So, Sarah, we meet again!' Luke greeted them. 'And Charles!' They shook hands. 'Good to see you both! I believe we're dinner companions.'

Lily touched her cheek first to Sarah's, then Charles's, her perfume enveloping them in its spicy thrall. 'Such a long time!' she murmured vaguely.

'Let me get you some drinks,' Luke said. 'What'll you have?'

After the initial awkwardness the atmosphere eased, helped when they were joined by other friends, with whom they stood chatting till they went through for dinner. Luke was seated directly opposite Sarah and, glancing up from her crab soufflé, she was disconcerted to find he was watching her. Something in his expression raised the hairs on her arm and as their eyes met he gave her a slow smile before turning to his neighbour. She quickly looked away, but her heart had set up an uncertain beat. Idiot! she told herself furiously. It's only Luke! But she was careful for the rest of the meal not to look in his direction.

The rest of the evening passed without incident; she and Lily were able to chat on a carefully censored basis, and Sarah was reasonably sure their table companions were unaware of any tension.

But later, in bed with Charles, she remembered the look in Luke's eyes when she'd caught him unawares, and gave a little shudder.

George and Cicely Fairfax lived in a substantial house on the outskirts of Sherborne. Both were prominent members of the community, he a school governor and member of the Town Council, she on the board of several charities. George had taken early retirement at the age of sixty and they were planning a round-the-world cruise later that year.

New acquaintances could be forgiven for thinking them mismatched, though in fact they were devoted to each other. Cicely was petite and immaculately groomed and, though herself approaching sixty, her hair was still gold and her face almost unlined. Renowned for never raising her voice, she was nonetheless a force to be reckoned with, seldom failing to achieve her aim. George on the other hand was a large, untidy man, a big softie to his family but known by previous employees to have a quick temper. Privately their son-in-law dubbed them 'Goldilocks and the Bear'.

It was starting to snow as Charles turned into the open gateway and parked next to Sarah's brother's Bentley.

'I hope it doesn't settle,' he commented. 'I've a meeting in Shaftesbury tomorrow.'

'Your daughters would love it!'

Her father was at the door. 'I see the weather's closing in! Come in, come in and get warm.' He took their coats and ushered them down the hall to the sitting room where the rest of the family was assembled. Sarah handed over the gift-wrapped package and Cicely exclaimed with pleasure, tearing off the paper to reveal the framed portrait.

'Oh, darling, it's lovely!' she cried, turning it round for the others to admire. 'Exactly what I wanted!'

'Worth all my suffering, then!' Sarah said, and turned to her brother and sister-in-law. 'How are you both? We haven't seen you since Christmas.' And she was struck again by how glamorous Imogen was, with her fall of chestnut hair and her enigmatic smile. She was the fashion editor of a glossy magazine and apparently making quite a name for herself.

'Before we begin catching up,' George said, 'a toast is in order.' He kissed his wife's cheek. 'Happy birthday, my love, and many more!' He raised his glass. 'To Cicely, Mamma and all other sobriquets that she answers to!'

They joined in toasting her health before, at George's gesture, seating themselves on the chairs round the fire.

'So, what's everyone been up to since we last met?' Sarah prompted.

It was Theo who replied. 'Actually we have a spot of news.'

'Oh?' Cicely turned to her son. 'Have they offered you a knighthood at last?'

He laughed. 'Patience, Mother! Seriously, you know we've been wanting to move to the country for some time now? Well, we spent last weekend with Guy and Anya in Bath, and while driving to a pub for lunch, by a stroke of pure luck we saw exactly the house we've been looking for – and it was for sale!'

'So we bought it on the spot!' Imogen finished.

'Subject to survey, I trust!' put in George.

'Of course, subject to all the necessary checks, but really, Father, it's perfect! An old converted farmhouse, with a fair bit of land so Imo can have the horse she's always hankered for!'

He took a folded sheet of paper from his pocket. 'These are the estate agents' particulars. It's been on their books for a while, so the owners were only too delighted to show us over that afternoon.'

The glossy brochure was passed round showing photographs of an attractive farmhouse, its kitchen, bedrooms and entertaining rooms. Charles and her parents were exclaiming with enthusiasm, but for Sarah the news came as a blow. She'd always been close to her brother and when younger had shared with him things she'd felt unable to discuss with her mother. Even recently she'd turned to him when a disagreement with Charles was slow in resolving itself.

'We'll miss you,' she said.

Theo looked up, meeting her troubled eyes. 'It's only an hour away, sis,' he said gently, 'not Outer Mongolia!'

She smiled reluctantly. 'It looks lovely,' she said.

But the news cast a cloud over the evening, and although the rest of it passed pleasantly enough, it was with a heavy heart that she returned home through a glistening white landscape.

The snow lasted several days, affording great enjoyment to the Drummond children among others and considerable inconvenience to their elders. The last of the slush had only just cleared by the following weekend, when Sarah and Charles had another engagement – this time a 'half-century' party for the twin daughters of Charles's boss, both of whom worked for the company and who were celebrating their twenty-fifth birthdays.

The party was in the form of a dance with buffet so there was no formal table plan, but Charles's colleagues, arriving ahead of them, had taken over one of the tables bordering the dance floor, and beckoned them over. Sarah had met them all before at office parties, so was looking forward to an enjoyable evening. What she was not expecting as she seated herself was to catch sight of Lily and Luke across the room. She'd not forgotten that fleeting but subtly worrying exchange of glances at the dinner, and Luke was positively the last person she wished to see. She could only hope they'd escape notice among the crowd.

But an hour or so later Charles returned from the free bar with the news that he'd met Luke, who'd wondered whether it would be OK if he asked her for a dance.

'I hope you said no!' she said quickly.

He looked at her in surprise. 'Well, of course I didn't! Be reasonable, love; I know Lily's not your favourite person but Luke's OK. He said he'll come over after supper, which they're setting out now. I suppose I'll have to do the decent thing and dance with Lily.'

'What are they even *doing* here?' Sarah demanded, her face flushed. 'He doesn't work for Bennett's and he can hardly be a friend of the twins!'

'Apparently he did some business with us over the Christmas period,' Charles said. 'The old man's clearly taking the opportunity to mix business with pleasure.' And he turned to reply to a query from one of his colleagues.

Sarah's appetite had deserted her and it was an effort to swallow enough of the delicious fare to avoid comment. It was only a dance, she kept assuring herself, and with all these people here what could possibly go wrong?

Sure enough, once coffee had been served and dancing began again, Luke came over, tall, handsome and very sure of himself, and gave her a mock bow.

'May I have the pleasure of this dance, Sarah?' he asked formally.

Since she'd no choice she came to her feet and into his arms, aware of the interest of the other wives. They moved into the centre of the room to join those already dancing, and Sarah felt his hand tighten on hers.

'This is very pleasant,' he said in a low voice. 'We should meet more often.'

Sarah's mouth was dry and her heart racing. 'I'm sure Charles—' she began, but he interrupted her.

'I'm not talking about Charles,' he said.

Her eyes flew to his face and she saw again the expression she'd caught at the golf club. His arm tightened round her waist, drawing her closer, and she gave a little gasp.

'Luke, please!'

'Please what?'

She didn't reply. *Why* hadn't she noticed it was a slow dance he'd claimed her for? She should have prevaricated, waited for a fast tune when couples danced opposite each other. *And yet*, whispered a treacherous little voice inside her, *what harm are we doing? It's a long time since Charles made me feel like this.*

The music was sensuous, dreamlike, and it was easier not to resist, to drift along with Luke's cheek against hers and his body pressing close, and to shut her mind to all else. She lost all sense of time until with a last lingering chord the music ended and everyone moved apart, applauding.

'I'll return you to your husband,' Luke said quietly, 'but I'll call you.'

Was that a threat or a promise? Blindly she turned and wove her way through the crowd towards her table. Only one couple was still seated, and they greeted her with a smile. Luke had followed her as protocol demanded and she flung him a quick glance over her shoulder.

'Thank you,' she said, and hastily sat down.

'Thank *you*!' he replied, and with another little bow merged back into the crowd.

Sarah reached for her glass and drank, trying to steady her hand. Something had changed in the last few minutes, something she knew to be momentous and possibly dangerous, and she felt powerless to prevent it. If, indeed, she wanted to.

By the next morning she had regained a sense of balance. It was highly unlikely that Luke would contact her – like herself, he'd have been temporarily seduced by the soft lights and sweet music. In fact, in the cold light of day, it seemed doubtful he'd ever intended to.

In the meantime life continued its normal pattern; the children were transported to and from school and nursery, the shopping attended to and all the other regular commitments fitted in – charity work, book group meetings and so on.

On the following Friday she strapped Mia into her car seat, collected Abby from school and drove to the hypermarket on the edge of town. She'd invited a couple of friends to dinner the following evening, and some ingredients needed for the meal weren't available locally.

She parked the car, transferred Mia into the trolley seat and, with Abby skipping alongside, braved the crowded interior, shopping list in hand. The store was huge, several times larger than their usual supermarket, and, unfamiliar with its layout, she found herself constantly dodging backwards and forwards rather than making steady progress, often finding that the next item on the list was in an aisle she'd already visited.

'Can I have an ice cream?' Abby begged for the third time, swinging on the handle of the trolley and causing it to lurch sideways.

'Stop that, Abby, you'll make us bump into someone! And I've told you, not till I've finished shopping – and not even then, if you ask again!'

'But I'm thirsty!' Abby complained, in the whiny voice that set her mother's nerves on edge.

'Well, you'll just have to wait!' Sarah snapped, her temper fraying. 'Now, hold on to the trolley properly so I know where you are!'

Abby promptly let her hand fall, and, deciding it was better to ignore her than cause a scene, Sarah turned back to the delicatessen counter. Frustratingly the particular cheese she needed didn't seem to be available and she was rapidly regretting having arranged the dinner.

'Abby!' said Mia suddenly.

'Abby's being naughty,' Sarah replied absently, deciding on one of the other cheeses. She watched while it was weighed out, took the package from the assistant and turned back to the trolley – and her heart stopped. There was no sign of Abby.

She looked up and down the crowded aisle. 'Abby! *Abby*!' she called, fighting down a rising panic. She turned back to Mia.

'Where did she go?' she demanded urgently.

Mia regarded her with wide eyes, lower lip trembling, and Sarah modified her tone.

'You said her name, darling. Did you see where she went?'

'With a lady,' Mia whispered, and Sarah stared at her aghast. This simply couldn't be happening! Both children had from birth had it drummed into them that they should never even talk to strangers, let alone go anywhere with them. But Abby had been cross with her. Oh God, where was she?

Impeded by the trolley, Sarah set off down the aisle, calling her daughter's name and frantically trying to see between other trolleys, baskets and people's legs, praying to catch sight of her.

'Has anyone seen a little girl with dark hair, in a blue coat?' she kept asking.

People moved sympathetically aside, shaking their heads as she blundered along, occasionally crashing into someone and apologizing. Oh God, Abby. *Where are you?*

Sensing her mother's panic Mia began to cry in earnest, adding to the nightmare. Up one aisle and down the next. This one was where she'd found the anchovies, where Abby had first asked for an ice cream. Oh God, God, God!

'Ask at the checkout,' someone advised. 'That's where they take lost children. There'll probably be an announcement any minute. Does she know her name?'

Sarah thanked her, nodding tearfully.

'They'll know if she's gone through the checkout,' added the woman.

Fresh horror! There was an endless line of checkout counters and, after a moment's hopefulness, Sarah's heart sank again. Where should she start? But surely Abby would never leave the store without her? It didn't seem credible, unless her abductor had given her no choice.

Sarah swallowed a sob. She'd try one more aisle before braving them. Please, God, let me find her *now*! Let her be safe!

Then, suddenly, there she was, seated at a table in the portion set aside for the café, a large knickerbocker glory in front of her. And opposite her sat a slim, neatly dressed figure with silvery blonde hair.

Abby saw her at the same instant, and a look of apprehension crossed her face. Seeing it, her companion turned, meeting Sarah's furious gaze.

'Oh, there you are!' Lily said, with a falsely sweet smile. 'We lost you!'

With a supreme effort Sarah took a deep breath. There were several things she wanted to do, all of them urgently: berate her daughter, smother her in kisses and, perhaps the most urgent, wipe that smile off Lily's face. Frustratingly she couldn't do any of them.

'Are you in the habit of kidnapping, Lily?' she asked unevenly.

'Oh, come now! Abby was looking lost, I couldn't see you, and she said she'd like an ice cream.'

'If you couldn't see me, how did you know who she was? You haven't seen her since she was three months old!'

'She looks so like Charles,' Lily answered smoothly, 'and when she told me her name I knew I was right.'

'Come here, Abby. Now!'

Abby glanced at the tall glass in front of her. 'Can I just—'

A quick look at her mother's face was answer enough. She slid off the chair. 'Thank you for my ice cream,' she said dutifully.

'A pleasure, darling!'

As she emerged from the café Sarah seized hold of her and, without looking in Lily's direction, set off grimly back down the aisle. The conflicting emotions of the last few minutes had drained her, and she knew she wouldn't refer to the matter again. Abby was aware she'd done wrong, frightening her mother in the process, and Sarah was satisfied she had learned her lesson.

It was only as, having abandoned any ingredients she still lacked, she paid for her purchases and led her daughters to the car, that it occurred to Sarah that Lily might have seen her dancing cheek to cheek last weekend and taken her revenge.

TWO

St Catherine's-on-Sea, present day

Henry Parsons seated himself in his usual chair, glancing appreciatively round the pleasant room and, through the window, at the garden beyond, already tinted with the colours of autumn. Rose Linscott, whose home this was, was a valued friend, and he enjoyed these weekly coffee mornings and their often in-depth discussions, though admittedly the item he had to impart today was scarcely intellectual.

He waited until she'd poured the coffee and offered a plate of shortbread before settling back in his chair and remarking, 'I have some news for you, my dear!'

'Excellent!' Rose returned placidly. 'What's the latest on the grapevine?'

He shook his head. 'Not gossip this time. A fact, no less, and of some significance, at least to me.'

'Oh?' She raised her eyebrows.

He held her gaze, relishing the moment of suspense. 'The name of the new resident has been announced!'

Having sold the family home following his wife's death ten years ago, Henry had moved into a small residential hotel that suited him very well. An inevitable downside, however, was that every now and again one of the elderly residents died and, to fill the vacancy, an outsider was thrust into their familiar circle, unsettling everyone.

'Well?' Rose prompted. 'Are you going to tell me who it is?'

'I think it will surprise you.'

She tutted impatiently. 'For goodness' sake, Henry, just tell me, and I'll let you know whether I'm surprised or not.'

He took a sip of coffee, patted his moustache with his napkin and, with the air of a conjuror producing a rabbit, announced, 'None other than the esteemed Mrs Fairfax!'

It was a satisfactory reaction. About to raise her cup, Rose's hand froze in mid-air. 'You're not serious?'

'Believe me, I am!'

'Cicely Fairfax is selling The Gables?'

'She is indeed. And moving to the Rosemount.'

'But that house is part of her!' Rose exclaimed. 'Her outer shell! How can she play lady of the manor without it? And where will everyone hold their committee meetings and garden fêtes?'

Rhetorical questions, as Rose was aware, but Cicely was indeed a leading member of St Catherine's society. Her late husband had twice been mayor; she was a church warden, chair of the Conservative Club, and had served as magistrate until, at the age of seventy, she'd been required to step down.

'She won't just be joining you,' Rose said flatly, 'she'll be taking over!'

Henry nodded glumly. 'My own feelings exactly.'

For Cicely Fairfax, as they both knew, habitually wielded an iron fist in a velvet glove. Never raising her voice, always smiling sweetly, she managed to rout her opponents and achieve her own ends in all she did, leaving those who'd opposed her wondering how they'd been outsmarted.

Mentally Rose reviewed the residents of the hotel, whom she'd come to know from the monthly lunches to which Henry invited her: two married couples; two unmarried ladies; three widows; Henry; and another gentleman, Mr Warren. They'd be a walkover.

'Perhaps we shouldn't be too surprised,' Henry added. 'After all, we've downsized ourselves.'

It was true; three and a half years ago, when her son-in-law Owen was offered the post of deputy headmaster at the college, Rose had made over her long-time home to him and her daughter. But she could see its roof two garden lengths away; it was still in the family, and she liked to think she retained a link with it.

'I remember when they arrived,' Henry was musing, 'she, George, the nanny and the little girls. Must be a good fifteen years ago, well before my wife died. They bought the house from the Harrisons, didn't they, when Arthur relocated to Scotland?'

'That's right. And the children caused considerable interest, since no mention was made of their parents. We learned later they'd both died, but that was all.'

Henry's mouth twitched. 'Most frustrating!'

Rose flashed him a suspicious glance but he remained impassive and she returned to the main item of news. 'So when's she moving in, do you know?'

'The end of the month, I believe.'

'And what will you call her?' The Rosemount was known to be set in its ways, the residents addressing each other formally as 'Mr' or 'Mrs' So-and-So.

Henry returned her smile. 'There'll be no problem as I've never been on first name terms with the lady. We didn't move in the same circles.'

'Well, just don't let her bully you!' Rose said darkly.

*   *   *

Mia Fairfax could scarcely believe her luck. Since leaving school a couple of months ago she and two friends had been searching with increasing desperation for a flat they could afford, and time had been running out. Her grandmother, with whom she'd lived for as long as she could remember, had decided to put her house on the market and move into a hotel.

'You'll find somewhere, darling,' she'd assured Mia, 'just as Abby did.'

Mia's elder sister had left The Gables on finishing school a year ago, but in her case the flat above the dental practice where she'd be working had just become vacant, and she and another trainee nurse were able to move in. The bookshop where Mia worked had no such useful attribute.

She'd been close to tears that evening three weeks ago when, over supper, her grandmother calmly announced, 'I've found you a flat, dear.'

Mia had stared at her open-mouthed, and Cicely gave a laugh. 'You didn't think I'd turn you out on the streets, did you?'

She went on to explain that she'd bought an apartment in Regent Road where several large Victorian houses had been converted into flats, and since it happened to be the show flat she'd also been able to purchase the furnishings and fittings, with the result that it was ready to move straight into.

'I made enquiries as to a reasonable rent, which the three of you can split between you,' Cicely went on, breaking off with a little gasp as Mia jumped up from the table to fling her arms round her neck.

Her friends were almost as ecstatic as she was. The apartment, they agreed, was perfect, not only because, in keeping with its age, it had spacious, beautifully proportioned rooms not usually available to young flat-hunters, but as an added bonus it over-looked Linden Park, a green space in the centre of town.

Standing at the window that Saturday morning, mug of coffee in hand, Mia had a bird's-eye view of the tennis courts where a game was in progress, of a group of fathers with their small sons sailing boats on the pond, and of a couple strolling hand in hand by the stream that wound through the park. Later, she decided, she'd take a paperback across the road, find a shel-tered spot in the rose garden and spend a relaxing afternoon before a planned outing this evening. The flats' one drawback was their lack of garden, but the park provided the ideal alternative.

Her musing was interrupted by the chime of her mobile and she glanced at it to see her sister's ID.

'Hi, Mi. Can you talk or are you at work?'

'It's OK, it's my free weekend.' Her job in the bookshop, which she loved, involved working alternate Saturdays.

'I've just been speaking to Grandma and she'd like us to go for lunch tomorrow, twelve thirty for one.'

'Oh, rats! We've just arranged a picnic!'

'Tough! As you well know, Grandma doesn't *ask*, she *tells*. She's moving next weekend and she wants us to choose a memento before it all goes to auction.' She paused, then added reflectively, 'Odd to think it'll be the last time we're there – the end of an era, I suppose.'

Mia bit her lip. The Gables was the only home she'd known – a mental shutter blocking what had gone before – and as such the only anchor they had. And now they were being cast adrift.

'I must go, Steph's waiting. See you there.' And Abby ended the call.

In sudden need of reassurance, Mia tapped out another number, relaxing as a well-loved voice answered.

'Mia! Hello, sweetie! How are things?'

'OK, thanks.'

'You don't sound too sure!'

'Grandma's moving out of The Gables next week.'

So that was it! Nina Phillips – 'Nanny Nina' as she'd been throughout the girls' childhood – said gently, 'And you're feeling a bit unsettled?'

'Yes,' Mia admitted, perching on the arm of a chair. 'I know it's pathetic, but it was our base, somewhere we could go if things went wrong, which we won't be able to at the hotel.'

'You could always come to me!' Nina said.

Mia smiled. 'Rob and Danny mightn't agree!'

Nina had stayed on in the town when her job as nanny ended, taking the post of school nurse at St Catherine's College. A year or so later she'd met and married Rob Phillips and they had a son.

'Anyway,' Mia continued, 'Abby and I are going there tomorrow to choose something before the house is cleared. It'll . . . be for the last time.'

Nina, who remembered the first time, was silent for a moment. 'Suppose you come here for tea afterwards?' she suggested then. 'You could tell us what you've chosen.'

Mia brightened. 'That'd be great. I'd love to, but I'm not sure about Abby. She might have arranged something.'

'Well, either or both of you would be very welcome. See you then.'

Nina was thoughtful as she switched off the phone. The Gables had been her home, too, for nearly ten years, and her mind went back to that traumatic spring when she'd first met the Fairfaxes.

Since that had been the only surname mentioned it never occurred to her, when she'd applied for the position of children's nanny, that there was any connection with the sensational Drummond case that had dominated both press and television, and at her interview Mrs Fairfax did not enlighten her. She was merely informed that she'd be required to care for her two grandchildren aged three and four, and that the family would shortly be moving to St Catherine's-on-Sea, a town fifty miles away.

Nina, who'd been expecting to continue living at home, had been on the point of withdrawing when the children were brought in, two pale, wide-eyed little girls clinging to the hands of a stout matronly woman introduced as Mrs Bell, who Nina gathered was the housekeeper. And her heart immediately went out to them.

Having been formally offered the post, which with some trepidation she had accepted, she was returning to her car when to her surprise Mrs Bell came hurrying after her.

'Excuse me if I'm speaking out of turn, miss,' she began a little breathlessly, 'but I think there's something you should know, and I'm guessing Mrs Fairfax was too upset to mention it.'

And it was then, to her horror, that Nina learned exactly who the children were, that the four-year-old cried every night for her mummy and the little one hadn't spoken since what was euphemistically termed 'the incident'.

'I'm that worried about them,' Mrs Bell had continued. 'I won't be going up to Somerset, so it seemed best to warn you, ask you to try to get them help of some kind.'

'But surely they're having counselling?' Nina had asked, and the woman shook her head.

'Mrs Fairfax won't hear of it. Says it would do more harm than

good to keep going over it, and that in new surroundings they'll
soon settle down.' Seeing Nina's shocked expression, she added,
'Don't judge her too harshly, miss; all this has knocked her for
six and I reckon she can't even bear to think of it. But they're
such helpless little mites, they shouldn't be left to fend for
theirselves.' Her eyes filled with tears.

Nina touched her arm in sympathy. 'Try not to worry,' she'd
said. 'I'll take care of them, I promise.'

And with a sniff and a nod, Mrs Bell had returned to the house.

And she'd done her best, Nina thought now. Though slightly in
awe of her employer, she'd begged repeatedly for the children to
receive counselling, but Mrs Fairfax remained adamant and eventually, knowing she was grieving herself, Nina felt unable to persist
any further, concentrating instead on giving the children all the
love she could muster.

It was some weeks later that, walking home from the park, Mia
had suddenly said, 'Can I have eggy soldiers for my tea?' – her
first words in over six weeks – and it had taken all of Nina's self-
control not to burst into tears of thankfulness.

'Ready for the weekly shop?'

She turned to see her husband in the doorway and gladly abandoned her reminiscences.

'Coming!' she said.

Sunday morning, and Cicely Fairfax was walking through the
rooms of her home, where a few labels were already attached to
table legs and stuck on picture frames. The bulk of the furniture
would be removed on Friday, leaving only the bedrooms, bathrooms
and kitchen till the following day. Theo and Imogen, who'd been
a great help these last few weeks, would be coming on Friday to
oversee things and spend the night here. Then, when the house
was finally emptied on Saturday, they'd accompany her to the
Rosemount and see her settled in.

They'd already removed several portable items such as lamps,
rugs and pictures, and it was a comfort to know that they were
taking the dining suite and corner display cabinet, and that she'd
still see them when she visited their home. She herself would be
keeping only a few items – her bed, the small rosewood table that
had been her mother's, some ornaments and pictures and a few
books, the vast majority of which had already gone to charity

shops. There was no point in keeping anything else, she told herself firmly; she'd have no use for it and storage would be an unnecessary expense. The children were coming to lunch today and could pick what they wanted, after which the rest could be dispatched, with little regret, for auction.

Following the trauma of Sarah's death she and George had chosen St Catherine's as their refuge because they'd spent several pleasant holidays here and it was a safe distance from the unwelcome gossip and speculation of Sherborne. Her grief had still been raw and her hatred of Charles pulsed through her with every heartbeat. Yet all these years on, she was no nearer understanding what had happened.

The autopsy reports cited manual strangulation as the cause of death in Sarah's case and a stab wound to the chest in that of Charles, found lying beside her. There was nothing to suggest a break-in or the presence of any third person. Since Charles's prints were on the knife, it followed that the coroner's verdict was uncompromising: unlawful killing and suicide.

'But *why*?' Cicely had cried repeatedly, and no one could answer her. To the best of her knowledge their marriage had been happy. God help her, she'd been fond of her son-in-law, and try as she might, she couldn't understand how the man she thought she'd known could have killed his wife and then himself, knowing their two young children were asleep upstairs. If he'd only left a note it would have helped, saved them eternally wondering.

'He wouldn't have been thinking logically,' George had tried to explain. 'He must have been at least temporarily insane.'

'Then why couldn't he just have killed himself?' she'd sobbed. 'Why take Sarah with him, when he'd promised to love her till death did them part?' And, realizing what she'd said, she'd stared at her husband, stricken.

'Perhaps he did,' George had replied.

Cicely took a deep breath, brushing an impatient hand across her face. No point wallowing in misery; it hadn't got her anywhere then and it wouldn't now. And St Catherine's had been good to her; it had allowed her to rebuild at her own pace and gradually become a person of influence in the town, as she'd been in Sherborne. Her abiding comfort was that no one here knew their history. Having changed the children's surname to their own, they'd sworn Nina, the new nanny, to secrecy, a promise she'd faithfully kept. Cicely still saw her occasionally about the town and they exchanged Christmas cards, but she knew the girls were in closer contact, which was only natural.

She paused to run her hand lovingly over a carved mantelpiece. She'd made full use of this house, she thought with satisfaction, offering it to various societies for their meetings, giving lavish parties and opening the garden for fêtes and firework displays. But after George's death it had become more and more of an effort. Looked at dispassionately, The Gables was too big for one person and there were rooms she didn't go into from one month's end to the next. She was also finding the stairs difficult as her arthritis worsened, and it was becoming increasingly hard to find a live-in housekeeper; the present incumbent would be leaving shortly to live with her recently widowed sister. Reluctantly, but with an undeniable sense of relief, she'd decided it was time for her to move.

It had come as a surprise, when she'd mentioned her intention to Theo, to learn that he'd foreseen this possibility some years ago, and had taken the precaution of reserving a provisional place for her at the Rosemount Hotel. She'd been both touched and grateful. It was a pleasant little hotel which she knew from the times she'd had lunch or tea there with Molly, who'd sadly died last year. And shortly after their discussion the death of one of the residents created a vacancy. It was as though it was meant to be.

The front doorbell roused her from her reminiscences. Her granddaughters had arrived.

Theo and Imogen Fairfax were enjoying a pub lunch with their friends the Burnsides.

'So you're going over to help dismantle the ancestral home?' Guy Burnside remarked idly, spearing a piece of smoked salmon.

Theo took a drink of beer. 'Well, it's not quite that, since as you know I've never lived there myself. But I'll be glad to give a home to some of the furniture, which I've known all my life.'

'How does your mother feel, giving up her home?'

Theo smiled affectionately. 'She's a lot tougher than she looks. It'll be a wrench, but she'll survive.'

'To tell you the truth,' Imogen confided to Anya as the men continued talking, 'I was terrified, when George died, that she'd want to move in with us, which is one reason why Theo contacted this hotel. Because quite frankly, though I adore Cicely, if we'd tried to live together we'd have killed each other!'

Anya laughed. 'Lucky you've both been spared, then! But surely she's a pussy-cat? Not like my spiky mother-in-law!'

'A pussy-cat who unfailingly gets the cream,' Imogen replied. 'And, let it be said, with never a cross word spoken. God knows how she does it!'

If Imogen spoke from experience, Mrs Fairfax senior had Anya's respect. For Imogen was a strong character in her own right, fashion editor for a prestigious monthly, forthright in her opinions and inclined to be dismissive of others. In fact she and Theo were a formidable pair, both highly successful in their careers and, with no family to consider, able to give their ambitions full rein. They lived in a converted farmhouse on the outskirts of Bath that Anya had secretly coveted for years.

'Theo's earmarked the dining suite,' Imogen continued. 'You'll be able to admire it next time you come. I've been bored with ours for years but had no excuse to get rid of it.'

'I look forward to seeing it,' Anya said.

Cicely and her granddaughters were at that moment seated round the table in question, enjoying their roast beef. The girls were slightly subdued, she noted, and was surprised. Both had been eager enough to claim their independence and move on once school was over, but before lunch they'd gone on a pilgrimage, a 'farewell tour', as Abby described it, and memories seemed to have been triggered. Their voices had floated down to her as they moved from room to room. *Remember hiding in the airing cupboard and not being able to get out? Remember wrapping apples in newspaper and storing them in the attic?*

For the girls, the tour was a bittersweet experience. The whole ambience seemed to have changed – as though, Mia thought, the house knew it was being abandoned. Some items had already been removed – by Uncle Theo, presumably – and there were marks on the walls where once-familiar pictures had hung. Suitcases stood in Grandma's room ready for her personal possessions, but their mother's photo still stood in pride of place on the dressing table. She'd paused to look at it, her eyes moving over the smiling face, and realized with a tug of the heart that her memory of her mother was now confined to this single image. Abby had come to join her and they'd both stood silently for a moment before, by unspoken consent, they moved on.

Abby remembered asking, at the age of six or seven, why there were no photos of their father, and Grandpa explained that he hadn't liked being photographed. But surely, she thought now, it was odd there wasn't so much as a snap taken on holiday? She could barely remember what he looked like, only that she used to enjoy being carried round the garden on his shoulders.

Glancing at their solemn faces, Cicely said brightly, 'The next meal we eat together will be at the Rosemount, when I invite you to lunch!'

'Are you looking forward to going?' Mia asked.

'Not the actual going,' Cicely acknowledged. 'I shall shed a few tears when I leave The Gables, but Theo and Imogen will help me over the move, and once I've settled in I'll be fine. I have a lovely room, which I'll enjoy showing you.'

Patsy, the last in a long line of housekeepers, came in to clear their plates. She had come to Cicely three years ago, glad of somewhere to live after giving up her home following divorce, and now she was going to her sister in Cirencester. Cicely was out a great deal and, after Abby had moved into her flat, Mia had spent many evenings in Patsy's cosy bedsit watching black and white films on Netflix. It was another goodbye, and she felt a fleeting sadness.

The meal over, the girls were invited to choose their mementoes. Abby picked an art deco mirror that had hung in her bedroom and a white furry rug, Mia a couple of Royal Copenhagen ornaments, and it was arranged that Theo would deliver them the following weekend when the house had been cleared. It only remained to wish Patsy well and their grandmother a trouble-free moving day, before walking down the path of The Gables for the last time, thankful they had tea at Nina's to look forward to.

It was only a ten-minute walk from The Gables to the Phillipses' home, but it could have been a world apart. They lived in a neat semi in a road of neat semis, the front gardens still ablaze with flowers, the gravel paths neatly raked. A man was cleaning his car in one of the driveways and farther on a woman was doing some weeding. Both smiled at the girls as they passed, and they turned into the familiar gateway with a palpable sense of relief.

Nina always joked that the house was like Dr Who's Tardis – bigger on the inside – an impression accentuated by the kitchen extension they'd built a few years back and the conservatory beyond the sitting room, where Rob Phillips now stood to greet them, a tall, broad-shouldered man with a thatch of fair hair that would never lie flat. After The Gables' dark furnishings, the house seemed filled with sunlight.

'Danny's at a school friend's party,' Nina was saying. 'It's his first without mothers and I was worried he wouldn't stay when I left, but he knows Julia and, of course, the other children and, thank goodness, there was no problem.' She gave a little laugh. 'So our son's social life has begun in earnest at the age of not quite six! No doubt the Phillips taxi service will be called on for many years to come!'

'You always collected us from parties,' Mia reminded her, and Nina bit her tongue; the Fairfax girls had had no parents to perform such duties.

'It's to be hoped he's not over-indulging on jellies and cake,' Rob interposed smoothly, 'or we'll have trouble getting him to settle tonight.'

'And talking of cake,' Nina went on, flashing him a grateful glance, 'I've made a lemon drizzle in your honour! Have you had time to digest Patsy's roast, or would you like to wait a while?'

'We've always room for lemon drizzle!' Abby told her.

At Rob's gesture they settled themselves on the wicker sofa with the squishy cushions, relaxing for the first time that day. The doors to the garden were open, giving on to the paved patio and, beyond it, the lawn. The sun had already moved off the swing and slide at the far end, leaving them in shadow.

Nina returned with a tea tray and set it on the glass-topped table, glancing at these girls who were almost as dear to her as her own child – Abby with her cap of dark hair and slightly anxious expression, an aftermath perhaps of that trauma in early childhood, and Mia, her long pale hair streaked with gold from the summer sun, whom the same trauma had rendered silent for two long months. The memory of the children they'd been still tugged at her heart.

'Now,' she instructed, distributing plates, napkins, mugs and cake, 'tell me about your visit. How did it go? How was your grandmother?'

'Sad, I think,' Abby replied, biting into her cake. 'And it was weird – the house felt different, somehow. I think she'll be glad when the move's over.'

'Moving's a big step at any age,' Rob commented. 'Bound to be a strain.'

'Theo and Imogen will be there to help.' Abby, unlike Mia, had dropped the 'aunt' and 'uncle' when she reached eighteen.

Nina nodded. 'That's good. And what did you choose as your mementoes?'

Mia smiled. 'The Copenhagen mermaid and baby robin, which I've always loved.'

'And I chose the mirror and rug from my old room,' Abby added. 'They'll be a welcome addition to the cell I call my bedroom!'

The flat above the dental surgery was indeed basic, a fact that Mia, with her own spacious apartment, felt guilty about, though her sister showed no signs of envy.

'Excellent choices all round!' Nina approved. 'And don't forget, if you ever feel the need for a bolthole, you can always come here! So, any other news? Jobs going well? Still enjoying pulling people's teeth out, Abby?'

'Still enjoying helping to!'

Nina laughed. 'And Mia? How's the book world?'

'Oh, I love it. The only drawback is working alternate Saturdays.'

'And the Creep!' Abby prompted.

Nina raised her eyebrows. 'And who might he or she be?'

'Suzie's partner,' Mia said a little unwillingly. 'He's started coming into the shop every day.' Suzanne Maybury was the owner of Maybury Books.

'And why is he a creep?'

She flushed. 'He thinks he's God's gift! And he invades your space, always coming and standing too close.' She gave a little shudder.

'So why has he appeared now, if he never used to? Has he started working there?'

'Not officially, thank goodness! He's between jobs and the new one doesn't start till October so he's at a loose end. He says he's "helping out" but he spends most of his time in the back room on his laptop.'

'Well, at least there's an end in sight!' Rob commented.

Abby helped herself to another slice of cake. 'What about you, Nina? Anything exciting at coll?'

Both girls had been at St Catherine's and were interested in any gossip Nina might pass on.

'Not really. We have two new members of staff, one male and one female, but as I don't come into contact with them I rely on Julia to fill me in. If you remember, she teaches a Year One class and her little boy's a friend of Danny's. In fact it's his party that he's gone to.' She glanced at her watch. 'Which reminds me, Rob, it's almost time to collect him.'

'Don't worry, I'm keeping an eye on the clock.'

'Is Mrs Allan still there?' Mia asked. 'Last term we were sure she was pregnant!'

Nina laughed. 'You were right; she'll be going on maternity leave at half term. One of the new staff is standing in for her, and the other, James Monroe, is taking over from Mr Grantham who, as you know, retired at the end of last term.'

Abby, less up to date with recent college history, was only half-listening. She'd been unsettled all day; the farewell tour of The Gables had, to her surprise, been not only nostalgic but upsetting. Things were changing, and there was nothing she could do to stop them.

She glanced across at Nina, laughing over a school anecdote, and with a sense of relief realized that she was and had always been their rock. Despite the changes in their lives, as long as they had her and her family to turn to all would be well.

THREE

The party was over and the last child had been collected. Richard, who had retreated to the golf club for the duration, was still not back and the boys were running off their high spirits in the garden. It would doubtless end in tears, but for the moment she was able to make a start on the clearing up.

Julia Coulson walked slowly round the table collecting paper plates and cups, trying to avoid tipping any cups with dregs of squash in them. It had gone well, she thought with satisfaction, thanks in part to Mrs Davis, who, on dropping Ben off and real-izing she was alone, had insisted on staying to help. Richard's absence was not commented on, though fathers' support at such events was more or less a given.

Well, Julia thought with a touch of wry humour, not *her* husband's, as the school and those connected with it had learned. Meetings or business trips frequently prevented his attending parents' evenings and sporting events – though in the latter case those 'meetings' usually took place at the golf club. Yet he was an affectionate father and enjoyed his sons' company provided it didn't impinge on his other interests.

And the same criterion applied to her! The sudden realization disconcerted her, though subconsciously she'd always known it. Richard would fall in with her requests and suggestions if they didn't put him out in any way; if they did, they were a lost cause. Perhaps, she thought philosophically, that came of marrying a man who, being so much older, was set in his ways. Granted he'd been married before, but his divorce seemed to have overridden consid-eration for others' opinions.

As she carried the tray to the kitchen she reassessed their meeting from this new perspective. At the time she'd been teaching at St Olaf's for a year, her first job since qualifying, and had gone home to spend the weekend with her parents. A two-year romance had just ended and, hoping for some much-needed tea and sympathy, she was not best pleased when her father announced he'd invited a visiting business associate to dinner.

Richard Coulson seemed nearer her father's age than hers and she was prepared to sit in near silence while they discussed mutual interests. She was certainly not prepared for the immediate interest he showed in her, continually drawing her into the conversation and listening to her replies and opinions with flattering attention.

And that was the crux, she thought now. She'd been flattered; flattered that this older but undeniably attractive man was so obvi-ously interested in her. It was balm to her bruised ego, providing the comfort she'd come home to find. Even more gratifying was that on leaving he'd asked for her phone number, ostensibly so he could text some information on a subject they'd been discussing.

'You want to watch that one!' her mother had warned. 'Looks as though he's in search of wife number two!'

She had laughed it off, but Richard proved a determined suitor, telephoning, texting, arranging meetings and eventually winning her round. Within six weeks they were engaged, within six months married, and she left her job, friends and family in Gloucestershire to move down to Somerset.

Well, she concluded, despite his failings and no doubt many of her own, their marriage had survived and next month, unbelievably, it would be their ninth anniversary.

An indignant yell from the garden reclaimed her attention and, tipping the disposable tableware into the bin, she went outside to restore harmony.

A row of hotels stretched for almost a mile along the promenade at St Catherine's – large, solid buildings, many incorporating saunas, swimming pools or gyms. In the road immediately behind them the Rosemount offered none of these. Originally converted from a private house, it was considerably smaller, boasting only ten rooms, but it enjoyed an excellent reputation and was much sought after by those approaching retirement, ensuring that there was always a waiting list.

Margot Teale, one of the proprietors, put a mug of tea in front of her husband, who was checking the accounts. He looked up with a smile.

'Ah, that's welcome! Come and join me, or are you still hovering?'

'I'm just waiting till Mr and Mrs Fairfax leave. I want to check that everything's in order.'

'Can't see why it shouldn't be.'

'Nonetheless.' Margot hesitated. 'I do hope we're doing the right thing in accepting her, especially when to all intents and purposes she's jumping the queue.'

Roy Teale shrugged, picking up his mug. 'Since her son had the foresight to reserve a place, we could hardly refuse.'

'Several of the residents have voiced doubts,' Margot said worriedly. 'She's been used to organizing things, hasn't she? If she tries any of that here, there'll be a few ruffled feathers.'

'The trouble is they're used to being a closed circle. There's always a blip when someone new moves in – it happens so rarely we tend to forget. Sit down, love, and have your tea. We'll hear when they come downstairs.'

As though in confirmation, the sound of voices and footsteps reached them and Margot hurried from the room. With a resigned shake of his head Roy returned to the accounts.

As always at the change of occupancy, the room had been completely redecorated and new curtains hung, presenting a clean slate for the latest occupant to stamp his or her personality.

Cicely drew a deep breath and looked about her. The room already had a semblance of home; her own bed was in place, neatly made up by Imogen with its familiar covering, and Theo had even hung one or two pictures on the walls. Her clothes hung in the wardrobe and her toiletries were on a shelf in the en suite. Less immediately essential belongings could be unpacked at leisure, when she'd decided where to put them. Finally, Theo had driven her Volvo down and parked it behind the hotel in the space allotted to her. Now, after all these years, no trace of her remained at The Gables.

It was a sobering thought, and to dispel it she walked to the bay window, appreciating the wide semi-circular view it offered. Immediately below her, the front garden with its lawn and flowerbeds reached down to the road, where a seemingly endless succession of cars was moving in both directions. The buildings opposite, of a similar style to this one, stood back to back with those on the promenade, and between the roofs wedges of sparkling blue sea were visible. To her left she could see the frontages of neighbouring houses and their gardens stretching in a row down the road. A shorter section to her right ended in a T-junction with Marine Drive, which stretched from the town centre to the beach and pier. Cicely had walked down it many times with Molly, who'd loved the sea and spent an hour or two each day sitting on the prom – in one of the shelters if wet – reading, knitting or just watching people pass by.

Thinking of Molly, Cicely accepted that she'd had very few friends in her long life. Acquaintances, yes, a host of them, whom she'd entertained on a reciprocal basis. And there were colleagues connected with the charities she sat on, and people she met frequently at church or at functions. But friends, with whom she could exchange confidences or turn to in distress? Very few.

Not that she'd missed them. Having been spoiled as an only child, she'd continued to be indulged by an adoring husband

and, apart from one overwhelming tragedy, had had a happy and fulfilled life, achieving all she set out to without, she congratulated herself, riding roughshod over anyone. And now, in these comfortable surroundings, she was about to embark on its latest phase.

She turned back into the room. She'd been told that it was the custom on a new resident's first evening to gather in the lounge before dinner, so that introductions could be made over a glass of sherry. Mrs Teale had offered to meet Cicely in the hall at six thirty and accompany her into the room.

It was now almost six – time to freshen up and change for dinner. With a pleasant feeling of anticipation, Cicely began to prepare for the evening ahead.

'So what did you think of her?'

Miss Derbyshire sniffed. 'She was very *gracious*, wasn't she? Like the Queen being introduced to factory workers!'

Miss Culpepper smiled protestingly. 'Oh come, that's hardly fair! What was the poor woman supposed to do? Behave like a new girl at your old school and wait to be spoken to?'

'Well, she *is* a new girl, relatively speaking. She'd better not start throwing her weight around, that's all.'

'I'd heard of her, of course,' Miss Culpepper said reflectively, 'but never met her. She's smaller than I expected, and – prettier, I suppose, with that soft gold hair. Probably out of a bottle, but it suits her.'

Miss Derbyshire moved impatiently. 'Are we going to spend the rest of the evening discussing the new arrival, or have this game of Scrabble?'

'Sorry, yes, of course.' And Miss Culpepper, reserving judgement, tipped the tiles on to the board.

Some hours later Cicely lay awake in her new milieu, her brain too active for sleep. It had been an emotional day, waking for the last time in her familiar room at The Gables and remembering other awakenings over the years, both happy and sad. It was a comfort to know Theo and Imogen were just across the landing.

But the whole day was a series of 'lasts' – a hasty breakfast before the return of the removal men, packing her personal belongings and laying the photograph of Sarah in her case. Sarah, who'd never known this house, but whose death had brought her parents and children here.

To escape the general disruption they'd gone to the Swan for lunch, but she'd had little appetite and not done it justice. She hadn't slept well the previous night and was beset with a combination of apprehension and nostalgia that lasted all day. And so to the Rosemount, settling in, saying goodbye to Theo and Imogen, then meeting the other residents over sherry. Some she knew slightly – Mr Merriweather had been a school governor, Mrs Hill was a member of her bridge club, though they'd never played together. Others she knew by sight, from church or the library or just about town. They'd been somewhat reserved, but that was only to be expected.

Then dinner in the restaurant with its separate tables, the majority of them laid for one. The Merriweathers and Latimers were obvious exceptions, and two of the single ladies, she noticed, shared a table. It would surely be more sociable if the tables were larger, so no one was forced to dine in solitary splendour. Possibly they could even move from table to table during the week, like in duplicate bridge? In fact, there were one or two tweaks she'd suggest over the coming days, which, she was sure, would improve the ambience.

With a sigh Cicely switched on the lamp and the room leapt into view, door and windows in different positions from those she'd subconsciously expected. She'd read for a while and perhaps then she'd be able to settle. Plumping up her pillows, she reached for her library book.

The Montpellier restaurant was regarded as one of the best in town, though Julia secretly preferred La Flambée in the Horseshoe, which in her view was less pretentious. Still, Richard was treating her to a special meal in celebration of their nine years together and she resolved to enjoy it to the full. The proprietor, Crispin Hynes, was hovering at his elbow making suggestions as they discussed appropriate wines for the courses already chosen.

Richard looked very handsome, she thought dispassionately. His dark hair was liberally sprinkled with silver, but there was no trace of the double chin or paunch which often bedevilled men of his age. The lines round eyes and mouth, far from ageing him, added character to his face, as did his frown of concentration over the wine list, and she'd noted with proprietary satisfaction the flickers of interest directed at him by other women in the room.

The choice of wine agreed, Hynes, with a little bow, moved away to instruct his minions and Richard turned to her with a smile.

'You're looking very lovely this evening, Mrs Coulson!' he said.

She smiled back. 'Why, thank you, Mr Coulson!'

'Especially considering you've endured nine years' hard labour in the role!'

She laughed. 'Oh, it's not been all bad! There've been quite a few perks for good behaviour!'

'Glad to hear it! So no regrets about marrying an old man?'

'I prefer the word "mature"!'

'Come to think of it, so do I! Nevertheless, I'm well aware I haven't as much patience these days, particularly with the boys.'

'They worship you,' Julia said.

He looked at her shrewdly. 'I know, for instance, that you think I'm too harsh with Jamie, but it's for his own good. We don't want him labelled a cry-baby.'

'Richard, he's only six!'

'Even so, the sooner he stands on his own feet the better for everyone. You've always babied him, which hasn't helped.' He glanced at her, saw her flush and bite her lip. 'And there I go, upsetting you on our anniversary.' He laid a quick hand over hers. 'Sorry, darling, let's talk about something else. And here, thank God, comes the first bottle of wine!'

Mia enjoyed her walk to work; her route took her through the park, and at eight thirty she had it more or less to herself, the occasional jogger or dog-walker the only other occupants. In a week or two the leaves would begin to turn and the trees explode into a riot of red, brown and gold. She must take some photos and compare them with last year's.

Taking the Marine Drive exit she crossed the road and turned into the main shopping area, where, after the solitude of the park, she was immediately engulfed in the hurly-burly of commerce. Blinds and shutters were being rolled up as supermarkets and chain stores prepared to open, vans were unloading supplies for the indoor market and cafés were setting up chairs on the pavement in readiness for early morning trade.

A little way along a turning to the left widened into the Horseshoe, a U-shaped pedestrian precinct with beds of flowers and shrubs down the centre. It was here that the more up-market premises were situated – designer dress shops, boutiques, jewellers, a wine bar, a couple of restaurants and, at the far end, Maybury Books. Mia often wondered how Suzie, who conducted a successful but modest business, could afford what must be a prohibitive rent, especially since the shop was in prime position in the bowl of the U, with a view looking up the length of the precinct.

She felt a surge of affectionate pride as she approached it, mentally checking the window display to ensure it fulfilled its function of tempting passers-by to pause and, with luck, to enter the shop. The interior was also inviting, its various alcoves offering a modicum of privacy in which to browse, while the ever-present coffee pot and scattering of easy chairs added to the welcoming atmosphere. Mia, who had always been a compulsive reader, could think of no better place to spend her time.

'Morning!' Suzie called from the back room as she let herself in.

'Morning.' Mia went to join her, finding her unwrapping a newly arrived parcel of books. No sign of Terry, thank goodness.

'We'll need more shelf space in New Releases,' Suzie went on. 'Could you start moving some of the older titles to the higher shelves? You'll need the steps.'

'Right.' Mia hung her jacket on a hook, deposited her bag in the corner and went to collect the ladder. The working day had begun.

It was break, but Julia was still in the classroom resolving an issue with the interactive whiteboard. A tap on the door interrupted her and she turned to see a man in the doorway, his hand resting lightly on the shoulder of her small, tear-stained son.

'Jamie!' she exclaimed, in exasperation as much as concern, and the child ran to her, clasping her round the knees. She turned to his companion, to whom, she remembered, she'd been introduced in the staff room, and fumbled for his name.

'James Monroe,' he said, coming to her assistance. 'We met briefly last week. I believe this young man is yours. Things were getting a little boisterous in the playground and . . . Jamie here

. . . wasn't too happy.' He smiled at the child. 'So we share the same name! I used to be Jamie too.'

'Thanks so much for rescuing him. My husband says he must stand on his own feet, but he finds it hard.'

The bell rang for the end of break and she gave her son an encouraging little pat. 'Back to your classroom, then. And say thank you to Mr Monroe.'

'Thank you,' muttered Jamie obediently, and scuttled from the room.

'You have another one, I believe? He's in my class.'

'Adam, yes.' She smiled. 'Chalk and cheese! Nothing ever fazes Adam!'

James smiled back. 'Thanks for the tip! Well, I'd better be on my way. Good to have met you again, Julia.'

'And you,' she said.

Terry Fenchurch arrived at the bookshop mid-morning, to Mia's consternation and Suzanne Maybury's relief. There'd been a slight altercation over breakfast and she feared he'd gone into one of his sulks, which were becoming more frequent. The fact that he was seven years younger than herself hadn't mattered in their thirties, but when she moved up a decade the age gap seemed to stretch, and she suspected he'd started to look for someone younger. She had, in fact, confided her worries to her friend Babs, even though it laid her open to an unspoken *told you so*; Babs had never liked Terry, though after an initial warning, she'd loyally kept her doubts to herself.

It wasn't ideal to have him lounging around in the shop; Mia was clearly uncomfortable with him, and he was inclined to hassle browsing customers. Still, at least she knew where he was and, thank God, his new job was due to start in a couple of weeks.

It was ironic, she reflected, that she'd the reputation of being calmly in control, whereas in truth she was a prey to uncertainties. Her divorce ten years ago had left her with a dread of being alone, of having to live out her life with no one to care whether she lived or died. The clock continued to tick, and if Terry left her she mightn't find anyone to replace him. Better, perhaps, to hold her tongue and put up with his childish foibles.

He was coming towards her now, coffee mug in hand, just as a customer who'd been hesitating over an expensive coffee-table book was approaching the counter. To head him off she said quickly, 'Terry, could you give Mia a hand? She's moving a stack of books to higher shelves, and some are quite heavy.'

He paused, a frown forming at the diversion, but then, to Suzie's relief, he shrugged and turned into the adjacent alcove where Mia was balanced on the ladder. Nice legs, he thought.

'Need a hand?'

She turned to look down, wobbling slightly. 'I can manage, thanks.'

'I've been instructed to help you.'

Mia bit her lip. 'Then perhaps you could pass me up the next pile?'

There were a dozen or so books on the table behind them, several, as Suzie had said, substantial tomes. Terry deposited his mug, collected an armful and moved to the foot of the ladder. But as he reached up and Mia bent to receive them he stumbled, his foot knocking against it and causing it to teeter precariously. Dropping the books, he made a grab for it, but too late. It crashed to the ground taking Mia with it, her head bouncing off one of the table legs as she landed.

The noise brought Suzie and several customers rushing to the scene, aghast to see her on the ground with her eyes shut.

'My God!' Suzie gasped, dropping to her knees beside her. 'Mia! Mia, can you hear me? *Mia!*'

There was a tense moment while everyone held their breath. Then, to universal relief, she moved her head slightly and gave a little murmur of distress.

'Get a glass of water, Terry,' Suzie said over her shoulder. She put a hand under the girl's head and gently raised it. Mia opened unfocused eyes.

'Mummy, wake up!' she said clearly. 'Wake *up*, Mummy!'

'It's all right, sweetie. It's Suzie, and I've got you. Can you sit up?'

Mia stared blankly at her. Then she gave a little gasp, a hand going up to her head.

'She's concussed!' someone said. 'Shouldn't she go to A & E?'

'Not for the moment,' someone else replied. 'I did a first-aid course; she just needs monitoring for a while. As long as she's not sick and doesn't develop a headache or fall asleep she should be fine.'

Terry returned with a glass of water and Suzie held it to Mia's lips. After a few sips her head seemed to clear and she looked about her, registering for the first time the concerned crowd around her and Terry's anxious face.

She struggled to get to her feet, but Suzie held her back. 'Take it slowly, sweetie. You should sit quietly for a while.'

'I'm all right,' Mia protested, embarrassed now at being the centre of attention, but at Suzie's insistence she allowed herself to be led away and the crowd began to disperse.

'She's one of the Fairfax girls, isn't she?' said the woman who'd suggested A & E. 'I've never heard of any mother – they used to live with their grandparents.'

Her companion shrugged. 'She probably didn't know what she was saying.'

'Bit odd, all the same. You'd think she'd have mentioned her grandmother.'

The other one snorted. 'Have you *met* Cicely Fairfax?' she asked.

Cicely herself was at that moment seated at the rosewood table checking through her diary. Every person and organization on her not inconsiderable address list had been notified of the move, given contact numbers and assured she'd be fulfilling her engagements as usual. The only difference was that she'd no longer be hosting them, as everyone was already aware. Nonetheless she intended to keep as firm a hand on matters as she always had, and it was essential that no one should interpret this move as the prelude to her retirement.

There was a tap on her door and Margot Teale's slightly anxious face peered round it. 'You wanted to see me, Mrs Fairfax?'

'Oh, yes, Mrs Teale. Please come in.'

She did so, closing the door behind her. 'I trust everything's all right?'

'Yes, indeed. It's just that it struck me at dinner last night how much more convivial it would be if we were seated at larger tables.'

'Convivial?' Margot repeated doubtfully.

'It seems a little austere to sit alone – like a punishment at boarding school! Surely it would make for a more friendly attitude if we sat together? Either that, or we could migrate from one table to another during the week, so we'd be sitting with different people?'

Margot pursed her lips. 'Thank you for the suggestion, Mrs Fairfax, but the seating arrangement in the dining room has never changed over the years, nor up to now has anyone suggested it might.'

'Well, it often takes a fresh eye to spot these things. People are inclined to accept the status quo rather than suggest improvements.'

'The point is, Mrs Fairfax, I'm not sure what you suggest would be considered an improvement. The single ladies in particular value their privacy, and they can and do spend time together if they wish during the daytime and especially the evenings, as I'm sure you'll find.'

She hesitated, glancing at Cicely's pleasantly unperturbed face. 'However, if you feel you'd like company in the dining room, I could ask if—'

'No, no, that was not my meaning at all. I'm perfectly content with my own company!'

'As, I think you'll find, is everyone else. However, I appreciate your suggestion and will bear it in mind if the opportunity offers.'

Roy Teale looked up as his wife came into their office.

'What's up, love? You've got a face like thunder!'

'It's started!' she said.

FOUR

Before leaving her hotel room Lily checked her appearance in the full-length mirror: boxy jacket in heather tweed, knee-length skirt, navy tights, high-heeled shoes. It was a matter of pride that she look her best when meeting her ex-husband, and with a nod of satisfaction she picked up her briefcase and left the room.

During their marriage she and Luke had made investments in several properties that had reaped dividends over the years, and, to maintain personal interest in them, they'd fallen into the habit of meeting once a year while in London on other business, to enable them to exchange views without the presence of their agent. And, as a bonus, these discussions were unfailingly followed by an excellent lunch. Today they were keen to look into plans for a proposed new development.

At forty-five, Lily's appearance did not differ greatly from the days of their marriage. Her fair, naturally curly hair had no hint of grey and her weight remained largely unchanged. In her youth she'd considered herself 'skinny', envying her better-endowed friends. Now, in early middle age, it was she who was envied, and admittedly the designer clothes she favoured fitted her to perfection.

Luke was awaiting her in the foyer and he too had aged well. With all due modesty, Lily reckoned they made a handsome couple. As usual he'd reserved a small room where they could hold their discussion, and booked a table for subsequent lunch in the restaurant.

'Lily!' He bent to kiss her cheek. 'Good to see you, as always.'

'You too, Luke.'

She meant it. They had, after all, been married for nearly ten years and their parting was not acrimonious, merely a growing apart. In fact she'd been on the point of suggesting a separation when two of their friends had died tragically, and she put it on hold for eighteen months. Luke had taken their deaths badly; at one time he'd been close to Charles, and Lily blamed herself for the estrangement that had robbed him of that friendship during Charles's last few years of life.

Now, he took her elbow and led her down a corridor to a small lounge with a 'Reserved' notice pinned to the door. Inside, a table was set with a tray of coffee and biscuits. Setting her memories aside, Lily seated herself. Luke did the same, and they both opened their briefcases.

An hour or so later, seated opposite each other in the restaurant, they turned to more personal subjects.

'How's the family?' Lily enquired, sipping her glass of champagne.

'Growing apace – in stature, not numbers!'

She laughed. She'd never wanted children, but was glad Luke had acquired some in his second marriage. She herself had not remarried, preferring the less restrictive relationship of a series of lovers, or 'partners' as they were now euphemistically called. Their statuses had risen as her career steadily advanced and the present one, Sebastian, was the Chief Executive Officer of an international consortium, with a title attached.

Luke, well aware of this progression, gently teased her about it. 'And Sebastian?'

'Flourishing!' she said.

He shook his head humorously. 'Just as well you ditched me, Lil! I could never have kept up!'

'We were great for quite a while. I've no regrets.'

'Nor I,' he said.

Suzie had requested Mia's flatmates Lola and Tamsin to keep an eye on her for the next twenty-four hours, and if in any doubt to drive her to A & E. She had picked at her food over supper and now, though the television was on, it was clear her mind was elsewhere.

'Sure you're OK, Mi?' Lola asked anxiously.

'Yes, fine.'

'Headache?'

'Just a slight one.' She raised a hand and gingerly felt her head. 'Not surprising, it's quite a bump. Though actually . . .'

'Yes?' Tamsin switched off the TV.

'It's not the bump that's bothering me,' Mia said slowly. 'I could only have been out a few seconds, but . . . I don't know, I seemed to have some kind of dream.' She shuddered. 'A horrible one.'

Both girls leaned forward anxiously. 'What about?'

'That's just it – I don't know! All I remember is a feeling of—' She broke off again. 'Sorry!' she said with a smile. 'Put it down to the concussion!'

'Talking of which,' Lola put in, 'I suggest a couple of paracetamols and an early night. We're taking it in turns to sit in your room, and I'm doing the first shift.'

'There's really no need!' Mia protested. 'I'm fine, honestly!'

'No arguments! We promised Suzie.'

And truth to tell it was a comfort to know that if the dream, whatever it was, should recur, she wouldn't wake up alone.

'Then thanks,' she said. 'I promise not to snore!'

*   *   *

Every few weeks Rose was invited to Sunday lunch with the family in what had once been her home. She enjoyed these occasions, though recently the participants had dwindled in number; her eldest granddaughter now lived in Bristol and the middle one was away at university. Which left Verity, the youngest, who, for reasons Rose would deny, was secretly her favourite.

Her relationship with her son-in-law was fine-tuned; she admired him and was proud of his achievements, but at times his strongly held opinions were at odds with hers, which unfailingly raised her hackles. And she was not above deliberately provoking him.

'Have you stamped out that bullying you had last term?' was her opening salvo over lunch, and she saw his jaw tighten. 'It came up at the Rosemount when I was there recently, with Mrs Hill's grandson being at the college. Do you know him, Owen? I believe his surname's Ferris.'

'Dominic Ferris,' Owen said evenly. 'Yes, I know him.' He forbore from pointing out it was his job to know all the pupils. 'As I told you at the time, Rose, the bullying – such as it was – was dealt with quickly and stringently and was in any case limited to only two or three offenders. There has been and will be no repeat of it, so you may reassure Mrs Hill on that score.'

Rose looked at him sharply. 'I trust your optimism isn't misplaced,' she said blandly. 'It can scar a child for life.'

'You were saying Mrs Fairfax has moved to the Rosemount, Ma,' Fleur said quickly. 'Have you heard how she's settling in?'

Rose, having shot her bolt, allowed herself to be diverted. 'According to Henry, *she's* settled in well, at the cost of unsettling everyone else!'

'How's that?'

'She keeps suggesting "improvements" to established routines. Henry says what most annoys people is that they're actually good suggestions, but they'd rather die than put them into effect!'

'Would you like to live at the Rosemount, Gran?' Verity asked, scraping her plate.

'No, dear, I should not,' Rose said firmly. 'My little bungalow suits me very well. It's an excellent hotel, mind. Ideal for single or widowed men like Henry and Mr Warren, though the majority of the residents are women. I'd have expected them to prefer their own homes.'

'I'd like to live in a hotel,' Verity remarked. 'Never having to clean my room or do the dishes or even the shopping!'

'I wasn't aware you did any of that now!' said her mother drily.

Although there were no other after-effects of her fall, the memory of the 'dream' continued to haunt Mia, the more so as she suspected that she might have had the same experience before, though in the manner of dreams it had faded from her memory. Nor could she understand why she'd apparently called for her mother, whom she remembered only as the image in her grandmother's photograph. So what, during that brief spell of unconsciousness, could have brought her to mind?

She needed to talk it over, but though Abby was her first thought she was hesitant, since by some tacit agreement they never spoke about their parents. And fond though she was of her grandmother she could never confide in her. Which left Nina, who was always ready to listen. Reaching a decision, Mia phoned her one day after work.

'I was wondering if we could meet for a chat,' she began hesitantly. 'There's something I'd like to discuss with you.'

'Of course, sweetie. Pop round.'

Mia hesitated. 'Could we possibly meet somewhere else?'

Nina frowned. 'If that's what you'd prefer,' she said slowly. 'Where do you suggest?'

'The Bacchus Wine Bar, if that's OK? In about half an hour?'

'I'll be there,' Nina said.

As she ended the call she heard the front door open and close, heralding Rob's return from work, and called him into the kitchen. 'I've just had a rather strange phone call from Mia; she wants to see me, but not here, for some reason. Our meal's in the oven, but would you mind bathing Danny and giving him his supper if I'm not back?'

Rob kissed her cheek. 'I've had a good day, thanks,' he said jokingly.

'Sorry, love, but the phone call threw me. Why won't she come here? She's always said it's her second home.'

'Something private, perhaps. Where are you meeting?'

'The Bacchus in Regent Lane.'

He went to the fridge and took out a can of beer. 'Your usual?'

'No, I'll wait for the Bacchus, thanks.' She reached up and kissed him. 'And I'm so glad you had a good day!'

Mia had been gazing pensively out of the window and turned as Nina joined her bearing two glasses of cider.

'Oh, sorry! I should have got those.'

'Be my guest. Now, what's this all about?'

'I'm sorry about coming here,' Mia began awkwardly. 'It's just that I didn't want Rob or Danny to overhear anything.'

'Right, let's start at the beginning, shall we?'

'Well, last week I fell at work and knocked myself out for a few seconds—'

'Hold on!' Nina interrupted. 'You had concussion? Were you checked out?'

'My friends monitored me through the night, bless them, though I only had a bump and a slight headache. But . . .' She stopped again before taking a deep breath. 'But Suzie says that as I was coming round I . . . seemed to be talking to my mother,' she ended in a rush.

Nina stared at her with deepening concern. This was more serious than she'd assumed. 'Could she make out what you were saying?'

'I was trying to wake her up.'

A chill spread over Nina, totally unconnected with the ice-cold glass in her hand.

'And there was something else,' Mia continued, when she didn't speak. 'I was having a really horrible dream, which is silly because there wasn't time for one, but I knew something was terribly wrong. And I can't get it out of my head.'

Concealing her mounting anxiety, Nina laid a hand over hers. 'Poor you! Even the mildest concussion can knock you for six; no wonder you're having nightmares.'

Mia looked at her hopefully. 'You think that's all it is?'

Please God! 'What else could it be?'

After a moment she shrugged. 'I suppose you're right. I – just wanted to tell someone, that's all.'

'And now you have! Feel better?'

'A little, I suppose.' Mia gave her an uncertain smile.

Nina slanted the conversation to a less disturbing level. 'How did you manage to fall, anyway?'

'I was up a ladder rearranging books and – and the Creep knocked against it.'

Nina smiled. 'Not redeeming himself, then?'

'No. Thank goodness he'll only be there for another couple of weeks. I can't imagine how Suzie puts up with him!'

'Love is blind, and it helps if it's sometimes a bit deaf too!'

Mia laughed, and Nina breathed a sigh of relief. She was coming out of it, bless her, but in offloading her worries she'd passed them on to Nina herself. In spades.

It was several hours later. Danny was in bed, they'd had their meal, cleared it away and were sitting over coffee in the conservatory, wrapped in another of the silences that had punctuated the evening. Rob had had enough.

'When are you going to tell me what Mia wanted? It's obviously upset you.'

She glanced at him quickly, about to deny it before accepting it was useless. 'I can't, Rob,' she said simply. 'I wish I could.'

'Signed the Official Secrets Act?'

'Something like that.'

'Oh, come on, Nina! Since when has there been anything we can't discuss?'

'I'm sorry, but this really is the exception.'

'Why, for God's sake?'

'Because I made a promise a long time ago, and I can't break it.'

He studied her troubled face. 'Look, sweetheart, something's really got to you and I want to help. You know anything you tell me will go no further.'

Her eyes filled with tears and he quickly moved to join her on the wicker sofa, his arm round her shoulders. 'You made a promise?' he prompted.

He'd almost given up expecting an answer when she said suddenly, 'Yes. To Mrs Fairfax.'

'Ah. Then can't you ask her to release you from it?'

She shook her head. 'It would cause her distress and I don't want that.'

'So in the meantime it's Mia who's distressed?'

'Yes,' Nina admitted unhappily.

'Why?'

'She banged her head at work,' she said slowly, 'and was

briefly unconscious. And as she was coming round, she . . .' Nina paused and moistened her lips. 'She seemed to be talking to her mother.'

'Her *mother*? Who, with her father, was killed in a car crash shortly before you went to work for them?'

Nina nodded, looking down at her tightly linked hands. 'I'm not sure if I told you, but she hadn't spoken since their deaths and didn't for several more weeks. Unfortunately Mrs Fairfax wouldn't allow them to receive counselling.'

Rob thought for a moment. 'That's all common knowledge, though. There's more, isn't there? You think this talking to her mother might be a throwback of some kind?'

Nina shrugged, afraid of where this was leading.

'Asking her to "wake up" sounds almost as though Mia saw her dead body, but that's not possible, is it, because the children weren't in the car. Or,' he went on, following a new line of thought, 'wasn't that how their parents died?'

He put a finger under her chin and turned her face towards him. 'Nina?'

'That's what everyone was told,' she said in a low voice.

'But it's not true?'

'Oh God, Rob!' Nina pleaded. 'Don't make me say it!'

'Was there something – shocking about the way they died?'

'It was in the papers for weeks.' She was speaking barely audibly and he bent closer. 'But when I went for the interview I'd no idea, with it being a different name, that it was the same family. Their housekeeper told me after I'd accepted the position.'

'What did she tell you?' Rob asked softly.

'That it was the Fairfaxes' daughter at the centre of the publicity. Her husband seemed to have strangled her, then committed suicide.'

'God, how appalling!'

'We were all living in Dorset then, but, having changed the girls' names to theirs, they were on the point of moving here to get away from the gossip. They swore me to secrecy and I've never told a soul until this minute.'

'And the children? How did they react?'

'That's just it! No one knew for sure if they'd seen the bodies – they were still in bed when the police arrived – but surely they *must* have! Why else would Mia refuse to speak? Staying with her grandparents and being told her parents were on holiday wouldn't cause a trauma, would it? And it was eight thirty when they were found. They should have been ready for school; it was one of the mothers calling to collect Abby who raised the alarm. But it seems no one was allowed to question them, on the ridiculous premise of "least said, soonest mended". Even the police had to pussy-foot their way round the interviews.'

She sighed. 'I think it was a form of denial, insisting that moving away and starting a new life would ensure that all would be well. Mrs Fairfax was probably terrified the girls would start talking about it, which was more than she could bear. But it was always a ticking bomb, and now I'm desperately afraid it's about to explode.'

Saturday afternoon, and Julia was alone in the house. Richard, as usual, was playing golf and both boys had been invited out to tea. Admittedly there were things she could do: the laundry needed sorting, the vegetables had to be prepared for tonight's meal. But it was Saturday! she thought rebelliously. She'd no intention of doing housework, and neither was she in the mood for reading or gardening.

To add to her restlessness she was still unsettled after last night's argument with Richard. Jamie had again come home from school in tears, insisting he was never going back, and over dinner – perhaps unwisely – she'd reported the incident to Richard, who'd lost his temper.

'That boy's turning into a snivelling little coward!' he stormed. 'We all have to do things we don't like, and the sooner he accepts that, the better. And it's not as though he has no friends; he enjoyed his party, didn't he?'

'Yes, but that was in the environment of home, which is very different.'

'My God! So we have to consider his "environment" now!'

'You're not even trying to understand!' Julia had flared.

'I understand that the root of the trouble is that you've always babied him! He thinks if he's faced with anything not to his liking, all he has to do is run to Mummy!'

'That's grossly unfair!' she flung back.

'Then why did we never have this problem with Adam?'

'Because Adam's a completely different kettle of fish! Jamie's much more sensitive, and it's nothing to do with me "babying" him, as you put it!'

Richard flung his napkin on the table and rose to his feet. 'If you say so, but please don't come to me with any more tales of woe because I'm rapidly losing interest!' And he left the room, leaving her sitting, close to tears, at the deserted table. And although normal conversation was resumed for the rest of the evening, the exchange had left a feeling of animosity that had not been resolved.

Julia straightened. She was *not* going to waste a free afternoon moping round the house. The art gallery was staging a month-long Monet exhibition, and this was the ideal chance to view it. Decision taken, she lost no time in slipping on her jacket, retrieving her handbag and leaving the house.

James Monroe saw her before she was aware of him. She was on one of the benches gazing straight ahead of her, presumably at the large depiction of waterlilies on the opposite wall. Yet judging by her expression her mind wasn't on the painting and it struck him that she looked unhappy.

He hesitated, wondering whether an intrusion might be unwelcome. Since their brief conversation in her classroom they'd barely spoken, exchanging only the odd word in the staff room, and he was well aware that the reason he'd not approached her was that he found her attractive. In any other circumstances he'd have made a move, but married mothers, especially among the staff, were very definitely out of bounds.

Unable to stop himself, he moved forward. 'Julia, hello! Managed to escape the family?'

She turned quickly. 'Oh, hello, James. Yes, I'm making the most of my freedom!'

He came round to join her on the bench. 'I have to say I'm most impressed with this gallery. On a par with the London ones, I'd say.'

'St Catherine's has high standards!' she said mock-seriously.

'So I'm learning. Have you always lived here?'

'No, my family home's in Gloucestershire. My husband's job's based here so we moved down after our marriage, though as he's in the wine industry he does a fair bit of travelling. In the early days I visited the vineyards with him, but that had to stop once the children arrived.'

James nodded sympathetically. He'd been surprised, a week or two ago, when someone had pointed out her husband, whom he'd almost have taken for her father. The received wisdom was that Richard Coulson showed little interest in his sons' education, seldom turning up at parents' evenings or sports events.

'Talking of the children, what have you done with them?'

She smiled. 'Out to tea with friends, hence my free afternoon.'

'And your husband?'

'Oh, he's at the golf club, but that, to coin a phrase, is par for the course!'

It didn't sound like his idea of family life. 'So you took the chance to soak up a bit of culture!' he said lightly.

She laughed. 'Quite!'

'Have you been round the rest of the exhibition?'

'No, actually. I seem to have taken root!'

'Are you interested in seeing it?'

'Definitely. Now I'm here, I want to see it all.'

'Then perhaps we could go round together? It's much more enjoyable having someone to compare notes with!'

'Yes, that would be good.' She stood up. 'Let's make a start, then.'

For the next hour or so they moved slowly through the three rooms of the exhibition, comparing the various canvases and occasionally disagreeing. Julia found him an interesting and amusing companion, and moreover one who gave consideration to her viewpoints, which Richard seldom did.

When they'd come full circle James said, 'I noticed a café as I came in. Don't know about you, but I'm ready for a cup of tea!'

'Not to mention sitting down for a while!'

The café was crowded, other visitors having reached the same conclusion, but they managed to find a vacant table. After a quick consultation, James ordered a pot of tea and two toasted teacakes and sat back in his chair, able to look her in the face for the first time.

'It'll be some time before I'll want to see another waterlily!' he remarked.

Julia laughed. 'Me too! But I'm so glad I came, and as you say, it was much better to have someone to bounce opinions off.'

'Actually painting's a hobby of mine. I'm only average, but it's a great way to relax, especially after a week of handling obstreperous young boys!'

'My son among them! What kind of painting do you do?'

'Landscapes mostly, in watercolour. My family home's in Cornwall so I've stacks of brooding cliffs and stormy seas, though I try my hand at portraits too. Mostly people's pets, but the occasional human being!'

'I should think it's extremely hard to get a good resemblance. Or do you paint your impression of the sitter rather than a photographic likeness?'

He grimaced. 'A bit of both. Trouble is my own impressions don't always go down well with my sitters – who, I hasten to say, are all family members.'

'Your harshest critics, then!'

He nodded. 'Have you any siblings?'

She shook her head. 'No, that's something I've always missed, especially as a child. I had a series of best friends as I was growing up, but it wasn't the same.'

'Well, they can be a mixed blessing!'

Their tea arrived and conversation was interrupted as it was poured and teacakes eaten. Julia glanced at her watch. 'I should be getting back. In any case the gallery closes at five.'

'Did you drive here?'

She shook her head. 'I needed the walk, and parking round here's a nightmare anyway.'

'Whereabouts do you live?'

'Sheldon Drive, which won't mean much as you're new to the area. What about you?'

'I've a flat near the school. I was lucky to find it – one of the masters tipped me off that it was becoming vacant.'

'We'll be going in opposite directions, then.'

James called for the bill, dismissing her attempts to pay her share, and they walked together out of the building, pausing on the pavement.

'Well, thank you for your company,' he said. 'It was an even more enjoyable experience than I was expecting!'

'I enjoyed it too. And thanks for my tea!'

They exchanged slightly awkward smiles. 'See you on Monday, no doubt!'

'No doubt. Hope my son isn't too obstreperous!'

He laughed and stood watching her as she crossed the road. Then, with a sigh he didn't analyse, he turned and set off for home.

FIVE

Mrs Nash had a visitor to lunch, Cicely noted. Which reminded her that she'd been at the Rosemount for almost three weeks now and it was time she invited the children, as she'd promised. Despite her suggestion for a more sociable arrangement the residents were still seated at separate tables, and she felt a flicker of annoyance. She'd mention it again to Mrs Teale; surely she must see the advantages?

She glanced across at the visitor – the youngest person in the room by a good thirty years – and found the young woman looking in her direction, though her eyes dropped as they met Cicely's. She'd probably been pointed out as the newest resident, Cicely assumed, and returned her attention to her lamb chop. She might have been less dismissive had she caught the conversation between Hester Nash and her niece.

'I don't recognize the name,' Madelaine was saying, 'but I'm sure I've seen her before. I just can't remember where.'

'Well, she's quite well known around here,' Hester replied. 'Her photo's often in the paper for one reason or another. Being in that business yourself that's probably where you've seen her.'

Madelaine shook her head. 'I've a feeling I've seen her in the flesh, but a while ago. I think she was involved in some kind of . . . incident.'

'Well, I'm afraid I can't help you there, dear.'

Madelaine smiled and shrugged. 'No matter,' she said. 'So, what have you been up to since I last saw you?'

Hester smiled back. 'Oh, you know, the usual riotous living! Rave parties, drug busts – is that the right expression?'

'I hope not! Seriously, Auntie, I worry about you being bored out of your mind in this backwater! You had such an exciting life with Uncle Jack, going all over the world—'

Hester looked at her fondly, at the high cheekbones, the tangle of fair hair, the earnest expression in her hazel eyes, and felt, as she often did, that she could have been looking at her beloved younger sister, who'd died ten years ago and whose daughter Madelaine was.

'Darling girl,' she replied, 'it's because I had such a wonderful life that I'm now happy to take things more easily! But I'll have you know St Catherine's is far from being a backwater! There are all sorts of things to do and places to go.' She smiled. 'And I in my turn worry about you! It does seem rather a cut-throat profession you've chosen! So what are *you* doing at the moment?'

Madelaine was a freelance journalist, another fact that worried her aunt, who would have felt happier were she affiliated to (and paid by) a regular newspaper.

She grimaced. 'Between scoops!' she admitted. 'I need a nice juicy story to get my teeth into!'

'Well, just be careful what you take on,' Hester advised. 'Now, have you thought what you'd like for dessert?'

'Thank God it's half term next week!' James commented, seating himself next to Julia in the staff room. 'I don't know about you, but I'm shattered! Are you going away?'

'We can't, unfortunately – Richard's working. It's a pity really that it's not the week after, when he'll be touring the French vineyards and I could have taken the children to my parents'.'

'If it's any consolation there's a Turner exhibition at the gallery. Perhaps you'll get the chance to see it?'

She shook her head. 'I very much doubt it.'

'Talk the boys into going with you! *The Fighting Temeraire* and all that! Sterling stuff!'

She laughed. 'Not a hope!'

'Pity. I enjoyed our tour of the Monet.'

Julia didn't reply but her heartbeat had quickened. It almost sounded as though he'd hoped they could repeat the experience. She'd replayed it in her mind so often that she could almost remember their conversation verbatim – like a teenager reliving her first date, she thought mockingly. And as the words registered her face flamed and she hastily bent to pick up a handkerchief she'd not actually dropped.

'Roll on half term!' exclaimed Daisy Ferris, plonking herself down beside them, mug of coffee in hand.

'Just what we were saying!' James replied, with a glance at

Julia's flushed face. 'Let's hope we come back with "renewed vigour", as the dog-food ads used to say.'

Saturday morning and Nina, focused on her shopping, didn't see Abby until she reached out and touched her arm.

'Oh, Abby, I'm sorry!' she apologized with a laugh. 'I was miles away!'

'So I saw! Are you busy, or have you time for a coffee?'

'I'd love one. Just let me pay for this lot and I'll be right with you.'

Mandy's Café was two doors down from the supermarket and renowned for its home-made scones. 'How's your grandmother settling in?' Nina enquired, unloading her carrier bags on to a spare chair.

'Fine, as far as I know. We've not seen her yet, but we're going for lunch tomorrow.' Abby paused. 'There was a removal van outside The Gables yesterday. It's strange, thinking of someone else living there.'

'I know, sweetie, but it'll be easier once you've seen your gran in her new surroundings and you can picture her there. Now, can I tempt you to one of those gorgeous warm scones?'

As they ate they chatted about Danny and about Abby's dental work, but meeting her had reminded Nina of Mia and the fact that she'd not made any attempt to see her since their meeting in the wine bar. The trouble was she'd no idea what, if anything, she could do, but she could at least check with Abby now.

'I trust Mia's none the worse for her fall?' she said lightly as they were about to leave – and immediately realized her mistake. Abby turned sharply.

'What fall?'

Damn! 'Oh, just a mishap at the shop a couple of weeks ago. Nothing to worry about.'

'But you said a fall. Did she hurt herself?'

Abby, though only fourteen months older, had always been fiercely protective of her little sister. When Nina joined the family after the tragedy she wouldn't allow Mia out of her sight, and it had taken weeks of patient understanding before she began to trust Nina to take care of her.

'She slipped off a ladder and bumped her head,' Nina said reluctantly.

'No one told me. How did you hear of it?'

'Look, Abby, it's no big deal, but it might be better if you had a word with her yourself.'

'Oh, I shall!' Abby assured her.

'Are you at work?' Abby on the phone.

'No, it's my Saturday off.'

'Good, because we need to talk.'

'Well, I'll see you tomorrow.'

'No, before that.' Abby paused. 'I've just had coffee with Nina.'

She'll have heard about the fall, Mia worried. Though she hadn't asked Nina not to mention it, she wished she hadn't.

'I'll call for you after lunch,' Abby went on, 'and we can go for a walk in the park. OK?'

'OK,' Mia said resignedly. 'See you then.'

The leaves were turning colour and in the chill wind quite a few had fallen, to lie crisp beneath their feet.

'So what happened?' Abby prompted as they started down one of the paths.

'I was up a ladder rearranging books and the Creep accidentally knocked against it. I fell and briefly knocked myself out.'

Abby halted abruptly. 'You lost consciousness? Nina said it was no big deal.'

'Well, it wasn't really. I was only out a few seconds.'

'Were you checked over?'

'The girls monitored me for twenty-four hours. They were great.'

They walked in silence for a few moments. Then Abby said, 'There's more, isn't there?'

Mia sighed. She might have known she couldn't hide anything from her sister. She said reluctantly, 'As I was coming round I seemed to be talking to Mummy. Telling her to wake up.'

'Were you dreaming?' There was urgency in the question.

'I don't know.' And as her sister looked at her expectantly, she added, 'I hadn't really time to dream, but I do remember being afraid.'

Abby drew a deep breath. 'We've never talked about it, have we?'

Mia shook her head, her eyes on the ground.

'Not that there's much *to* talk about, since we don't remember anything.' Abby paused. 'At least, I don't. Do you?'

Mia shook her head again.

'If there *was* something,' Abby said thoughtfully, 'our minds must have blocked it out – to protect us, I suppose. But it hasn't stopped us dreaming.'

Mia turned to face her. 'You too?'

'Of course, but like most dreams they don't make sense when you try to analyse them.'

'What do you dream about?' Mia asked, almost fearfully.

'Usually that I'm in some sort of cage, looking out through the bars. I can see . . . shapes, a man's and a woman's, but not their faces. The woman might be Mummy, but the man's not Daddy. I'm sure of that.'

They still used the diminutive form when speaking of their parents; it was by those names that they'd known them.

'And that's all?'

'Yes. But I've dreamt it over and over. I still do occasionally. What's in your dream?'

'It's more a feeling, really. A – a presence. That's the only way to describe it. I know someone's there, someone who shouldn't be, but I can't really see him.'

'Him?' Abby repeated sharply.

'Oh yes, it's a man.' She paused. 'Perhaps the one in your dream.'

Abby started walking again, kicking the dead leaves ahead of her. 'Where were we, do you suppose, at the time of the accident?'

Mia shrugged. 'With Grandma and Gramps?'

'It's odd Gran's never told us about it.'

'We never asked,' Mia said simply.

'Perhaps we should, to put an end to the dreams.'

Mia looked doubtful. 'If she wanted us to know, she'd have told us. She probably thinks the less we know, the better.'

'But we're not children any more! I feel stupid sometimes when people ask about our parents, not knowing any details. For instance were they killed outright, or did they die later in hospital?'

Mia gave a little shiver. 'I'm not sure I want to know.'

'I've the feeling Gran blames Daddy for some reason,' Abby said slowly. 'His name's never mentioned, is it, and there are no photos of him, even holiday snaps.'

'If he was driving I suppose he *was* to blame, in a way.'

'We can't know that! Something might have crashed into them.'

She gave an exclamation of annoyance. 'That's what I mean! We don't know *anything*!' She looked at her sister almost defiantly. 'That settles it; I'm going to ask Gran tomorrow. We have a right to know.'

Suzanne Maybury lived in a village further down the coast, a half hour's drive that allowed her time in which to separate the two halves of her life, to review the happenings of the day and plan the evening ahead. Today, though, the worries she'd managed to keep buried during a busy day now crowded in, jostling for position, and as usual it was Terry who came uppermost.

But, surprisingly, there was also Mia; the girl had seemed withdrawn all week, often not hearing Suzie speak to her and making careless mistakes when ordering that were totally unlike her. And when Suzie reprimanded her, her eyes had filled with tears. She wondered uneasily if this aberration was linked with the fall, though she'd seemed fine enough the previous week.

But to go back to Terry and the row they'd had last night: he'd started the new job on Monday, but her relief was tempered by the realization that it hadn't put an end to his fractiousness. He was if anything even more taciturn, scarcely bothering to answer when she enquired after his day, ignoring her interested questions about the job and either immersing himself in some vacuous television programme or endlessly consulting his mobile. And as usual she was torn between wanting to slap him and attempting to pander to his mood.

Finally, tired and depressed, she had lost her temper and listed a number of changes she intended to implement, including his paying his share of household expenses and taking his turn with the housework.

'These last few weeks you've had nothing to do,' she ended, 'but it never seemed to occur to you to clean the house or offer to do the shopping. And now you can hardly be bothered even to be civil! It's just not good enough!'

He'd heard her out uninterrupted, an infuriating smile on his face, and when she finally came to a halt, merely commented, 'So, now we know where we stand!'

'And what does that mean?' she'd demanded, breathing heavily. But, still smiling, he'd merely returned to his mobile and, defeated, she'd gone to bed. She wasn't looking forward to the weekend ahead.

Her eyes on the winding coast road, she thought back to their meeting seven years previously. At the time she was part-owner of a small bookshop in Clevedon but the venture, entered into too hastily following her divorce, was not proving a success. It was becoming increasingly clear that she and her co-owner had diametrically opposing views, both on the stock and on how the business should be run – salient points neither had appreciated – and since Liz was the senior partner, it was her viewpoint that prevailed.

They'd gone to a pub one evening intending to talk through their differences, but were making little headway when a group of four came in. One of them was a friend of Liz's and came over to speak to her, and when he asked if he and his friends could join them, the women, abandoning their business discussion with relief, agreed.

Suzie tried to think back to those first impressions, discounting the irritating traits that the present Terry had acquired and focusing on the instant attraction that had flared between them and her growing sense of excitement. Because back then Terry was *fun*, and there'd been little fun in her life for the last couple of years. With his curly dark hair and laughing eyes he was totally unlike her ex, and the expression in those eyes when they met hers lit instant fires inside her. Within the week they were lovers and three weeks later he moved in with her.

Remembering those heady early days brought a tightness to her throat. Though uncertain about her job, having Terry in her life overrode all else and she'd been happier than she could ever remember. And when, about a year later, her wealthy godfather died leaving her a totally unexpected legacy, the first thing she did was move out of her rented flat and buy the cottage where they now lived. They redecorated it together, and over a period of months visited auctions and showrooms to find exactly the furniture that would complement it, turning it into her ideal home.

Also, with more options at her disposal, she began to consider asking Liz to buy her out of the bookshop and investing in one of her own, so when she read that premises had become vacant in the much sought-after Horseshoe in St Catherine's she hadn't hesitated.

Delighted by all the extra space at her disposal, Suzie chose a colour scheme to emphasize it, with pale blue walls and bleached wood shelving. She also invested in some easy chairs and sofas which, with an ever-ready coffee pot, she hoped would encourage browsing. With her increased range of stock and some judicious advertising, Maybury Books launched itself with considerable panache and soon had a steady stream of satisfied customers. By the end of the first summer and with her accountant's approval, she was able to take on a 'Saturday girl' to help on the busiest day.

Then COVID struck, and with it came disaster. As a 'non-essential' shop, Maybury Books was forced to close and Suzie embarked on a perilous existence trying to run it as a mail-order business. Terry meanwhile had to work from home, which meant he took over the sitting room with his files, his phone and his computer, leaving Suzie to conduct what business she could from the kitchen. Furthermore he refused to tidy his work away at the end of the day when she wanted to relax with the television.

'It's like living in an office!' she'd complain, but he insisted it wasn't worth clearing everything, only to have to set it all up again the next morning.

Being cooped up together twenty-four hours a day also took its toll. At first there was a sense of novelty, and though they were allowed out only once a day for exercise or essential food supplies, the glorious weather meant that in the evenings and at weekends they could spend time in the garden, tending their plants and marvelling at how loud the birdsong sounded without the constant drone of aeroplanes. But as time moved on with no sign of an ease in lockdown, cracks began to appear in their relationship and, she realized now, they had never been satisfactorily addressed.

As she drove into the village she began to regret her outspokenness of the night before. But she'd held her tongue so many times in order to avoid a row, and enough was enough. She could only hope it had cleared the air and they could now resume on a more compatible basis.

Turning into her driveway she noted that she was the first one home. It would give her a chance to make a start on supper, for which, as an olive branch, she'd chosen one of his favourite meals.

Happily engaged in preparing it, it was another half hour before she went upstairs to change, coming to a halt on entering their bedroom. Terry's wardrobe door stood open on an empty space and his backpack was missing from its usual place on top of it.

Hardly breathing, Suzie walked slowly into the room, catching sight of the note propped on her dressing table.

It was fun while it lasted, she read. *Take care.* And a single kiss.

She sank down on the bed, the note in her hand and her mind numb with shock. What had she done? Oh God, what had she done?

Abby said without preamble, 'Granny, where were we when our parents were killed?'

They'd enjoyed a Sunday roast in the Rosemount dining room before repairing to Cicely's room for coffee and the special biscuits she'd bought for them. She was pouring from the well-remembered silver coffee pot and her hand jerked, spilling liquid on to the tray. She recovered quickly.

'Goodness, dear, what a question!' she said lightly, though there was a slight quiver in her voice. 'What brought that on?'

'Mia knocked herself out, and when she came round she was trying to wake Mummy.'

Cicely put the pot down abruptly, keeping hold of its handle and staring at the tray. Then she raised her head and the girls were shocked by her face.

'Knocked herself out?' she repeated faintly. 'How did that happen?'

They exchanged glances. Was she going to ignore the original question?

'I fell off a ladder at work,' Mia replied. 'It – wasn't serious.'

'Gran?' Abby prompted. 'Where were we?'

Cicely straightened and met her eyes. 'At home in bed,' she said.

'It was at night, then? Must have been a shock for the babysitter! How did she hear what had happened?'

'There wasn't a babysitter.'

A pause, then Mia ventured, 'You and Grandpa were there?'

'No.' Cicely lowered herself on to the upright chair behind her.

Her face had paled beneath her make-up and her hands, loosely clasped in her lap, were trembling. 'I very much hoped we'd never have this conversation,' she said.

Her granddaughters stared at her, curiosity giving way to unease, and Mia reached for her sister's hand.

'But since you've asked,' Cicely continued expressionlessly, 'it's only right that I should tell you.' She lifted her chin, her eyes going from one of them to the other. 'The truth is that your parents died at home.' She paused, moistening her lips. 'Charles strangled your mother and then killed himself.'

For long moments the only sound was the ticking of the little clock by the bed. Then Abby said explosively, '*No!*' and Mia burst into tears.

Their reaction pierced the protective shell Cicely had erected and her face crumpled. She rose quickly and knelt in front of them, gathering them into her arms.

'Oh, my darlings, that was brutal but there was no other way to tell you. I've tried to shield you all these years – and, I admit, myself in the process – but you have a right to know. I'm so very sorry.'

'I don't understand,' Abby whispered.

'None of us did. They seemed so happy together. It was beyond belief.'

'But – what happened?'

Cicely released them and sat back on her heels. 'All we know is that Charles was at a meeting that evening, and according to his colleagues in good spirits. One item on the agenda was postponed, so it ended earlier than expected. And that was the last anyone saw of him. What happened when he arrived home, God alone knows.'

Abby dabbed at her eyes. 'How did he . . .?' Her voice tailed off.

'Stabbed himself,' Cicely said. 'With a knife from the kitchen. Oh, darling—'

'There wasn't a note?'

'No. No explanation whatever.' She looked at them pleadingly, but they remained silent and after a moment she continued.

'Since they were fairly well known in the town there was a lot of publicity and speculation, and when it got to the stage that we couldn't bear it any longer, we left and came here.'

'And changed our name to yours,' Mia said. 'I did wonder about that.'

Her grandmother nodded. 'To avoid anyone making the connection.'

'Did Nina know?' Abby asked after a minute.

'I never told her, but I suspect she soon realized. I don't know how we'd have got through that time without her.'

'So who – found them, and who told us?' Abby asked.

'Someone called to take you to school the next morning, and when you didn't appear she looked through the sitting room window and . . . saw them. When the police broke in a few minutes later, they found you both in Abby's bed. That wasn't particularly unusual,' she added, seeing their exchanged look. 'Although you always started off in your own beds, you often ended up with each other.'

'Were we still asleep, then?'

'It seemed so, and since it was always a major task to get you up in time for school, we hoped that was the case. You were bundled into a police car and driven straight to us.'

She paused. 'As to who told you, the simple answer is no one. At first we explained that your parents had gone on holiday and you seemed to accept it. But you cried every night, Abby, and needed a night-light, and Mia didn't speak for weeks. Later, when you began to ask when they were coming home, we said they'd been killed in a car crash – no one's fault; it seemed the kindest way.

'In my defence, I was blind and deaf with grief and refused to listen when people urged me to get you some counselling. I insisted you were too young to take it in and would soon forget, but it was partly to spare myself. With hindsight it was both wrong and selfish, as your grandfather tried to tell me at the time.'

'But after my fall I was trying to wake Mummy,' Mia said in a little voice. 'That sounds almost as though . . . I saw her.'

Cicely nodded soberly. 'That struck me too, darling. I think perhaps you should have counselling after all.'

Mia shook her head violently. 'No, you were right. I don't want to have to go through it, whatever it was.'

'Well, we can talk it over when you've had time to come to terms with everything.' She looked at their subdued faces. 'Now, if you've no more questions for the moment, how about a cup of restoring coffee and one of these special biscuits?'

And with the answer to their query being so much more momentous than they'd expected, they were only too ready to agree.

SIX

Dorset, March, fifteen years ago

The dinner party for which the ingredients had been hard to find was not an unmitigated success. From the minute the couple arrived it was clear they were in the middle of a row, and Sarah, who had spent most of the day preparing the meal, felt her heart sink. The husband, Toby, was an old friend of Charles and Mia's godfather, while Sarah had known Dinah since teenage days at the tennis club. They'd never been close friends, and it was the two men who kept up the connection.

'Is there anything I can do?' Dinah asked brightly, as Charles started to pour the drinks.

'No, thanks,' Sarah replied, 'everything's under control.' She preferred to be left to her own devices in the kitchen, where everything was to hand and she did not have to keep making detours round a would-be helper. But Dinah, she sensed, wouldn't take no for an answer and, when she excused herself some ten minutes later, followed her to the kitchen.

'Really, Di, I can manage,' she protested half-heartedly, aware that there was no way of dislodging her.

'Then I'll just keep you company while you slave over a hot stove!' Dinah seated herself at the kitchen table and crossed her legs. Sarah noticed she had brought her glass with her, and regretted having left her own in the sitting room.

'So, how are things?' Dinah enquired, her voice brittle.

'Fine, thanks.' Carefully she refrained from passing the question back, but the ploy was useless.

'Wish I could say the same!' Dinah replied, and took a large gulp of gin and tonic.

'Oh?' Sarah bent to lift the casserole out of the oven.

'Toby's having an affair!' Dinah said bluntly.

Sarah, taken by surprise, turned to face her. 'Oh no! Are you sure?'

'Yes, though of course he denies it. Someone from the office – such a cliché!'

'I'm so sorry, Di. Have you just . . . found out?'

'I've suspected for some time, but I tackled him about it this evening and it was pretty clear from his reaction that I'd hit the nail on the head, so to speak.'

He could merely have been shocked by the accusation, Sarah thought, but refrained from saying.

Dinah took another gulp of gin. 'Has Charles ever strayed?'

Sarah stared at her, dumbfounded. How *dared* she? They weren't even close friends! And as if she'd tell her, if he had!

'Certainly not, as far as I know,' she answered stiffly.

'Um. Probably the faithful type. Lucky you!'

The kitchen pinger sounded a welcome interruption and Sarah returned with relief to her cooking. 'I hope everything works out,' she said.

The meal was doomed from the start. Toby looked miserable and Dinah kept up a ceaseless monologue, seamlessly switching from one topic to another without affording anyone else the chance to insert a comment. Sarah caught Charles's puzzled frown, and after a while he determinedly broke in. Dinah, seeming to take the hint, stopped talking and some semblance of normality continued for the rest of the evening.

'What the hell was that all about?' he demanded, the minute the front door had closed behind them.

'She thinks he's having an affair,' Sarah said tiredly.

'What? Bloody nonsense!'

'You can't know that!' she protested.

'I know Toby, and I'd say it's highly unlikely. In any case, why did they have to inflict it on us, and when you'd gone to so much trouble with that meal? It was delicious, by the way, darling. I'm sorry they didn't do it justice!'

'Well, at least you did!' Sarah said with a smile.

But later, while getting ready for bed, a sudden memory of Luke's face close to hers brought a shiver of excitement that she hastily dispelled. Was she, like Charles, the faithful type? she wondered, and, not daring to pursue the thought, went to brush her teeth.

Faithfulness or the lack of it must, however, have remained in her consciousness, because that night she dreamt Luke was making passionate love to her and awoke bathed in sweat with a pounding heart. For several long minutes she lay in the darkness, fighting the lingering desire and the feeling of shame that came with it. Eventually she crept out of bed, went to the en suite and sluiced her face under the cold tap before carefully inserting herself back under the duvet beside her sleeping husband.

On the second Thursday of every month Sarah's book group met to discuss the novel they'd read. The evening was social as much as literary and they took turns in hosting it. That month it was held at the home of Emily Barton, whose daughter went to the same school as Abby, and they were discussing *Anna Karenina*.

'Pretty steamy, wasn't it?' Wendy Grey commented.

There were murmurs of agreement.

'I don't know about you,' observed Gemma King, 'but I could just do with a handsome cavalry officer! Harry's doing my head in at the moment!'

Everyone laughed, but Louise Price, who enjoyed analysing real-life emotions as well as literary ones, leaned forward. 'Seriously, though, have any of you ever had an affair?'

'Hey!' Emily protested. 'What is this, truth or dare?'

'But has anyone? We're all friends here, surely we can be honest?'

'You be as honest as you like!' declared Cathy Reid. 'I'm keeping schtum!'

Louise leaned back triumphantly. 'So you have!' she exclaimed.

'I didn't say that!'

'As good as!' Louise surveyed them defiantly. 'All right, if you're all being coy I'll be the first to own up. I dabbled myself several years ago, before we came here.'

Everyone spoke at once.

'Really?'

'Who was he?'

'Did Jeff find out?'

Louise smiled. 'He was one of the instructors at the gym I went to, and no, Jeff never knew. We'd been going through one of those humdrum phases and basically I was bored. Brad started flirting with me and as he was a gorgeous hunk whom all the girls fancied I responded. At first it was just drinks after the session, then it got a bit more heavy. Quite a lot more heavy, actually, but neither of us thought it was serious. Then I discovered he had a wife and baby, and though it was totally illogical, considering I was in a similar position, that put the kibosh on it.'

There was a brief silence, then Wendy chose her words carefully. 'And did you never feel at all . . . guilty? About Jeff?'

'Of course, but it was *because* we were doing something wrong and slightly dangerous that it was so exciting. Forbidden fruit!' She looked from one to the other. 'Anyone else going to confess, or am I the only sinner?'

Cathy sighed. 'OK, I can see you're all agog, so yes, I did have a little flutter a few years ago, and I have to admit I don't regret it. It didn't last long but it was out of this world at the time and added a spice to life that bizarrely carried through to my marriage. From then on David and I were much closer. And before you ask, no, he never found out either.'

'What would have happened if he had?' Gemma asked.

'He'd have been deeply hurt,' Cathy said soberly. 'It was a risk, but at the time it seemed worth it.'

'Would he have divorced you?' That was Wendy.

'God, I don't know. Possibly. We hadn't any kids then.'

'How about you, Louise? Did you regret your fling?'

'No. Like Cathy, it actually improved our marriage.' She gave a short laugh. 'In fact I'd recommend it if your love life lacks lustre!'

'You're very quiet, Sarah,' Emily observed. 'Have you ever strayed?'

Sarah felt herself flush. Why, suddenly, was everyone talking about affairs? And did she almost envy them?

'No,' she answered quietly, 'I've been boringly faithful. Obviously I've missed out!'

'You should try it some time!' Louise advised.

Emily stirred awkwardly. 'OK, can we get back to discussing *Anna*?'

And a little reluctantly they picked up their books.

*　　*　　*

Later that week, as Sarah was belatedly setting out to keep a dental appointment, the house phone rang and with a muttered curse she snatched it up on her way to the front door. 'Yes?'

There was a pause, then, unbelievably, Luke's voice. 'Sarah – Luke. Is this a bad time?'

Her heart leapt into her mouth, memories of her dream flooding back. God, why did he have to ring now of all times, when she was desperately struggling to put him out of her mind? She said breathlessly, 'Yes, it is, yes, actually; I'm already late for an appointment.'

'Give me your mobile number and we can talk while you're en route.'

Her mouth went dry. 'Luke, I really don't—'

'Please.'

'I have to go—'

'Number?'

She gave it rapidly, adding 'Goodbye!' in the same breath. Then, heart hammering, she hurried out of the house.

Her phone rang as soon as she reached the car and a second time as she was parking at the surgery. Switching it to silent she hurried into the building, but in the waiting room a text came through.

You seemed surprised to hear from me, but I said I'd be in touch. I've been away on business for a couple of weeks but I'm back now and I'd like us to meet. I'll call again in an hour or so, when hopefully you'll be free.

She'd just time to read it before the receptionist called her name and, buffeted by a welter of conflicting emotions, she went into the surgery. So that explained the silence; he really had meant to contact her, and had done so on his return – all of which added unwelcome weight to those moments on the dance floor.

Above the drone of the drill, voices from the book group echoed in her head: *It was* because *we were doing something wrong and slightly dangerous that it was so exciting . . . added a spice to life . . . You should try it some time . . . it actually improved our marriage.*

'Thank you, Mrs Drummond. You may rinse now.'

She looked at the dentist in some surprise. The treatment was apparently finished and she'd been totally unaware of it.

*   *   *

Having parked the car in his drive, Luke reread the text he'd sent Sarah. Could he have phrased it better? She'd not seemed exactly delighted to hear from him, and had ignored his last two attempts to speak to her. He hoped he'd not misread the signals. She'd been on his mind constantly since the night of the party – or rather, he corrected himself, since the golf club dinner, when he'd first felt that unexpected surge of attraction which, over the weeks that intervened, he'd tried and failed to explain.

Sarah, for God's sake! Sarah, whom he'd always thought of first as his wife's friend and second as Charles's wife. She was an attractive girl, yes, and he'd always liked her, but she'd lit no fires in him until that night a few weeks ago. But boy! he thought feelingly, had she made up for it since! The business trip had come at totally the wrong time; if they could have met within a week or so while she was still responsive they might now be on an altogether different footing, albeit a clandestine one. He just *had* to see her again!

A tap on the car window made him jump and he swiftly pocketed his phone before looking up to see his wife regarding him, her head quizzically on one side. He forced a smile and opened the door.

'I've been wondering if you were ever going to get out of the car!' she said.

He gave her a quick kiss. 'Sorry, hon, I was just checking something.'

'Something engrossing, by the look of it!'

'No, just a business meeting that went belly-up. But you're back sooner than expected, aren't you?'

Lily had been on a business trip of her own.

'Yes, but unlike yours, my meeting went extraordinarily well. We landed the contract in record time so there was nothing to keep us there.'

'Congratulations!' He opened the boot of her car and lifted out her matching luggage. 'I only got back myself this morning, so I'm afraid there's no food in the house.'

'Fine. I'd no intention of cooking anyway. You can take me to L'Aperitif!'

They walked up the path together and he unlocked the front door. His own case was still in the hall and the house, on a reduced heating programme, felt distinctly cool. He turned up the thermostat, swearing under his breath. Lily's unexpected return meant he couldn't phone Sarah as promised; all he could do was send another text from the privacy of the bathroom, postponing the call and hoping she'd understand.

Sarah received the text with mixed emotions: part relief, part frustration at the delay in putting an end to any contact between them. If she refused to meet Luke as he suggested, he would safely revert to his role of lapsed friend, and their rapport on the dance floor could be dismissed as a meaningless exchange generated by romantic music and too much wine. But was that what she wanted? Or was she secretly longing to relive the sensations he'd stirred in her, and which, during the last couple of weeks, she'd forced herself to discount?

It was as if she was being torn between her conscience and this totally unwanted but surprisingly strong attraction, but of one thing at least she was certain: Charles was the man she loved and intended to spend the rest of her life with, and whatever happened he must never be hurt.

But then, that treacherous little voice reminded her, he need never know – Cathy and Louise had proved that. And even if she did agree to meet Luke it wouldn't be serious, just a brief fling, and perhaps the best way to get him out of her system once and for all. It would be *wrong* – of course it would – but provided they were careful and no one was hurt, what harm could it do?

She went through the weekend like an automaton, her thoughts in turmoil, one minute determined not to meet Luke, the next aching to see him, and by the time the call came on Monday morning she felt physically sick.

A text had preceded it, asking if she was free to speak, and before replying she settled herself at the kitchen table with a cup of coffee to steady her. Then the phone rang.

'Sarah?'

'Hello.' Her voice shook.

'I wasn't mistaken, was I? You would like to meet?'

'I'm honestly not sure, Luke. I still love Charles, you know,' she added, in a last desperate bid to deflect him.

'Of course you do.' Luke, too, had given his erstwhile friend some thought, his conclusions being similar to Sarah's: Charles wouldn't be hurt because he'd be in blissful ignorance – and damn it all, he *lived* with Sarah! Surely he could share her for a brief period, albeit unknowingly?

For himself, he accepted that his marriage would fizzle out within the year. Lily was away more and more often, and, he had reason to suspect, was sleeping with fellow delegates at conferences. What surprised him was that he didn't really care. He guessed they stayed together because they were still fond of each other and, with no alternative in view, it wasn't worth the hassle of divorce.

'Anyway,' Sarah added, voicing her greatest fear, 'we'd be sure to be found out. We're both fairly well known around here.'

'I have the perfect solution. There's been a mix-up over an order at work; it should have been booked for tomorrow but for some reason wasn't and the intended recipient isn't happy. So as he's an important client I offered to deliver it personally, and he just happens to live in Swanage – where, you might remember, Lily and I have a holiday home. I suggest we meet at the Shell petrol station, you leave your car there and we drive down, deliver the order and go on to the cottage for a picnic lunch, which I'll provide. There are gas fires so it shouldn't be too cold.'

A picnic lunch and what else? Sarah's mouth was dry. 'But Mia's only at nursery in the mornings.'

He swore under his breath. 'Surely someone could look after her? It's the perfect opportunity and God knows when we'll get another.'

She moistened her lips. 'Actually a friend and I have an arrangement that gives us each a free day. Once a week we collect each other's child and look after her till about four. Tuesdays happen to be Hannah's free day, but I – could ask if she'd swap this week, though it's very short notice.'

'Perfect!' He seemed to take it for granted she'd agree. 'What time do you drop your daughter?'

'Any time after eight thirty. Several of the mothers go on to work.'

'Great! Then suppose we meet at the petrol station on the A352 at eight forty-five? It will be roughly an hour and a half's drive, then once the delivery's made the time's our own.'

She heard a phone ring and he spoke briefly into it. Then, 'I must go, Sarah, a meeting's just about to start. See you tomorrow.' And he rang off.

She sat unmoving for several minutes. Then, before she lost her nerve, she phoned her friend. 'Hannah, something's come up for tomorrow. I know it's awfully short notice, but is there any way you could do me a favour and swap days this week?'

'Of course, I've nothing planned,' Hannah answered cheerfully. 'Going somewhere nice?'

'I don't know – I've not been before.'

Hannah laughed. 'Enjoy yourself anyway, and I'll see you around four.'

Sarah drew a deep breath. Everything felt totally unreal, but one thing she knew beyond a shadow of doubt. She, Sarah Drummond, the most conventional of women, was on the brink of an affair – and she was looking forward to it!

The following weekend the family drove up to Bath to see Theo and Imogen's new house. Contracts had been exchanged and alterations and redecoration were now nearing completion.

'It'll look bare without any furniture,' Theo had warned them, 'but at least you'll get an idea of the layout, its position and so on.'

It was a lovely March day with blue skies and scudding white clouds that seemed to mirror the lambs in the fields bordering the road. Sarah, buffeted by recurring memories, was in a state of suspended animation, only a part of her consciously in the car with Charles and the children, answering their questions and requests on autopilot. Ahead of them Theo's Bentley led the way, the back of her parents' heads visible in the rear seat. Oh God, she wished Theo wasn't moving, now of all times, when she needed some stability in her life.

As it was, a welter of emotions continued to batter her as her mind relentlessly replayed those hours in Swanage: the slightly musty smell of the closed-up house, its drawn curtains, the stripped bed – and Luke and the wild, uncontrollable sensations he awoke in her, along with the scald of shame. What had she been *thinking* of? Had she been out of her mind? It was the only explanation, a temporary madness that must never be repeated. Nor had the lovemaking been the pleasurable experience she'd expected, more an intense need that had to be satisfied.

She shuddered, forcing her thoughts back to the present as Theo's car started to slow down, signalling they'd reached their destination.

They'd been told it was a converted farmhouse, and this was immediately apparent from the five-barred gate that initially blocked their entrance and the buildings surrounding the courtyard, presumably former byres and stables. Imogen, having opened the gate, waved them through before closing it again behind them.

'Are there any animals?' asked Abby, who had caught the word 'farmhouse'.

'No, sweetie, but I think if Auntie Imogen has her way there'll be a horse here next time you come!'

'Will I be allowed to ride it?'

Charles laughed. 'We'll have to see nearer the time.'

Ahead of them George and Cicely were getting out of the car, and Sarah frowned as her father paused for a moment, resting his hand on the door frame as though for support.

'All right, Dad?'

He turned to smile at her. 'Fine, fine, just a little stiff after the journey. Well!' He looked about him. 'I think "bucolic" is the word!'

'It's certainly one of them!'

They looked about them at the fields stretching on all sides, a distant spire the only sign of habitation. Imogen had gone ahead to unlock the front door while Theo and Charles started to unpack what looked to be a substantial picnic lunch from the Bentley's boot. Sarah was relieved to see they'd also brought some folding chairs; at least they wouldn't be reduced to sitting on the floor for their meal! Holding her daughters' hands, she followed the others into the low panelled hallway.

'One country custom we won't be keeping is using the back door as the main entrance!' Theo joked, coming up behind them with one of the hampers. He directed them down a long tiled passage to the kitchen, where the others had gathered. It was a large room with an efficient-looking Aga, at present unlit, the only item of furniture.

'The units we've ordered are completely in keeping with the age of the house,' Imogen was saying, 'and we'll be bringing our own kitchen table, which originally came from a farmhouse anyway.'

George had wandered over to the folding chairs stacked against the wall. He set up two of them and touched his wife's arm, nodding towards them, but she shook her head, going over to look out of the window, and after a minute's hesitation he sat down himself.

'So,' Theo said, 'let's start in the hall and I'll explain the alterations as we go. The floors are pretty uneven, by the way, and there are unexpected steps to look out for, so mind how you go. There are also odd buckets and ladders lying around – the decorators will be back on Monday.'

Dutifully they followed him, the children, Sarah noted anxiously, already restive. Perhaps before lunch they could be turned into the garden to run around for a while. Meanwhile the tour slowly proceeded. What had been grandly known as the butler's pantry had been converted into a bathroom, the room next to it into an extra bedroom. 'For when the stairs get beyond us!' Theo joked.

So to the two front rooms, designated sitting and dining rooms, then up the shallow, hollowed-out stairs to the first floor, where signs of work still in progress were more apparent – a stepladder and a pasting table in pride of place in the main bedroom. Sarah glanced at her father and saw him bite his lip. She looked round, hoping for somewhere he could sit, but the windowsills were narrow and there was nowhere.

She slipped her arm through his. 'Don't know about you, but I'm ready to sit down!' she whispered. 'I think we're coming to the end of the tour!'

He nodded, just as Theo said, 'Well, there you have it! It will all look very different next time you see it, but at least you'll be able to picture us here when we move in.'

'It's going to be lovely, darling!' Cicely exclaimed. 'Thanks so much for showing us over.'

The others murmured agreement, and Theo led the way downstairs, again cautioning them to take care.

'Not the house for kids!' Charles murmured in Sarah's ear, and she nodded agreement.

The children duly had their run around, supervised by their father, an enjoyable picnic lunch followed and then it was time to drive home.

'I'm rather worried about Dad,' Sarah said, as they followed Theo out of the farmyard and waited while Imogen closed the gate behind them. 'He didn't look himself, and kept needing to sit down.'

'Can't say I noticed,' Charles replied. 'What did you think of the house? It has great potential, hasn't it?'

'Yes, though as you said, not for us. I wouldn't have a happy moment with the children running up and down those stairs.'

Sarah was in the middle of a dream about Luke, and the persistent ringing wove its way into it as someone at the door about to discover them. On another level she was aware of Charles slipping out of bed and moving out of the room. The next moment, so it seemed, he was gently shaking her awake.

'Wake up, darling. Bad news, I'm afraid. It seems you were right about George; he's been rushed into hospital with a suspected heart attack and your mother wants you there.'

'What?' She struggled awake, shaking off the strands of the dream and blinking in the light he'd switched on. 'Dad? Oh God, no!'

'It was Theo on the phone. He's with them, but it seems Cicely's insisting she needs you. And I can't even take you, unless we drag the kids out of bed, which doesn't seem fair. They'd be terrified.'

She was sliding out of bed. 'No, of course not. You stay with them.'

This was her fault, she told herself, fumbling in her haste to get dressed, her punishment for what she had done. But not Dad! Oh, please not Dad!

Collecting the car keys carelessly dropped on the hall table in another existence, she let herself out of the silent house.

The next few hours seemed like a nightmare – the drive through dark, deserted streets to the hospital, the echoing corridors. Then her mother's white face and Theo's reassuring presence.

'What happened?' she demanded, looking from one anxious face to the other.

'He wasn't feeling well when we got home,' Cicely explained jerkily. 'Said he had indigestion and didn't want anything to eat. We went to bed a little earlier than usual, and the next thing I knew he was complaining of a pain in his arm and chest. So I dialled nine-nine-nine and then Theo, and he followed the ambulance. I wanted you here, darling, just in case . . .'

Her voice trailed off in a sob and Sarah put her arms round her. 'Of course I should be here,' she said.

So, in the soulless waiting room and fortified by cups of

indifferent coffee, they waited almost in silence for two long hours. Sarah phoned Charles as instructed, but could tell him only that there was no news. And finally, when their nerves were stretched almost to breaking point, their ordeal came to an abrupt end. They were informed that the attack had been mild and no permanent damage appeared to have been done. Once the doctors had seen him in the morning, subject to a number of restrictions, George would be allowed home. Sarah and Cicely promptly burst into tears and it was left to Theo to thank the staff for their care of his father.

When Luke phoned on the Monday, Sarah refused to make any further plans, using her father's illness, shamelessly exaggerated, as the reason for her prevarication. But though she'd convinced herself she could resist him, the sound of his voice dried her mouth and tightened her stomach muscles and with a despairing sigh she had to accept that she was not yet free of him. She'd bought herself some time, that was all, and for the next week or two she did indeed spend time with George, helping Cicely carry out the list of instructions the hospital had provided.

Meanwhile, the date fixed for Theo and Imogen's move was coming ever nearer. He had at once offered to delay it in view of George's illness, but his father wouldn't hear of it.

'Your mother's taking excellent care of me and I'm making good progress,' he insisted. 'You go ahead, and once you're settled in we'll be over to see you again.'

Sarah, however, was dreading the move. Her brother had always been her rock, and his leaving seemed one more instance of the instability of her life.

During lunch at their parents' house on the Sunday before the move, Theo noticed she was subdued, and when she carried a pile of plates back to the kitchen he followed and slipped an arm round her.

'Everything OK, sis?' he asked, and felt her briefly lean against him as though for support.

'Except that you're deserting me in my hour of need!' she answered lightly.

'And what need would that be?' he teased, and was concerned to see her eyes fill. 'Sarah? What is it, honey?'

She brushed away her tears. 'Oh, nothing, I'm just being silly.'

His eyes searched her face. 'Seriously, is anything wrong?'

'Nothing that can't be fixed.'

'Look, you're worrying me. This isn't like you. If there's anything I can help you with—'

'No, Theo, really. I'm fine! Sorry, it's just . . . the time of the month.'

He didn't believe her, but she gave him a bright smile, loaded the plates into the dishwasher and returned to the dining room and, since she'd refused his help, all he could do was follow her.

SEVEN

Present day

M adelaine said, 'I've got an idea for a piece.'

Her companion raised his eyebrows. 'You're never going to *tell* me about it?'

Steve was a fellow journalist and ideas were closely guarded, but he and Maddy had been friends since childhood and she trusted him not to pre-empt her.

'If you give me the chance! It's a cold case; I've read up all the gen but since you always have an ear to the ground you might be able to add something.'

'Go on, then,' Steve said resignedly, 'but you can buy me another pint first.'

Maddy obliged, returning to their table with two brimming glasses. 'I was visiting my aunt a couple of weeks ago,' she began. 'She lives in a hotel in St Cat's, and there was a woman there I recognized but couldn't place. Her name's Fairfax, which didn't ring any bells, but when I got home I asked around and guess what I discovered?'

'No doubt you're going to tell me.'

'It was a cause célèbre, way back. You probably remember it – the Drummond case? Couple found dead, woman strangled, man stabbed. Everyone swore they were happily married, two kids, no apparent motive. Anyway, to cut to the chase, this Mrs Fairfax was the mother of the dead woman. I was a cub reporter at the time and attended the inquest as part of my initiation. I *knew* I'd seen her in the flesh and not just a photo!'

'Have you told your aunt?'

'Of course I haven't! It would make things awkward for her, not to mention upsetting Mrs Fairfax. Though if I *do* come up with a new angle, I should think she'd want to know.'

Steve took a drink of his beer. 'So what *are* you going to do?'

'Well, you know I hate loose ends, and in a case like that there must have been plenty of theories, rumours and so on.'

'Which the police didn't follow up at the time?'

'All right, smart alec, but they might not have had enough evidence back then. A fresh look could reap dividends.'

He shook his head. 'You're on a hiding to nothing with this one, kid.'

'Humour me; I'm intrigued. For one thing, they looked such a nice couple; in one of the photos he had his arm round her.'

'No doubt Dr Crippen cuddled his wife on occasion.'

She sat back with an exasperated sigh. 'OK, if you're not interested, forget it. I'll poke around on my own.'

'Didn't say I wasn't interested, just that you haven't a hope in hell of coming up with anything.'

'You might be surprised!' she said.

After a weekend of abject misery and self-recrimination Suzie had finally pulled herself together, even convincing herself she was well rid of Terry. He'd been a source of increasing worry over the last eighteen months and it was a strain continually having to walk on eggshells or risk having a row.

Now she was free to move on. At forty-two, half her life should still lie ahead of her and she determined to make the most of it, reminding herself that, as her mirror confirmed, she was still attractive. She was also a successful businesswoman with her own home and a job she loved, so what was she whinging about? She'd treat herself to a new autumn outfit and embark on life post-Terry with confidence. And if she didn't meet someone else in the normal course of things, she'd try online dating.

On Thursdays during the school holidays an area in the children's section of the shop was set aside for Storytime, the under-fives catered for from ten o'clock till eleven, the five to tens from two till three. On rare occasions Suzie had been lucky enough to

persuade a children's author to do the honours, but usually volun-
teers from the amateur dramatic society were happy to step in for
a small consideration.

The event had the advantage of bringing in mothers new to the
shop who'd heard of the readings from friends and who, while their
offspring sat enthralled, enjoyed a cup of coffee before browsing
round the shelves and unfailingly leaving with at least one
purchase. Standing at the counter, Suzie would catch snatches
of stories involving dragons and princesses and magic islands
that brought back memories of her own childhood, invoking a
sense of nostalgia.

This was half term and they were unusually busy, exacerbated
by the fact that Mia had left early for a dental appointment. It
seemed every child in St Cat's had decided to visit the shop at the
same time and she was hard-pressed to deal with them, in particular
with two hyper little boys who ran amok between the shelves,
shouting at the tops of their voices while their mothers sat placidly
chatting on the easy chairs.

Closing time had seemed a distant dream, but it came at last
and with profound relief she went to lock the door and draw the
blinds before cashing up, a task she usually shared with Mia. But
as she bent to draw the bolt the door was pushed open, temporarily
knocking her off balance, and she found herself face to face with
a middle-aged man.

'I'm sorry,' she said, 'we're closed.'

He glanced irritably at his watch. 'For God's sake, it's only just
five thirty!'

'Believe me,' she answered tartly, 'it feels like midnight!'

The retort took him aback, and after a minute he commented
more amicably, 'Like that, was it? Well, meet a fellow sufferer
and grant me a bit of leeway.'

'We open again at nine,' Suzie said implacably.

'When, naturally, I shall be at work. As it was, I had to leave
early to get here.'

Not early enough, it seemed. 'I'm sorry,' she repeated.

A flash of annoyance, then he changed tactics. 'Look, I'm only
asking for an extra five minutes, and it'll be worth your while if
I buy something, won't it?'

He glanced past her at the discarded mugs she'd not had time
to clear. 'And I'll help with the washing up!' he added.

The smile came before she could stop it, and they both knew she was lost.

'Five minutes,' she said, moving aside, 'and the washing up!'

'Done!'

He waited while she pulled down the blinds and locked the door. If he's an axe-murderer, she thought fleetingly, too bad!

'Now, can you point me in the direction of books by Michael Haywood?'

She did so, wearily seating herself at the counter and watching him as he moved along the shelf, occasionally taking down a book to read the blurb before replacing it. And it struck her that ironically he was just the sort of man she'd fantasized about – tall, confident, good-looking, roughly her own age. And presumably spoken for. Ay, there was the rub!

She stood up as he approached the counter, book in hand. 'I think this should fit the bill,' he remarked, handing it to her.

'It's had good reviews.' She swivelled the card-reader to face him. 'And there's a sequel due next month.'

'Ah! Perhaps you'd let me know when it's available?' He slid a business card across the counter. 'And before we start clearing up, is there any coffee left in that pot? Or am I pushing my luck?' He made a sudden negating gesture. 'No, forget it! I've held you up long enough and there'll be someone waiting for you.'

'No one's waiting,' she said, and as the phrase echoed in her head she was horrified to feel tears come into her eyes.

'Oh God, I'm sorry!' he said quickly. 'It was selfish of me to force your hand like this.'

She shook her head, reaching for a handkerchief. 'No, *I'm* sorry. Most unprofessional!'

'In all seriousness, though, a coffee might help you unwind, and I could certainly do with one!' He smiled for the first time and she thought again how attractive he was.

Too tired to resist any further she capitulated. 'All right,' she said.

Which is how, five minutes later, they came to be sitting opposite each other, mugs of coffee in their hands – a totally surreal scenario. Suzie envisaged recounting it to Babs, and remembered she'd not yet told her of the split with Terry. Time to rectify the omission. In the meantime her tardy customer was surprisingly easy to talk to, and she found herself discussing books in general – finding, not unnaturally, that they had widely differing tastes – before moving on to weigh up candidates in the local by-election and exchanging views on the latest block-buster TV series.

Coffee finished, he insisted on keeping his promise, helping her to clear away and drying the collection of mugs as she washed them before finally taking his leave with repeated thanks.

It was only when, after again locking up, she returned to the counter to cash up and saw the card he'd left. Printed in burgundy type, it was headed *Distinctive Wines*, with an address and contact number. And, beneath it: *Richard Coulson, Sales Executive*. She tapped it thoughtfully with one finger, wondering if he'd come back for that sequel. And if so, whether he'd stay for coffee.

In fact, Richard's visit to the bookshop had been a spur of the moment decision. Julia had been on his conscience lately; he knew he'd been short-tempered with her, particularly with regard to Jamie, and he also knew how much she'd enjoyed accompanying him on his trips to the Continent. Next week he'd be visiting a region of France she particularly loved, and despite it being a business trip he felt a twinge of guilt.

Originally he'd thought of buying some flowers or chocolates as consolation, before dismissing both as clichés. Then, the previous evening, he'd overheard her speaking to a friend on the phone; they'd been discussing a book by Michael Haywood that they'd both enjoyed, and Julia remarked that she'd not read any of his later work. Which was why he'd checked the publica-tion dates of several on the shelf before selecting the latest. It struck him as the perfect peace offering, and her delighted surprise when he handed it to her confirmed that.

'Oh darling, that's lovely! How clever of you!'

'You've not read it?' he asked anxiously.

'No, and I've been wanting to for some time. It came out last year, I think.'

'The woman in the shop says there's a sequel due next month.' He thought back to that nameless woman, her eyes soft with tears, and wondered fleetingly what had caused them.

They made love that night for the first time in a while, and Richard resolved to keep his temper in check, particularly regarding his younger son. But he did wish Julia would stop pandering to

Jamie. He gathered from Adam that the boy hadn't wanted to join in planned outings over half term, preferring to lie on the sofa watching television or playing a video game. In his father's opinion a game of rounders would have done him more good, but he'd not been around to enforce it.

He sighed, turned over and went to sleep.

'Maddy?'

'Steve – hi!'

'About that cold case you mentioned?'

'Yes?'

'There just might be something worth following up.'

'You're a star! What have you gleaned?'

'Well, there was a rumour the wife had been seen with another guy.'

'Ah *ha*! Who was he, do you know?'

'Nope, you'd have to ask around. I warn you, though, it was looked into at the time but nothing came of it.'

'So where was she seen?'

'On the coast somewhere. Not around here anyway.'

'And who spotted her?'

'Oddly enough, a local woman who was visiting her sister. But she wouldn't commit herself to a positive ID; said she'd only seen her from a distance and in any case didn't know her well. It sounds as though she regretted mentioning it, because she clammed up when the police tried to question her.'

'Any info on this woman?'

'Sorry, again you'd have to do some digging. Look, don't get your hopes up. It might be nothing, but you asked me to keep an ear open.'

'Understood. Thanks so much, Steve. At least it gives me a starting point.'

'Good luck!' he said.

Lola, Tamsin and Mia had been friends all through their schooldays, and her two flatmates were worried about her. Something had been on her mind ever since she'd banged her head, and regular gentle probing had achieved no result. But since the previous weekend, when she'd had lunch with her grandmother, she'd seemed really upset and they didn't know what to do. When she left for work that Saturday, they settled down at the breakfast table for an in-depth discussion.

'So what do we actually *know*?' Tamsin began, refilling their coffee mugs.

'It all started, didn't it, with her being knocked unconscious at work and having some sort of dream, though she was only out a few seconds.'

'We've all had bad dreams, but we don't go on thinking about them for weeks afterwards.'

Lola sighed. 'Well, if she won't tell us what's wrong, let's try to take her mind off whatever it is. How about the theatre? We know she enjoys that. What's on locally, do you know?'

Tamsin checked online and pulled a face. 'It's a Chekhov at the Maggie Smith. Hardly a bundle of laughs.'

'What about Bristol, then? Make it a matinée instead of the evening? Next Saturday will be her free one.'

Tamsin brightened. 'That's a thought. Let's hope for a comedy, but whatever it is, with luck it'll jolt her out of her doldrums.'

And, hoping they'd thought of something that might alleviate the problem, they abandoned their discussion and belatedly began to clear the breakfast table.

Cicely was seated at her bay window watching for Theo's car. He and Imogen had invited her for lunch, 'to see your dining suite in its new home', and although she was looking forward to the outing, her erstwhile furniture was if anything a downside rather than an inducement. She frequently dreamt she was still at The Gables, sometimes seated at that table for Christmas dinner or a birthday tea with George and the girls, and the thought of it in another setting, albeit still within the family, brought a dull ache of nostalgia. Which, she told herself roundly, was extremely stupid and once she'd seen it in its new location such reservations would vanish.

Her talk with the girls last weekend also weighed on her mind, and she was anxious to discuss it with Theo. Since George's death two years ago she had increasingly come to rely on her son's opinion and was hoping he could offer her some advice. And here, she thought, leaning forward slightly to confirm it, was Theo's car turning into the driveway. Banishing her doubts, she picked up her coat and handbag and went down to meet him.

*   *   *

She had to admit the dining suite looked good in the low-ceilinged room at the farmhouse, as did the matching corner cabinet, now filled not with her own Crown Derby but with Imogen's collection of Staffordshire. And, after all, this house had become a second home to both her and George; the furniture had simply moved from one home to another.

She thought fleetingly of the first time she'd been here, when they'd all come over to see Theo's new house – Sarah, Charles and the children, George and herself. Her nails dug into the palms of her hands. Thank God they hadn't known, then, what lay just ahead. At the time George had been her main concern – he'd suffered a heart attack that night, and she remembered the gnawing anxiety of that frantic drive through the dark to the hospital. Luckily, though, they'd had another thirteen years together before the second attack that claimed his life. Whereas Sarah . . .

'And you say you're settling down well?' Imogen asked later that afternoon as they sat over tea.

'Oh yes. Some things aren't entirely to my liking, but that's only to be expected.'

'Have you made any friends?' Theo enquired.

'I wouldn't say friends exactly; that takes time.' A lifetime, perhaps, she thought privately, acknowledging her own lack of them through the years. George had always been enough for her. 'And I have rather been thrust among them,' she added, feeling more was required. 'Alliances were formed long before I arrived, but I'm sure I'll find my slot.'

'No regrets, though?' Theo probed anxiously. 'About leaving The Gables, I mean? I didn't force your hand before you were ready?'

She smiled at him affectionately. 'No, darling, you didn't. You never even mentioned the Rosemount till I told you I was thinking of moving.'

He nodded, satisfied.

'And speaking of the Rosemount, I should be getting back. You don't want to be late for your friend, Imogen.'

Though Cicely had her own car, Theo always insisted that one or other of them should collect and return her. Today, it was arranged that Imogen would run her home, then go on to visit a friend who lived in St Catherine's.

She stood up. 'I'll just visit the bathroom before we leave.'

The floors of the old house were on slightly different levels, and halfway down the passage, as she'd been reminded many times, there was a step leading to a bathroom and bedroom that had been used by Imogen's father when he'd stayed with them following an operation. Cicely negotiated the step with care, used the bathroom, and started back. But as she reached the step one of her heels caught in the carpet and she pitched forward with a cry, one ankle twisted beneath her.

Theo and Imogen came running, exclaiming with concern, and Theo attempted to raise her, stopping at her gasp of pain. 'What is it, Mother? Where's the pain?'

Her face was white. 'My ankle,' she whispered.

'Lean on me, then. Now, can you put your foot to the ground?'

It was immediately clear she could not. Between them, he and Imogen half-carried her back to the sitting room and lowered her on to a sofa, carefully positioning the injured leg on its cushions.

'You will wear those ridiculous heels!' he scolded gently, removing her shoe while Imogen hurried in search of a bandage The ankle was already swelling ominously.

'I'm so sorry!' Cicely murmured. 'How careless of me!'

Imogen returned with an ice pack. 'Try this first, and we'll put on the bandage later.'

'Well, one thing's for sure,' Theo remarked, watching her. 'There's no way you can go back to St Cat's this evening.'

Cicely looked up in alarm. 'But darling, I must! I'll be all right when I get there!'

He shook his head. 'This will take at least a week to heal, during which you wouldn't be able to go down for meals or even hobble round your room. You'll be much better here, where we can keep an eye on you.'

'But I can't put you out like this! You'll both be going to work on Monday, and anyway I've nothing with me – no change of clothes or even a toothbrush!'

'We can take it in turns working from home,' Imogen said practically. 'As to what you need, I'll go to St Cat's as arranged and call in at the Rosemount to tell Mrs Teale what's happened. If you give me a list, I can collect what you want from your room. You won't need it till bedtime, by which time I'll be back from Jan's. Now I'll make up the bed in the downstairs room, so you won't have the stairs to cope with.'

'I'm putting you both to so much trouble!' Cicely moaned.

'Nonsense! It will be good to spend more time with you.'

She shook her head. 'It reminds me of that film, *The Man Who Came to Dinner*. He was invited for a meal and after injuring himself stayed for months!'

Theo laughed. 'Well, we might boot you out if it comes to months, but we'll certainly enjoy your company for an extra week or so.'

'A couple of days, surely,' she protested. 'Apart from anything else, I have several meetings next week, and it's the AGM of the Arts Society!'

'Then you'll have to send your apologies,' Imogen said firmly.

'Let's see how it goes,' Theo advised. 'Now, while Imogen sees to the bedroom I'll make a fresh pot of tea and you can take a couple of ibuprofen with it, to take the edge off the pain.'

And Cicely, used to giving orders, could only lie back and let her family take over.

EIGHT

Since her conversation with Steve, Maddy had wasted no time in embarking on her investigation. An hour or two poring over newspaper archives had furnished her with the names of several people she wanted to speak to, though whether they'd agree to be interviewed was by no means certain. Most important to her mind were friends of Charles and Sarah Drummond, from whom she hoped to learn whether they'd suspected that all was not well with their marriage. Loyalty could have kept them quiet in the aftermath of the tragedy, but with luck they'd feel freer to talk about it now.

Back at her desk, she glanced at the names she'd gleaned of friends and acquaintances who'd been interviewed at the time for their reaction to the tragedy: men at the meeting Charles attended that last night; employees from J.F. Bennett, the firm where he worked; fellow members of the golf club and other societies he'd belonged to. And for Sarah, women who'd been on the same school run, together with friends from the tennis club and a book group,

several names appearing on more than one list. Shock, horror and
disbelief were a universal reaction, but never a hint of a possible
reason for the tragedy.

Several names had to be crossed out after she discovered they'd
either died in the interim or moved away, but to her delight Maddy
had stumbled on the name of the woman who claimed to have
seen Sarah in Swanage before rescinding her statement – a Mrs
Alice Grogan, who lived here in Sherborne. Why had she changed
her mind, and would Maddy be able to persuade her to change it
back again? If so, it could possibly prove a big step forward in
the investigation.

Monday morning, and not just any Monday but the one after half
term. And to add to the stress Jamie was playing up again. He'd
had to be called three times before getting out of bed and now he
was making no attempt to eat his cereal.

'I don't want to go to school!' he whined. 'I've got tummy
ache!'

'Nonsense!' Julia said robustly, aware that Richard was coming
down the stairs with his cabin bag. 'No one wants to go back after
a holiday, but once you get there it'll be fine.'

'But my tummy hurts!'

'Then eat your breakfast, that'll make it better,' she said,
wondering if her class had written their holiday diaries.

Jamie burst into tears just as Richard came into the kitchen.

'That's enough, Jamie!' he said briskly. 'Eat your cereal or
you'll all be late for school.'

'My tummy hurts!' Jamie wailed again.

Julia looked at him more closely. 'He is a bit pale,' she observed
in an undertone.

'He's pale,' Richard rejoined, 'because he's been cooped up
watching television for the past week instead of playing outside
in the fresh air. I must go,' he added, bending to kiss her cheek.
'I'll be back at the end of the week, but in the meantime don't
stand for any nonsense from that young man. He might try it on,
knowing I'm away.'

'We'll be fine.'

Richard nodded. 'Goodbye, boys. Be good for your mother.'

And he was gone.

Julia glanced at the clock. 'Come on, Jamie, just a few spoonfuls.'

'Stop being such a wuss!' Adam said unhelpfully, reaching for the toast.

Jamie, still sniffing, moved his spoon desultorily round the bowl, managing to snare a few Frosties.

It was, Julia feared, going to be one of those days.

Monday morning was always quiet at Maybury Books. Suzie guessed her customers were either going back to work, doing the weekly wash or nursing a hangover. It gave them the chance to log in new deliveries and check orders before relaxing with a mug of coffee.

'How's Terry enjoying his new job?' Mia asked, appreciating his absence.

'Ah, thereby hangs a tale!'

Mia turned to look at her. 'Oh?'

'In a word, we're no longer together.'

'Oh!' Mia said again. Taken by surprise, she was unsure whether this called for congratulations or sympathy.

'It was never going to last,' Suzie said philosophically. 'I've always known that.'

'So you're . . . OK?'

'Definitely.' She smiled. 'As it happens, the man of my dreams came in on Thursday, while you were at the dentist. We had a coffee together!'

Mia's eyes widened. 'Really?'

Suzie laughed. 'Well, we had a coffee, but unfortunately it's not the beginning of a big romance. It's just that he's the kind of man I'd like to have in my life.'

'Perhaps he'll come back?'

'He might, because the sequel to the book he bought is out next month.'

'Well, there you are then!'

Suzie shook her head regretfully. 'From what he said, it's not his type of book at all. It'll be for his wife.'

'Ah!'

'Exactly. But I can dream, can't I?'

The word 'dream' had unpleasant connotations for Mia, but she smiled dutifully as Suzie drained the last of her coffee and stood up. 'Right, back to work. Did you put that Ian Rankin aside for Mrs Jacobs?'

And the working day began in earnest.

Listening to a recital of what her class had been up to during half term, Julia was impressed by the ingenuity of some of the parents and the trips they'd devised, aware that she herself had fallen short. But Adam had just wanted to play with his friends and vetoed several suggestions, while Jamie, as Richard had remarked, hadn't wanted to go out at all. She hoped that now, back in the familiar routine, he'd forgotten the stomach ache he'd complained about.

'Thank you, Simon,' she said, returning her attention to the class. 'That was very interesting. Did anyone else visit the SS *Great Britain* last week?'

A hand at the back went up, but before Julia could respond the phone on her desk rang.

'It's Nina, Julia. Sorry to interrupt you, but I'm afraid we have a problem. I've had Jamie with me for the last hour or so complaining of feeling unwell, and he's just been sick.'

'Oh Lord!' Julia's brain went into overdrive. If a child vomited during school hours the rule was clear: he or she must be taken home.

'Actually,' Nina continued, lowering her voice, 'he doesn't seem at all well. Was he OK when you came in?'

'He said he had tummy ache,' Julia admitted, 'but I thought it was an excuse so as to miss school. I'll get on to Mavis about cover and collect him as soon as I can.'

It took a while to find someone able to stand in for her, and then to hand over lessons for the rest of the day. She also had to arrange for Adam to be brought home at the end of the day. Consequently it was almost lunchtime before she was able to collect Jamie from Nina's office. He was lying on a bed in one of the little cubicles and Julia's heart lurched at the sight of him. As Nina had said, he didn't look well.

'It might be as well to pop into A & E and let them check him over,' Nina advised in a low voice. 'I'm not happy about that pain, which I'm sure is genuine enough, and it would set your mind at rest.'

'I feel guilty now about not believing him,' Julia confessed, 'but he's been making up all kinds of excuses not to come to school.'

'The little boy who cried "Wolf!"' Nina said with a smile. 'Good luck!'

James Monroe was coming along the corridor as they emerged from Nina's office.

'Oh dear!' he said sympathetically. 'Been in the wars?'

'A persistent pain,' Julia said briefly. 'We're off to A & E.'

'A wise precaution. I hope they can sort things out.'

Julia nodded and hurried past him, shepherding the tearful child ahead of her.

The hospital car park was full and it took several minutes of circling before Julia was able to find a slot. As she helped Jamie out of the car he vomited again and, hoping no one had noticed, she hurried him, now bent double, into the hospital. Whether because of his age or the obvious intensity of his pain, they bypassed triage and to Julia's relief were shown into a cubicle where they were shortly joined by a doctor, a tall, thin man who introduced himself as Dr Turner.

His calm voice soothed Jamie, whose crying subsided into hiccupping sobs as he tried to explain where the pain was. The doctor bent forward, gently pressing on his right side, and as he lifted his hand Jamie screamed and arched his back.

Dr Turner turned to Julia. 'Sorry I had to do that, but it's an infallible way of establishing appendicitis, and as you saw, there's not much doubt.'

Julia stared at him aghast. 'Appendicitis? Does that mean . . .?'

'An operation? Yes, I'm afraid so, and the sooner the better. From what he says it's been grumbling for some time and we need to act before it bursts.'

He turned to Jamie. 'When did you last have anything to eat or drink, sonny?'

Jamie went on crying, no longer trusting him, and Julia bent forward urgently. 'Have you eaten anything since breakfast, darling?'

He shook his head.

'And it was barely a mouthful then. What about a drink?'

'Nurse gave me some water when I was sick.'

The doctor looked at Julia. 'Which would have been when?'

'Roughly a couple of hours ago.'

'Good, then we're clear on both fronts. We'll just have to ask you to sign the assent form, Mrs—?'

'Coulson. My husband's abroad this week,' she added, suddenly aware she'd no one to turn to for support.

'Well, by the time he's home again,' the doctor said briskly, 'Jamie here should be well on the road to recovery. There'll be no need for you to stay once the form's signed; he'll be prepared almost immediately and you'll be told when to phone to enquire about him.'

'When can I see him?'

'It's open visiting in the children's ward but it would be wise to wait till tomorrow; he'll be drowsy after the anaesthetic and will probably sleep the rest of the day.'

Suddenly realizing he was to be left, Jamie reached for Julia's hand and hung on to it. 'I want to go home, Mummy! I'll be better in the morning!'

Julia fought back tears. 'Yes you will, darling, but only if we let the doctor take out your appendix, which is causing all the trouble. And you'll be asleep, so you won't know anything about it till it's over and the pain has gone.'

She turned to Dr Turner. 'How long will he have to stay in hospital?'

He was removing his stethoscope. 'Normally twenty-four to thirty-six hours, followed by a week at home to recuperate.'

'Then he can go back to school?'

'Provided he avoids any strenuous activity.' He drew back the cubicle curtain. 'And no contact sports for the next two months,' he added. 'I'll be speaking to you later, Mrs Coulson. Try not to worry.'

As he left a nurse came in and smiled reassuringly at Julia. 'I'm Nurse Hastings, and I've come to get this young man ready for surgery.' She turned to the child. 'Hello, Jamie. Say goodbye to Mummy, then you can tell me what you did over half term.'

Julia looked back at her son on the couch, his wide, tear-filled eyes fixed pleadingly on her face. 'See you tomorrow, darling,' she said quickly, bending to kiss him before her own tears caught up with her. 'Love you lots.' And as instructed she went to sign the form.

God, why couldn't Richard be here? She was having to take

sole responsibility for allowing her son's operation, and the thought filled her with terror. What if something went wrong and he never came round from the anaesthetic? It would be her fault!

With thundering heart she signed on the dotted line and stumbled back to the car. Jamie's satchel was in the footwell and, unable to hold back any longer, she broke down in a storm of tears. It was some minutes before she recovered enough to raise her head and fumble for a handkerchief but her breathing was still ragged and her throat thick with tears. It was, in fact, the worst possible moment for her mobile to ring.

She gazed at it in something approaching panic and, when she didn't recognize the number, considered letting it go to voicemail. But suppose it was someone from the hospital? For the next week or so she wouldn't dare ignore any calls.

Reluctantly she lifted it and said, a little indistinctly, 'Hello?'

'Julia? It's James.' A pause, then again, 'Julia?'

'Yes,' she said, her voice clogged. 'Hello.'

His voice sharpened. 'Are you all right? I was just calling to check Jamie's—'

'It's appendicitis,' she said. 'I've just left him to get prepped for the operation.'

'God, I'm sorry. Poor little guy! And poor you! Have you contacted your husband?'

'Not yet – he's in France this week.'

'Rotten timing! How about your family? Could they help?'

'My parents would come if I asked but I don't want to worry them – Dad had a cancer scare a few months ago. And I'll be fine once the operation's over. I'll have to be, for Adam. Charlie's mother's bringing him home this afternoon, but I can't keep imposing on her.'

'How long will Jamie be off school?'

'Two or three days in hospital, then a week at home. It'll be no problem while he's still here – I can visit in the lunch hour and after school – but once he's released, of course I'll have to stay home.'

'Couldn't your husband step in, work from home for a day or two? He'll be back by then, won't he?'

'Unfortunately I don't think that would work.'

James waited for elucidation but it didn't come, and from what he'd heard of Richard Coulson he didn't sound the caring type anyway.

'Mavis will probably get someone from an agency,' she continued after a minute. 'But I'll have to prepare all the lessons to hand over, which is an additional headache.'

'I can imagine. Well, in the meantime Jamie's in the best place and I'm sure he'll sail through the op and spend the rest of the term bragging about it!'

That sounded more like Adam, but Julia smiled. 'I'm sure he will!' she said.

It was some hours later and James stood at the window of his flat staring down at the darkening street. He was being a bloody fool and he knew it. He wished now he'd not phoned Julia, because hearing her voice clogged with tears had ignited a powerful desire to comfort her – let's not mince matters, he told himself: to *hold* her and comfort her – which set in train a host of conflicting emotions he'd been trying to suppress since that afternoon at the gallery.

She was *married*, for God's sake, and the fact that he didn't like what he knew of her husband had absolutely no bearing on the case. He glanced at his watch. Nine thirty. *I'll be fine once the operation's over*, she'd said, but would she, alone and prey to any manner of worries? She must know there was still the danger of unforeseen complications, and would be for the next couple of days.

He was wondering whether he could possibly justify another call when his mobile rang, and his heart lurched as he saw her name. Telepathy, or what?

'Julia?'

'Hello, James. Since you were kind enough to enquire after Jamie earlier, I thought you'd like to know that all went well. He's back in his ward now but still very drowsy, apparently.'

'That's excellent news. And how about you? Are you all right?'

A smile came into her voice. 'Well, I could have done without Adam asking if he was going to die!'

'God! Kids!'

'He was genuinely worried, James. I've never seen him so subdued.'

He made himself ask, 'And you've spoken to your husband?'

'Yes. He assured me appendicitis these days is very run-of-the-mill and nothing to worry about! Which is all very well for him, over two hundred miles away and with a plate of *andouillette d'Alençon* in front of him!'

Before he could stop himself, James said, 'Could you do with some company?'

There was a long pause, during which he cursed himself silently for his stupidity. Now he really had blown it!

Then she said quietly, 'I could, but I don't think that's a very good idea, do you?'

'Julia—'

'Goodbye, James. See you at school.'

He stood for several long minutes, the phone still in his hand. Did that mean she knew how he felt? Could it possibly mean . . . but no, that was wishful thinking and the sooner he stamped on it, the better.

He leaned forward, both hands flat on the windowsill, waiting for his breath to steady. For better or for worse, something had changed between them and he had no idea what would happen next.

The Maggie Smith Theatre was part of the prestigious Arts Complex, which, since it also embraced the library, the art gallery and the heritage museum, took up the entire northern curve of the area known as The Crescent, the southern curve accommodating the more functional buildings of Town Hall, Law Courts and police station.

Rose and Henry had season tickets, which ensured them their chosen seats in the dress circle for every production. Now, as the audience started to trickle in from the bar, Rose put down her programme and looked about her with a sigh of contentment. It was a pretty theatre, small enough to feel intimate but large enough to accommodate five hundred, and its décor of gold and cream gave an impression of unostentatious luxury of which she thoroughly approved.

A young couple came in and took their seats next to Henry, reminding her that she'd something to tell him.

'By the way,' she said, 'I've some family news: Jessica has just become engaged.' Jess was her eldest granddaughter.

'Oh? Time to buy a new hat, then!'

'She brought her fiancé to Sunday lunch to meet us all.'

'And do you approve?'

'I'll need to know him better before I can answer that, but he seems a pleasant enough young man. He moved into her flat after that unfortunate business in the summer.'

Trust Rose, Henry thought fondly, to allude to murder as 'an unfortunate business'!

'I've an item of news myself, as it happens,' he told her. 'We've been deprived of Mrs Fairfax's company this week, so you won't have the pleasure of seeing her when we lunch on Wednesday. She went to her son's for lunch, sprained her ankle and has been there ever since.'

'A brief respite, then!'

'Oh, she's not too bad. Likes to throw her weight around a bit, but it doesn't get her anywhere and she'll soon realize that. I believe they're bringing her back at the weekend.'

'She'll probably expect to be waited on,' Rose observed acidly, and Henry was spared making a reply as the safety curtain rose and a ripple of anticipation went through the audience. The play was about to begin.

Maddy said, 'It's very good of you to see me, Mrs Grogan. I really appreciate it.'

It was politic to stress her gratitude since considerable persuasion had been needed to secure the meeting.

'Well, you'd better come in, then.'

Hardly an effusive welcome, Maddy thought ruefully as she followed her through the hallway into the sitting room. No sign of coffee or tea either, she noted, taking the chair indicated. Mrs Grogan seated herself on the edge of the one opposite. She looked to be in her fifties, a tall, rather ungainly woman, and she was clearly nervous.

'As I explained on the phone,' Maddy began, 'there's been renewed interest lately in the deaths of Sarah and Charles Drummond – you might have seen articles in the press.' No need to admit they'd been at her instigation. She smiled. 'With all these programmes on television, people are becoming more interested in what are known as "cold cases", and of course there've been considerable scientific advances in the last decade or two, which help with DNA and so on. However, old cases are still more likely to be solved with the help of what people who were around at the time saw or heard or, in the intervening years, have remembered.'

She'd no evidence for that last assertion, which was probably untrue, but hoped it would encourage her hostess's reminiscences. Mrs Grogan knitted her hands together in her lap.

'But this wasn't a cold case, was it?' she said doubtfully. 'I mean, there wasn't much doubt about who did it.'

Maddy made a dismissive gesture. 'But they never discovered a motive. Your evidence might possibly provide one.'

Mrs Grogan looked even more alarmed. 'Look, I need your assurance that if you use anything I tell you, there won't be the remotest hint of where you got the information. My husband doesn't know I'm seeing you, and he'd hit the roof if he found out. He was angry at my speaking out at the time.' Which explained the nervousness. 'Said he didn't want us dragged into the case, it was nothing to do with us and I should have kept my mouth shut.'

Maddy felt a ripple of excitement. 'So that's why you back-tracked on your statement?'

Mrs Grogan flushed and nodded.

'Well, I promise you no names will be given. We never reveal our sources.' Maddy wondered how many times she'd said that. 'So, is there anything else you can add?'

The woman still looked worried. 'I honestly didn't know her well,' she prevaricated. 'I might have been mistaken.'

'But you don't think you were.' A statement, not a question, and it wasn't contradicted.

'So where was she when you saw her, Mrs Grogan?'

She twisted her hands in her lap. 'Well, as I said, she was with this man, whom I *didn't* recognize, and they were going into one of those holiday homes on the front.'

Gold dust! Maddy tried to keep the excitement out of her voice. 'Can you remember which one?'

'I'd need to see it again.'

Not a hope in hell of getting her back there, Maddy knew. 'Could you describe it then? For instance, was it by itself or in a row of houses?'

Mrs Grogan frowned, thinking back. 'As far as I recall it was the end one of three, with a blue front door.'

Which had probably been repainted a variety of colours over the years.

'On the front, you said. Can you be more precise?'

'My sister and I'd been to the Pier Café, and it was as we were leaving that I saw her. I remember saying to Eleanor, "Small world! That woman over there lives in Sherborne." I knew her by sight because she was on the committee of a charity I belonged to, and I'd seen her with her husband at one of their "dos".'

'And this man she was with; had you seen him before?'

A positive shake of the head.

'Would you know him again?'

She looked alarmed. 'I'm not going to any identity parade, you can forget that!'

'Heavens, of course not! I just wondered if there was anything about him you might recognize.'

'Not really. I mean, I didn't stand looking at them or anything; I just caught sight of them as they stopped at the house and went in. It did cross my mind it wasn't her husband, but I assumed he was a business colleague or something. As he might have been,' she added.

'So what do you remember about him?'

'Nothing really. He was quite tall, with darkish hair.'

And that, Maddy concluded reluctantly, was as much as she was going to get out of her. Nonetheless, it opened all kinds of possibilities, and her next step would be a trip to Swanage.

NINE

Rose couldn't now remember when these monthly lunches at the Rosemount had started, but they were a regular and enjoyable fixture in her calendar. They were always held on a Wednesday, partly to separate them as widely as possible from the Saturday coffee mornings, and partly to leave the more traditional Sundays free for family invitations.

Occasionally she and Henry met on other occasions, such as on theatre visits or a coach trip to a stately home, but somewhat to her surprise she was never bored in his company. He was an erudite, widely travelled man and she valued his opinion on a range of subjects, as she had valued her husband's but hardly anyone else's, being an opinionated woman herself.

She was aware that on his part Henry enjoyed her company, since she was far more on his wavelength than any of the residents at the hotel, though for the most part they were pleasant enough.

As was her custom, Rose chose to walk to the Rosemount; she usually allowed Henry to drive her home afterwards, especially now the nights were drawing in. The clocks would go back at the weekend.

As she turned the corner into Marine Drive she met the onshore wind full blast and shivered, drawing her coat more closely about her. The pier facing her at the end of the road had its bleak winter look. It was mainly the haunt of anglers at this time of year though some hardy people – mostly dog-walkers – went for bracing walks along it in all weathers. Rose was not among them, and she turned with relief out of the main thrust of the wind into the road that housed the Rosemount.

Henry was, as always, waiting in the foyer to welcome her. A fact that might have surprised her gossiping granddaughters was that in all the years she'd been coming here, Rose had never even seen his room. A gentleman to his core, he entertained her only in the public rooms.

'Let me take your coat,' he said now, helping her off with it. 'There's a log fire in the lounge, so that and your usual tipple will soon warm you up!'

Being a residential hotel, the Rosemount had no separate bar. Instead, a section at one end of the lounge was screened off and revealed every evening at six o'clock. Wine was available if required at lunchtime, as were pre-prandial drinks if ordered in advance.

Installed in an armchair near the fire, Rose sipped her dry sherry and looked contentedly about her: at Mr Warren engaged in the *Times* crossword; at Miss Derbyshire and Miss Culpepper, together as usual and both busily knitting; at Colonel Latimer and Mr Merriweather discussing a forthcoming rugby match while their wives chatted. It was, Rose thought, a world of its own, co-existing with but separate from the larger universe beyond its doors. There were certainly worse places to be if owning your own home was no longer an option, though, as she'd assured Verity, it was not for her.

'I had some good news at the weekend,' Henry informed her when they were seated at their usual table in the dining room. 'My son phoned to say that he and his family are planning to come to the UK for Christmas. What with COVID and everything, it's a while since I saw them.'

'That's wonderful, Henry!' His only son Edward lived in Toronto, had married a Canadian girl and had two children. 'How long will they be here and where are they making their base?'

'They'll stay in London for two weeks, and have invited me to join them at their hotel over Christmas. It will be a novelty to spend it with children again!'

'I'm so pleased for you. I imagine that hotel will be somewhat different from this!'

He laughed. 'Indeed! I'm told they have all kinds of festivities laid on.'

Rose divided her Christmases between her daughter and her son in Taunton; it had been a difficult year for Justin and his wife, happily now resolved, and it was right that this year Christmas should be celebrated with just their immediate family. She herself would be at Sandstone with Fleur, Owen and the girls. Cassandra was expected home from university, and Rose very much hoped that, despite her recent engagement, Jessica would also be with them.

It was the custom that coffee after lunch was served in the lounge, and by the time Rose and Henry reached it most of the chairs alongside convenient tables had been taken. Seeing them hesitate in the doorway, Mrs Nash, who was seated alone with a table at her disposal, called them across.

'Do please join me, Mr Parsons, Mrs Linscott. There's plenty of room here.'

Gratefully they complied, and Rose realized with some surprise that in all the years she'd been coming here, she'd never had a proper conversation with Mrs Nash. Feeling she should therefore make an effort, she cast about for an opening. It seemed tactless, without any background knowledge, to enquire about family, and she was still wondering how to start when Mrs Nash herself came to her rescue.

'I was speaking to my niece earlier,' she began. 'You might remember her, Mr Parsons, she occasionally comes to lunch.'

Henry nodded. 'She's a journalist, isn't she?'

'That's right. We're each other's only living relative – she's the daughter of my late sister – so we've become quite close. I admit I worry about her, sticking her nose into other people's business; people can turn quite nasty sometimes, when there are things they'd prefer to keep hidden. Still, it's her life and I try not to interfere.' Hester Nash smiled fondly. 'She's quite excited at the moment – she's on to what she thinks might be a scoop, and though she won't tell me what it's about, she says it will be of interest to me! I can't imagine what it might be!'

'How exciting!' said Rose dutifully. 'Does she work for a local paper?'

'No, she's freelance, but she lives in Sherborne. I don't know anyone there, so what it could be about is a mystery! Still, no doubt I'll find out in good time.'

'Let's hope it's a pleasant surprise!' Henry said.

Though reluctant to admit it, Cicely was bored. She'd finished the library book Imogen had retrieved for her, and although there was a wealth of both hardbacks and paperbacks on the shelf, none were to her taste. She'd read the *Daily Telegraph* from cover to cover and completed both crosswords; the idea of daytime television was anathema to her; and she was tired of Radio Four, when not all the programmes were of interest.

Theo and Imogen had taken it in turns working from home, which was good of them, but the fact remained that they *were* working, and therefore not generally available for a chat, let alone a game of Scrabble or whist. They brought her cups of tea or coffee at appropriate intervals, but lunch was a hurried affair and it was only during the evening that they could really be considered company.

It struck her for the first time that she'd become used to having other people around rather than spending time alone as she had at The Gables, and she was surprised to find she preferred it. She'd suggested returning to St Catherine's halfway through the week but had been overruled, partly because her ankle still needed rest but also because neither Theo nor Imogen could spare the time to take her. And she couldn't deny that the wretched thing still throbbed when put to the floor.

Idly she leafed through one of the glossy magazines from the table beside her, noting that on the table of contents her daughter-in-law's name was shown as fashion editor. Any pride she might have felt was, however, tempered by her opinion of the fashions featured, which she considered outlandish in the extreme. Certainly nothing, she was sure, you'd be likely to encounter away from the catwalk.

With a sigh she let it fall into her lap and closed her eyes. A nap would pass the time until the next cup of tea.

She was just dropping off when she was startled awake by the strident ringing of the phone on the table beside her and, struggling into a more upright position, she eyed it doubtfully. It was Theo's day to be home, but he was ensconced in his office at the end of the corridor and would probably not hear it. He'd kindly left her the phone in case she wanted to make a call, so she'd better answer it and take a message.

She was reaching for it when the answerphone cut in and she heard a man's voice, startlingly close at hand, which she vaguely recognized.

'Hi Theo, Guy here. I've mislaid your new mobile number, hence recourse to the landline. As you know, we're in Sherborne spending the week with the family, and we feel there's something you should know. A journalist down here has started digging into what they're calling the Drummond case, and apparently some new information has come to light, though I doubt if it's significant after all this time. Anyway, apologies for inflicting this on you but we thought you should be aware of it, forewarned being forearmed and all that. See you when we get back. Cheers.'

Halfway through the message Cicely's hand had gone to her throat, and as it ended she looked up tremulously to see Theo standing in the doorway. Across the room their eyes held, then he came in quickly and took her hand.

'Don't worry, Mother. As Guy says, it can't be anything significant.'

'But what good will it do, poking around again? Why can't they let her rest in peace?' *Her*, he noted, not *them*.

'You know the press,' he said with some bitterness. 'Anything for a story. I'm sorry you had to hear that message; please just try to forget it.'

Cicely gave a wry smile. 'I think you know you're asking the impossible. Sarah's been on my mind constantly since the other weekend when I told the girls the truth.'

'Then concentrate on the good times,' he advised gently. 'Now, we're just about due for a cuppa, and as I've finished the piece I was working on, I intend to call it a day so we can have a game of Scrabble. How does that appeal?'

She patted his hand affectionately. 'Very much,' she said.

Guy was frowning as he clicked off his phone. 'I hope I did the right thing, leaving a message,' he said. 'It's not the ideal way to pass on something like that. I should have left it and called back later.'

Anya threaded her arm through his. 'Don't worry; you wanted to warn him, and you have. As you said, there's probably nothing in it, but if he thinks Cicely should know, he'll find the right way to tell her.'

She glanced at the local paper on the table beside them. She and Guy sourced their daily news online, but his parents still depended on a wad of newsprint pushed through their letterbox. 'Do these newshounds ever pause to consider the hurt they cause, resurrecting old tragedies for the sake of a story?'

'And not only to the family,' Guy said ruefully. 'Us too; I'd known Sarah most of her life as Theo's little sister, always wanting to tag along, and she'd been your best friend since primary school, hadn't she?'

'Till we went to different unis,' Anya corrected. 'Then, of course, she met Lily.'

'But you were still one of her bridesmaids.' He ran a hand through his hair. 'I've never been able to get my head around it – Charles seemed such a decent bloke. It still gives me nightmares.'

'What gives you nightmares?'

They turned. Guy's mother had come into the room, and Anya, never at ease with her mother-in-law, bit her lip.

'Oh, this Drummond story, I suppose,' Mary Burnside went on, answering her own question. 'I must say, I hoped we'd heard the last of that. You'd already moved away when it happened, but it swamped the whole town, day after day the main item of news. I'm not surprised the family fled.'

'I just called Theo to let him know,' Guy said.

Mary plumped up the cushions on the sofa where they'd been sitting. 'I meant to ask, his mother's moved into a care home or something, hasn't she?'

Cicely would love that! Guy thought. 'Not a care home, Ma, a residential hotel. From what I hear, she seems happy there.'

'Well, I warn you, don't imagine you can bundle me off some-where if your father dies. I shall leave this house feet first or not at all!'

'I'll bear it in mind,' Guy said solemnly.

One reason why Julia had phoned James on Monday was because, although she'd been told the operation had been a success, she was still on edge and in need of reassurance. All evening she'd been expecting Richard to call and – unbelievably – he hadn't. Nor – even more unbelievably – had he been in touch since. They'd not spoken since she'd phoned in distress to report the appendicitis, which he'd more or less dismissed. Had he expected her to call him? But on business trips it was an unspoken rule that she'd only contact him in an emergency. This she had done. The rest was up to him.

James, whom she barely knew, had shown more concern, which was another reason why she'd phoned him. But it had been a mistake; somehow during that call things had shifted between them, and it was her fault. She'd been careful to keep her distance over the last couple of days, and it was almost a relief when Thursday came and, having collected Jamie from the hospital, she began her week-long absence from school.

To her relief, Jamie himself seemed none the worse for his experience – was in fact enjoying being the centre of attention – and she was touched to see Adam's pleasure at having his little brother back home. He was unusually solicitous, and she wondered how long it would last.

She also wondered how she'd greet her husband on his return. At first she'd been hurt by his seeming indifference, but as time passed with no word the hurt had hardened into anger. Admittedly he never contacted her when away on business – out of sight, out of mind – and she'd secretly envied friends whose husbands phoned nightly when away. But this time was different: his son had under-gone an operation – surely he must have felt a modicum of concern? Or was he perhaps embarrassed at his dismissal of Jamie's pain? But no; Richard didn't do embarrassment.

Julia sighed. Matters would resolve themselves as they always did and, since no amount of worrying would change the outcome, she might as well make a start on the boys' supper.

* * *

During the week Mia had become aware that the emphasis in her dreams was subtly shifting towards the male presence. Was this what Abby had been dreaming? *The man's not Daddy*, she'd said. Then, on the Friday morning, halfway between sleep and waking, such a startling thought came to her that she sat bolt upright in bed, both hands flying to her mouth. She desperately needed to speak to her sister, but since they both had a day's work ahead of them, there was no point in contacting her now.

On the way home that evening, however, she lost no time in calling her. 'Have you finished work?' she asked, as Abby answered.

'Yep, Steph and I are just clearing up.'

'Can you meet me at Mandy's?'

The café she was just approaching was only minutes from the dental surgery.

'When?'

'Now.'

Abby's voice sharpened. 'Why, what's happened?'

'I need to discuss something with you.'

'Then go ahead – discuss.'

'Not on the phone. Please, sis. It's important.'

She heard Abby sigh. 'All right, but I hope it won't take long; I'm meeting Archie at six.'

'Ten minutes max!' Mia promised as she turned into the café, welcoming its steamy warmth after the cool evening air. She ordered two lattes and carried them to a table. Minutes later her sister joined her.

'It's about the dreams,' she said, as Abby sat down and reached for her coffee. 'They seem to be – progressing.' She gave a wry smile. 'Probably because of the bang on the head!'

Abby eyed her warily over the rim of her glass. 'Progressing how?'

'I can see the man more clearly now and I'm wondering if he's the same as the one in your dream.'

'Oh, now look—'

'No, listen! The more I think about it, the more it makes sense. Suppose we woke that night – perhaps because of loud voices in the hall – and saw something or someone . . . unusual.' She paused. 'You said you dream you're looking through the bars of a cage; but could they be . . . bannisters?'

Abby's eyes widened and she slowly replaced her glass on the table. 'Are you saying what I think you're saying? That there really was someone there?'

Mia nodded. 'Someone who wasn't Daddy.'

'So . . .?'

'Yes.'

'Oh my God!' Abby breathed. They stared at each other for a minute, then Abby said again, 'Oh my God!'

'We'll have to tell someone,' Mia said shakily.

'Granny?'

'Perhaps not till we've thought it through a bit more. I was thinking of Nina in the first instance.'

Abby nodded. 'Yes, you're right.' She shuddered. 'This could have all kinds of repercussions.'

'I know. That's why we have to be sure. Pool what we seem to remember, and try to piece it together.'

'Phone her now,' Abby urged.

'But you're meeting Archie, aren't you?'

'Oh God, I'd forgotten!' She looked at her watch. 'Actually, I'll have to dash. Can I leave it to you to arrange it? Though how I'll be able to concentrate on James Bond after this, heaven knows!'

'You go. I'll try to fix something for tomorrow.'

Abby finished her latte, got to her feet and, taking her sister completely by surprise, bent down and kissed her cheek. 'Let me know what you arrange,' she said, and, dropping some coins on the table, she hurried out of the café.

Guy and Anya had made a detour on their way home from Sherborne to have lunch with their daughter, who was a GP living in north Somerset, and in the exchange of news she'd mentioned that her twin brother, who lived in Durham, had a new girlfriend. They were recapping on the conversation as they drove home.

'Do you think Matt really is serious about this girl?' Anya asked anxiously.

'God knows.'

'But surely he wouldn't get engaged or anything before we met her?'

Guy smiled. 'He doesn't need our permission, love!'

'You know what I mean. Perhaps we should invite them for the weekend?' Anya made a sudden exclamation. 'Guy, I've just realized – we don't even know her name! Meriel didn't mention it, did she?'

'Don't think so. Look, just leave it; he'll tell us all we need to know in due course.' He consulted the dashboard. 'I'll have to stop for petrol soon, and luckily I can see a filling station coming up.'

Anya was still following her train of thought. 'I just wish we knew her name,' she was saying as Guy, having turned off the road, drew up alongside a row of pumps.

He started to reply, then broke off abruptly. 'My God! Isn't that . . .? Yes, it is! Talk about coincidence!'

And before she could question him he'd left the car and was hurrying over to a man at a pump further down the line.

'Cool Hand Luke, as I live and breathe!'

The man turned quickly, recognition slowly dawning on his face. 'Guy Burnside! Good God! Hang on a minute.'

He disengaged the hose, hung it back in place and replaced his petrol cap before turning back to Guy. 'How are you, after all these years?'

'Fine, fine! And you?'

'Yes, can't complain.'

'What makes it so odd, seeing you like this, is that we've just spent a week with the parents in Sherborne.'

Luke gave a short laugh. 'Lord, living there seems like a previous existence! How is the old place?'

'Much the same.' Guy sobered. 'An odd thing, though. You knew the Drummonds, didn't you? Charles and Sarah?'

Luke went still. 'I did indeed,' he said after a minute. 'I was still down there when it all blew up. Terrible business.'

'Well, unfortunately it's in the news again.'

'What is?' His voice had sharpened.

'The tragedy. Some journalist or other has got it into her head that there were important facts that didn't emerge at the time. I phoned Theo to warn him, but there's a further development in today's paper. They're saying Sarah was seen with a man down on the coast, which might well put a different complexion on things. I hope to God it doesn't rebound on Cicely and the girls; they've made a new life for themselves and the last thing they need is to be dragged into this.'

Guy glanced at his companion, noting to his consternation that the colour had left his face. And realization dawned. 'Oh God, I'd forgotten! You were very friendly with them, weren't you, you and Lily? God, I'm sorry, Luke! Me and my big mouth!'

He paused, but Luke made no comment.

'How is Lily, anyway?' Guy pressed, hoping to backtrack.

Luke moistened his lips. 'She's fine,' he said after a moment, 'but we're not together. We divorced years ago.'

Guy spread his hands apologetically. 'I'd better shut up, before I make any more faux pas!'

'No, it's OK. We're still friends. We meet occasionally for lunch.'

'Well, give her my best.' He hesitated. 'Good to see you again, Luke. And now I'd better get on with what I came for, or Anya will be tooting the horn!'

Luke glanced at the car further along and raised his hand to the woman inside. After a moment she raised hers. Probably hadn't a clue who he was, Guy thought, as Luke went in to pay for his fuel.

He was replacing his own petrol cap when Luke re-emerged and, with a wave, got into his car and drove away.

'Who was that waving?' Anya demanded as Guy returned to the car. 'He looked vaguely familiar.'

'Cool Hand Luke, of all people, from Sherborne! Small world!' He started the car and filtered back into the stream of traffic, frowning slightly. 'I'm afraid I shook him up a bit, mentioning the renewed interest in the Drummond case. I'd forgotten they were close friends. He went quite pale, poor chap.'

'Your mother won't be pleased if it's going to dominate the news again,' Anya commented. 'As for Theo, you've put him in the picture so now let's just forget it and think of more pleasant things. If we hurry we should be just in time to collect Caesar from the kennels.'

TEN

Now that she was at last able to return to the hotel, Cicely was experiencing an unexpected reluctance. Though she'd chafed at the time, it had been pleasant to be cared for by her family and she'd particularly enjoyed the evenings spent together, when, after supper, they'd watch an interesting programme on television, or sit reading in companionable silence, or play three-handed whist; and the choice of occupation was chiefly left to her. She'd not have that much sway once back at the Rosemount.

'Promise me you'll get some more sensible shoes, Mother,' Theo entreated as he drew up in front of the hotel, accepting even as he spoke that his advice would be ignored. 'Your fall could have been much more serious, you know,' he continued, removing her suitcase from the boot.

'Yes, darling, I know, stop fussing. I promise to be more careful.'

And with that he had to be content.

One of the residents was coming down the stairs as they entered the foyer, and he smiled at Cicely.

'Welcome home, Mrs Fairfax!' he greeted her. 'How's the ankle?'

'Much improved, thank you, Mr Parsons. This is my son Theo, who's kindly been looking after me.'

The two men nodded to each other as Margot Teale came hurrying from her private room.

'Mrs Fairfax!' she exclaimed. 'So glad to have you back with us! And Mr Fairfax – good to see you!'

She preceded them to the lift and rang the bell to summon it. 'If you'd prefer to have dinner in your room this evening it could easily be arranged.'

'Thank you, no, Mrs Teale; I shall be quite happy to come down.'

'Just as you wish.' And, as the lift arrived, she returned to her room, duty done.

As arranged on Friday, Mia had phoned Nina after Abby left the café, and she'd invited them to supper the following evening.

'Rob has some do on at the bowls club, so I'll be glad of the company,' she said. 'Come as early as you like, and once Danny's in bed we can have a good old chat over a plate of spag bol! It'll be just like old times!'

As Mia was working that Saturday it was almost six by the time they arrived at the Phillips house. Their ring on the bell was followed by a thundering of feet and the door was flung open by six-year-old Danny.

'I've got a new dinosaur!' he shouted excitedly, waving it in the air.

Nina appeared behind him, laughing apologetically. 'Let them come in, darling!' she chided, moving him to one side. 'Sorry, it was half term this week, and I took him to an exhibition in Bristol. We've had dinosaurs non-stop ever since!'

'It's an Allosaurus!' Danny boasted.

'Oh, I can tell!' Abby assured him solemnly and he stared at her, slightly nonplussed.

'Hi, you two!' Rob greeted them, emerging from the kitchen. 'How are things?'

'Fine, thanks,' Mia said automatically, and it was true that she felt instantly better, surrounded by this happy family. A more detailed and truthful reply would be called for later.

The glass doors to the conservatory were closed this cold evening, and a thick curtain screened it from the sitting room, where a log fire was burning.

'How's your gran settling in at the Rosemount?' Rob enquired, as they settled on the sofa in front of it.

'Quite well, I think,' Abby replied, 'but she went to Theo and Imogen's for lunch and sprained her ankle, so she's spent the last week there. I think she's due back today.'

'I bet the heels were to blame!' Nina said, and they all laughed.

Danny joined them with a bag of plastic dinosaurs which he proceeded to set out on the carpet.

'Ten minutes, then bath time!' his father told him.

Mia leaned back against the cushions and closed her eyes, revelling in the family atmosphere and regretting that she and Abby must later introduce a note of disquiet. She wished fruitlessly that she hadn't banged her head; but then even if she'd not fallen off the ladder, Abby had been having similar dreams. Their possible authenticity had to be confronted.

It was an hour later. Rob, having bathed his son, had left for his engagement and Danny was in bed. Nina came into the sitting room bearing steaming bowls of spaghetti bolognese, which the girls balanced on their laps.

'To be eaten round the fire without ceremony,' Nina instructed. 'And to avoid giving ourselves indigestion, I suggest we postpone all serious topics of conversation until we've finished. So – *buon appetito!*'

Comfort food, Abby thought, remembering other times the three of them had needed it, though never for anything as far-reaching as today. So they chatted about their work, about her boyfriend and about Nina's latest hobby – crocheting; she'd embarked on a number of squares that she hoped would eventually comprise a patchwork quilt.

Then the meal was finished, the plates carried through to the kitchen, and Nina returned to her chair by the fire, regarding the two anxious faces in front of her.

'OK,' she said quietly. 'What's happened?'

The sisters exchanged a glance. Then Abby, her hands knotted together, said starkly, 'We think our dreams are linked.'

Nina's eyes widened. 'You've been having them too?'

'All my life.'

'Oh, darlings,' Nina said softly, 'why didn't I know about this? Why didn't you tell me?'

'It's only lately they've become clearer, but we didn't even tell each other till Mia banged her head.'

Nina turned to Mia. 'You seemed to be talking to your mother when you came round. Was that part of the dream?'

She shook her head. 'I don't remember seeing her, but since I banged my head the dream has changed, become clearer. Before it had always been vague, just a . . . presence really, but now I'm sure a man's there – I can even hear his voice, though not what he's saying.'

A cold hand closed over Nina's heart. Oh God, could they have seen something crucial? Something that could put a whole new slant on the tragedy?

She forced herself to ask, 'And you, Abby? What do you dream?'

'That I'm in a cage, looking out between bars. I can see a woman who looks like Mummy, talking to a man.'

'Your father?'

She shook her head. 'And we're wondering,' she went on after a minute, 'if perhaps it wasn't the bars of a cage I was looking through, but bannisters.'

There was a pause, then Nina said from a dry mouth, 'Can you describe this man?'

'No, it's all very blurry. But he took hold of her arm, and I somehow knew they were arguing.'

Nina said carefully, 'And now that you've compared notes, what have you come up with?'

Abby moistened her lips and glanced at Mia. 'That there might have been someone else in the house that night,' she said.

There was a long silence while the three of them considered the implications. Then Nina cleared her throat.

'Darlings, thank you for telling me this, but you'll appreciate I can't take sole responsibility. It should be passed to someone in authority.'

'They wouldn't take any notice,' Mia objected. 'They're not going to reopen the case based on a dream! They'd just think we were being hysterical!'

'Even so, someone should be told, probably your grandmother in the first instance. I presume she doesn't know anything about this?'

They shook their heads.

'Theo might be a better bet,' Abby suggested. 'He'd know what to do, and it would save upsetting Granny until we have to.'

Theo Fairfax. The white-faced man who had come to Sherborne in those first terrible days and helped pack up the family home for removal to St Catherine's. And who, according to the girls, had undertaken the same task for his mother when she again decamped to the Rosemount. She'd seen him and his wife, of course, over the years she was with the Fairfaxes – they'd been fairly regular visitors – but she usually stayed out of the way on family occasions, and she couldn't say that she knew him.

What interpretation would he put on his nieces' account? Probably that it stemmed from a subconscious build-up over the years, caused by lack of counselling at the crucial time. And he might be right.

'Nina?' Both girls were looking at her, awaiting her reaction to the suggestion.

She nodded. 'Yes, that's a good idea. I'd certainly feel a great deal happier if he knew about it.'

'I'll phone him tomorrow,' Abby said.

Alone in her room after Theo had left, Cicely's mind immediately returned to the phone call she'd inadvertently overheard. Hadn't journalists enough contemporary tragedies to report, she wondered angrily, without having to dig up those in the past? And what 'new information' could possibly have come to light after so long? Nothing could change the fact that Sarah and Charles were dead!

The tears that still overcame her from time to time caused her to sit down suddenly on the edge of her bed, reaching for a handkerchief. Oh God, why oh why did it have to happen? Why couldn't they have continued what had seemed their happy lives, watching their daughters growing into the lovely young women they now were?

She thought back, as she repeatedly did, to the last time she'd seen Sarah, when, after an afternoon's shopping, she'd called at her house to pass on an amusing mishap that had befallen Theo during the house move. And for a fleeting moment she'd wondered if Sarah had been crying. But she'd been her usual calm and welcoming self, and that brief impression was forgotten. Sarah rarely cried; could it, Cicely wondered now, have been significant?

They'd had a cup of tea, Mia perched on her grandmother's knee, until it was time to meet Abby from school, and as they said goodbye Sarah reminded her that she and George were expected for lunch on Easter Sunday. The lunch that was never to happen, the goodbye, though neither of them knew it, that was to prove final.

Enough! Cicely rose to her feet, carefully favouring her injured ankle. Time to wash and change, since she'd insisted on going down for dinner. And she was glad that she had; in her present mood, she was in need of company.

An hour or so later, she was gratified and a little surprised by the apparent pleasure her reappearance elicited. Colonel Latimer and his wife were in the foyer when she emerged from the lift, and he insisted she take his arm so he could escort her to her table.

Once she was seated, several people paused to enquire how she was, and in the lounge after the meal Mrs Hill came to sit beside her. The two women had known each other vaguely for years, belonging to some of the same clubs, but had never spent time in each other's company.

'It's good to see you back, Mrs Fairfax,' she began. 'I hope your ankle has quite recovered?'

'Almost, thank you, as long as I'm careful.'

'I believe you were with your son and daughter-in-law?' she went on, pouring the after-dinner coffee into the cups provided. 'They live nearby, then?'

'Just outside Bath, half an hour's drive away.'

Mrs Hill nodded. 'I feel so sorry for ladies with no family, like Miss Culpepper and Miss Derbyshire. I don't know where I'd be without my daughter and her family.'

Feeling she should make a reciprocal effort, Cicely asked, 'And are they local?' She recalled seeing a rather bossy, efficient-looking woman in her forties collecting Mrs Hill from the bridge club one afternoon.

'Yes indeed, and all very involved in community life. Daphne's President of St Barnabas Mothers' Union, Ronald's a member of the Council and the children go to the college. Dominic's just coming up to his GCSEs and Lisa's a year or so behind.'

Aware that some response was expected, Cicely, who could never remember Theo's job title, volunteered the information that he worked in IT. 'And my daughter-in-law,' she continued, on safer ground, 'is fashion editor of a glossy magazine.'

'Oh, how interesting! Is she very glamorous?'

'I suppose she is,' Cicely conceded, never having really thought about it.

'And your granddaughters?' Mrs Hill prompted gently, when nothing further was volunteered. She remembered the Fairfax family coming to St Cat's, and the interest in the absence of the children's parents. Perhaps, when she knew Mrs Fairfax a little better, she might make a tentative enquiry.

'Abigail, the elder one, is training to become a dental nurse and Mia is at present working at Maybury Books. I believe she eventually wants to become a librarian.'

Mrs Hill nodded, took a sip of coffee and moved the conversation on. 'Are you playing bridge on Tuesday?' she enquired.

'I am, yes,' Cicely confirmed, glad to move on from family topics.

'It occurred to me driving might be difficult, with your ankle still not at full strength. I'd be happy to give you a lift, if that would help?'

In her still vulnerable position the unexpected kindness took Cicely by surprise, bringing a lump to her throat.

'I should be extremely grateful,' she said.

* * *

That evening Maddy was in a pub with Steve, filling him in on her progress.

'I managed to run the Grogan woman to earth,' she told him.

'Yes, I read your piece in today's rag.'

'She was heavy going at first but she opened up eventually, and I thought I'd struck gold, because she saw Sarah and a man going into one of the holiday cottages on the front. She described its relative position and I found it on Google Maps, but as luck would have it the estate agents who handled it in the early 2000s have closed down and there doesn't seem to be any record of past occupants.'

Steve took a slurp of his beer. 'That's tough luck, but par for the course I suppose. It is quite a while ago.'

'I'm not giving up on it; I intend to go down next week and have a good prowl round, see if there's anyone in the house now, though since it's November there probably won't be. People often go back to the same place year after year, so someone might remember him. I know it's a long shot, but it's all I've got.'

'And if you do run them – or him – to earth, what are you proposing to do about it?'

Maddy hesitated. 'I haven't really thought that far ahead,' she admitted.

'I mean, you can hardly go up to him and say, "Were you having an affair with that woman who was murdered, and did her husband find out?"'

Maddy grinned. 'I'd think of something!' she said.

Sunday morning, and Julia was battered by a host of conflicting emotions comprising anger, disappointment and frustration. On his return the previous day, far from showing any contrition, Richard had swept aside her implied rebuke.

'I was surprised you didn't call to ask after Jamie,' she'd said, once they were alone.

He'd looked surprised. 'Julia, I was on business. I'd other things on my mind.'

'More important than your son?'

'Now you're being ridiculous. You'd told me he was in hospital and it was all in hand; what more did I need to know?'

'Richard, people *die* from appendicitis!'

'For God's sake!' He slammed his phone down on the table.

'Why do you have to dramatize everything? I've been on a difficult trip, meeting bolshie customers who needed treating with kid gloves – *in French!* – and correcting mistakes some idiot at head office made in their orders. And as soon as I get home, looking forward to a peaceful weekend, you start whinging about Jamie, which is exactly what you were doing when I left!'

A sound made them both turn, to see Adam standing in the doorway gazing at them.

'Darling . . .' Julia began, starting towards him, but he turned swiftly and ran back upstairs.

'He's all right,' Richard said dismissively.

'Do you *never* consider other people's feelings?' she flared, close to tears.

He stared at her for a moment. Then he said abruptly, 'I've had enough of this. I'm going to the pub.'

And he'd slammed out of the house.

He returned in time for dinner, which was eaten in almost total silence, and the atmosphere, frosty for what remained of the evening, was still unresolved this morning.

By which time Julia, too, had had enough. She needed space to clear her mind and find an acceptable way to restore the status quo.

'I need some groceries,' she announced abruptly. 'I shan't be long.'

And before he could object to staying in with the boys she hurried out of the house and into the car. She'd no clear idea of where she was going, but since she'd have to return with something to validate her excuse, she headed for the supermarket on the edge of town.

As she didn't normally shop on Sundays she was surprised to find the car park almost full, but after circling for a while she was able to slide into a newly vacated slot. She switched off the engine, welcoming the sudden silence, and sat unmoving, staring ahead of her.

Where was this going? This latest altercation wasn't, she accepted, unusual. Either Richard had become more difficult in the last year or so, or she less willing to accommodate him, but they were continually rubbing each other the wrong way and it had to be resolved, for the sake not only of themselves but of the boys. Adam's face in the doorway was etched on her memory, intensifying her guilt.

Suppose, she thought, her father hadn't invited Richard to

dinner that night nine years ago? How different would her life have been? For a start she'd have stayed on at St Olaf's, at least for a year or two. She and Nick might have got back together. Or she might have met someone completely new, fallen for him, married him and had children. But they wouldn't have been Adam and Jamie. She couldn't wish them out of existence.

She pulled herself up, slightly shocked at the direction of her thoughts. Was she wishing *Richard* out of existence, or at least out of her life? Had it really come to that? She took a deep breath, trying to still the accelerated beating of her heart, but her imagination, given free rein, wouldn't be silenced. Fate might even have brought her to St Cat's and the college, where she'd have met James. Then what? What if it was James, not Richard, to whom she returned home each evening?

A wave of undeniable longing swept over her and she had at last to acknowledge the fact that she loved him, wanted him, with every fibre of her body. And much good that would do her.

It was starting to rain, large, ponderous drops that were almost sleet. And she hadn't brought an umbrella. Great! She watched them sliding down the windscreen, welcoming the shield they gave her from prying eyes.

But not entirely. A tap on the passenger window startled her, and it was no surprise to see James standing there, the shoulders of his coat already darkened with rain. She had conjured him up, she thought dully; he always materialized in one form or another when she was at her most vulnerable.

He hesitated, possibly waiting for her to lower the window, then opened the door. 'Julia! I thought it was you!'

'Hello, James.'

A pause, then, 'Would it be OK if I got in for a minute? It's pretty grim out here!'

She nodded and he slid in beside her, pulling the door shut and turning to face her. 'So what are you doing out by yourself on a miserable Sunday morning?' he asked, half-jokingly.

She was too drained to prevaricate. 'I needed some space.'

He frowned. 'Is something wrong? God, it isn't Jamie, is it? I thought—'

'Jamie's fine.'

His eyes searched her face. 'You don't look happy,' he said gently.

'I'm not.'

He waited, and when she didn't elaborate, continued, 'I know it's been a strain, but at least your husband must be home now, so you'll have some—'

And stopped abruptly as without warning she burst into a storm of tears. Instinctively he reached for her, pulling her into his arms and holding her while she sobbed uncontrollably. After a while the sobs began to ease into a series of little gasps and he smoothed the hair from her face as she reached for a handkerchief. She seemed in no hurry to disengage herself from his arms, nor he to release her.

Eventually, with a final sigh, she straightened and gave him a shaky smile.

'Sorry!' she said.

'Don't be. You needed that.' He paused. 'Something's obviously very wrong; might it help to talk about it?'

'I don't see how,' she said wearily.

Again he waited, but when it became obvious she wasn't going to confide in him, he said, 'Well, since you're here I presume you've some shopping to do?'

She nodded.

'So have I, so suppose we go in, and when we've bought what we need we can have a cup of coffee and a biscuit?' He smiled. 'Shades of the art gallery!'

'That would be good.' She pulled down the vanity mirror. 'Do I look like the wrath of God?'

'No, you cry as elegantly as you do everything else!'

She laughed, as he'd meant her to. 'Well, at least it's stopped raining for the minute, so let's make a dash for it.'

Inside the welcome anonymity of the supermarket Julia struggled to restore her balance but her imagination still held sway. Her daydream was continuing, with James beside her going up and down the aisles, reaching down packets from high shelves, helping her find elusive items, and she was conscious of buying more than she'd intended, simply to prolong the contact.

His own purchases, she noticed, were modest: several ready meals for one, some tins of baked beans, a jar of instant coffee. Typical fare for a student or a bachelor, she supposed, and she ached to cook him one of her special recipes.

When at last she called a halt to her buying spree they made their way to the adjoining café and it was then, facing each other, that a certain reserve set in, relating back to their intimacy in the car. For the first time conversation between them was stilted, and it was finally a relief to them both when, their coffee finished, they could return to their respective cars.

Only as they parted was an oblique reference made to what had happened between them. Having unlocked her car, Julia turned back to him.

'Thank you, James,' she said.

When Julia turned into her driveway ten minutes later Richard was at the sitting room window, and he had the door open before she was out of the car.

'Where have you been?' he demanded.

'Shopping,' she replied, bypassing him as she walked into the house. 'As I told you.'

He followed her into the kitchen, watching as she unloaded her purchases on to the table.

'I'm sorry, Julia,' he said quietly. 'I've had an infernal few days, and I took it out on you. I'd no right to, and as you know I find it hard to apologize. But I do so now, unreservedly.'

'It's all right,' she said, wearily turning her face towards him as he bent to kiss her.

But it wasn't really; this particular contretemps might have blown over, but how long before the next one? Fleetingly, before she could clamp down on the thought, she remembered James's tenderness, and wondered whether he'd had any idea how much she'd wanted to throw her arms round his neck.

ELEVEN

Dorset, April, fifteen years ago

Even after Sarah's delaying tactics citing her father's illness, it proved almost impossible to arrange a meeting with Luke, an impasse that left her half-relieved, half-impatient to let the association run its course. How, she wondered, did married people ever manage to have affairs, what with family commitments, children, and friends who took an interest in your social engagements? Cathy and Louise, she recalled, hadn't touched on the more practical aspects.

And the affair, such as it was, was nothing like she'd imagined. The soft lights and sweet music were a distant memory; far from the romantic, light-hearted lover she'd expected, Luke turned out to be intense and selfish in his lovemaking, making her resent all the more the response he still evoked in her. Since Swanage they had managed only two rendezvous, both confined to Luke's car and highly unsatisfactory.

He too was finding the restrictions irksome, leading to his urging her to take risks that had the potential to expose them. His marriage, she knew, was virtually over, and with no children to consider he was more or less a free entity. For her, the stakes were much higher: after this brief lapse she fully intended to spend the rest of her life with her family, and refused to countenance any action that might compromise that.

Once, after one of their clandestine phone calls, she'd gone into the kitchen to find Mia crooning a lullaby to her doll, and promptly burst into tears. What the hell was she doing? This was home! This was her family! How could she risk threatening it? But even as she questioned herself memories of Luke's lovemaking flooded her mind, bringing a wave of weakness, and she accepted that her infatuation had not yet run its course. Just a little longer, she promised herself, then she'd end it. Just a few more meetings.

Meanwhile, somewhat to Sarah's surprise, life continued more or less as usual. She did her charity work, took her turn on the school run, met her friends at book group. If only her life were as normal and uncomplicated as it appeared!

One morning, when she was on edge expecting a call from Luke, the doorbell rang and she answered it to find Dinah, the friend who'd come to that disastrous dinner, on the doorstep.

'Hi!' she said brightly. 'I hope this isn't a bad time, but I'm in need of coffee and sympathy!'

Taken by surprise – they'd never been on dropping-in terms – Sarah had no option but to invite her in. Dinah went ahead of her to the kitchen, the scene of her last confidences, and seated herself expectantly at the table. Sarah silently filled the kettle.

'I just wanted to update you,' Dinah began, 'since you were in at the start of it, as it were.'

'I hope you've managed to sort things out,' Sarah said.

'Not exactly. It turned out Toby wasn't having an affair; I got the wrong end of the stick.'

Charles had been right, Sarah thought. 'That's good,' she said. 'So why the sympathy?'

'Well, he didn't exactly appreciate being accused of it. We had a blazing row and he moved out.'

Sarah turned and stared at her. 'But that was about a month ago!'

'I know.'

'A bit drastic, wasn't it? You must have had rows before?'

Dinah flushed. 'I said some pretty unforgivable things, which really got under his skin. Anyway, he's moved in with his brother for the time being, while we decide on the next move.'

Sarah poured coffee into the mugs. 'I'm so sorry, Di. I presume you've apologized?'

'Yes, once I found out it wasn't true.'

'But he'll come back, surely?'

'I hope so.' She gave a little laugh. 'The ridiculous thing is I'd rather he *had* been having an affair! Then at least he'd have deserved some of the things I said, and I could have been magnanimous and forgiven him!'

Sarah was wondering how to reply when her mobile rang, and she glanced down at it to see Luke's name. To her annoyance she felt herself flush as she switched it off, praying he wouldn't immediately ring back.

Dinah flicked her a glance. 'If that's a paramour,' she said jokingly, 'better not let Charles find out!'

The following week, at Luke's suggestion, she again swapped a free day with Hannah, but an unexpected business appointment forced them to cancel the meeting and she spent her 'special' day at home alone. He urged her to arrange another, but it seemed altogether too hit-and-miss to risk arousing Hannah's suspicions with repeated requests.

After several more unavoidable postponements Luke's patience finally gave out, and he startled her by suggesting they go to his house, Lily as usual being away on business.

At first Sarah demurred vehemently, the violation of Lily's home seeming to emphasize the sleaziness of the affair, but she was eventually forced to admit it seemed the only solution. However, her unease intensified when Luke parked further down the road instead of in his own drive, escalating minutes later into a furious outburst on discovering he proposed to use the marital bedroom.

She was actually on the point of leaving when he finally gave in and with bad grace made up the guest room bed, grumbling as he did so that it would have to be dismantled again almost immediately.

Having started badly, it was an unsatisfactory assignation. Sarah was on edge, fearing Lily might return unexpectedly, and Luke, possibly due to pent-up frustration, was even more impatient and demanding. But at least it served to finalize her decision, and she was able to admit to herself that the hunger had gone and she no longer wanted to be with him. Time to end the affair and try to pacify this overpowering guilt.

Which made it all the more galling when, just before lunch, she received a phone call from Gemma from the book group.

'And what exactly were you up to this morning?' she enquired teasingly.

Sarah went cold, then unbearably hot. 'This morning?' she repeated.

'That's right; with that handsome stranger!'

'I don't know what you're talking about,' she said faintly.

'Like hell you don't!'

What was Gemma even *doing* there? She lived on the other side of town! 'Really, Gem, it was nothing! I just—'

Gemma laughed. 'Methinks the lady doth protest too much!'

'All right, if you must know, he's someone I used to know. We just – happened to bump into each other, that's all.'

'In his house? I saw you coming down the path!'

Sarah closed her eyes on a wave of panic. Why did this have to happen now, of all times? 'Look, OK, but it was a one-off, and obviously I'd be very grateful if you'd forget it.'

'I bet you would!'

'Seriously, Gem. It was just a bit of fun and now it's over.'

'I must say you kept pretty quiet when Cathy and Louise bared their souls!'

'It hadn't started then! I mean, it wasn't—' She choked to a halt.

'Hey, I'm only teasing! Of course I won't say anything – what do you take me for? It was a surprise, that's all. You of all people!'

Sarah drew a steadying breath. 'You promise not to tell anyone?'

'OK, OK, I promise!'

'Thanks, Gemma. I owe you.'

There was a brief pause. Then Gemma said, 'See you at book group on Thursday.' And rang off.

This wasn't supposed to happen. Seducing Sarah, the erstwhile friend of his wife, had promised to be a pleasant pastime, neither side taking it seriously. He'd been totally unprepared for the insatiable craving she aroused in him, giving him no peace night or day and making him bitterly regret ever having started the affair.

Perhaps it had been a mistake, meeting at his house; she'd resisted the idea and he should have listened to her. There'd been undeniable tension between them, and although physical desires were gratified, emotionally they were poles apart.

In an attempt to rectify the situation he phoned in his lunch break, basically to apologize but also to arrange another meeting to compensate. But she immediately interrupted him.

'Luke, we were *seen*! A friend just called to ask who you were!'

He froze. 'What friend?'

'What the hell does it matter what friend? We were *seen*, that's the important part!'

'Hold on, Sarah! Seen where?'

'Coming down your path! I *knew* we should never have gone there!'

He forced himself to keep calm. 'Is this friend likely to say anything?'

'I hope not. I did make her promise, but she was treating it as a joke.'

A joke! 'Well, as long as she keeps that promise—'

'But you see what this means? God knows, we've always been on thin ice and now our luck's run out. We're lucky it was only Gemma, but this is a warning – a yellow card, if you like – and we can't ignore it.'

Panic gripped him. 'Let's not get this out of perspective, sweet-heart; OK, we were seen, which means that in future we must be more careful, but—'

Again she broke in. 'No, Luke, no "in future"! You must see it's too risky! It was never going to last – we knew that – and now's the time to pull the plug before anything more serious happens. It's been great,' she lied, 'but it's over.'

'No! Sarah, listen! OK, this is a wake-up call, but there's no need to—'

'I mean it, Luke. It's over!'

'Look, I'm tied up for the rest of the day, but can you slip out for half an hour this evening? Make some excuse – anything you can think of – and we can thrash it out, I know we can! We can't—'

'It's too risky,' she repeated. 'In any case Charles is out this evening so I'm stuck at home. Look, we had our time together, which was what we wanted, but now it's over, so please don't call again. Goodbye.' And she put down the phone.

He did call, of course, every free moment he had that afternoon, but she didn't pick up, nor did she answer his texts, and his frus-tration grew. OK, they'd had a close shave but that was no reason for such drastic measures. He was convinced that if they met face to face he'd win her round, that she was as much in thrall to him as he to her and she'd soon weaken.

But there was no time to lose; the longer she had to become entrenched in her resolve the harder it would be to shake her, and by the end of the afternoon he'd convinced himself there was only one course of action open to him: Charles would be out this evening, so he'd go round. She could hardly shut the door in his face.

With the weight at least temporarily lifted from his shoulders, Luke returned to the work on his desk.

Sarah remained on edge for the rest of the afternoon, principally because she was dreading meeting the other mothers at the school gates. Luckily Gemma's children went to a different school, but Emily and Louise would be there. Suppose Gemma hadn't kept her promise, and had already phoned them to report what she'd seen?

Her fears proved groundless; there was no hint of secret

knowledge in their manner and she silently apologized to her friend for doubting her. Back home she enjoyed the children's company more than she had for weeks, no longer half-listening for the phone and able to give her daughters her undivided attention.

Dinner was early to accommodate Charles's committee meeting, scheduled for seven thirty. 'I wish you didn't have to go out,' Sarah said suddenly as she passed him his plate.

He smiled. 'Why? Nothing decent on the telly?'

'I could do with the company, that's all.'

He raised an eyebrow. 'Had a bad day, love?'

She closed her eyes to block sudden tears. *Yes, indeed! I spent the morning in bed with Luke, then he wouldn't accept that the affair's over!*

How could she have been so shallow, so self-centred, so totally uncaring towards this man whom she loved with all her heart?

'Kids playing up?' he probed when she didn't reply.

'No, they've been little stars.' She reached out a hand and laid it over his. 'I do love you,' she said unsteadily.

'Glad to hear it, because I love you too. Now, give me my hand back so I can get on with my meal, or I'll be late for this blasted meeting!'

When he had gone Sarah cleared the table and carried the dishes to the kitchen, aware of drawing out each task in an attempt to fill in the time. What was wrong with her? she wondered impatiently. Charles often had meetings and she was used to spending evenings alone, yet tonight for some reason she felt uneasy.

She returned to the sitting room, switched on the television, glanced at it unseeingly for a minute, then switched it off again. Next weekend was Easter, and the parents would be coming for Sunday lunch. She could use her time by planning the meal and making a shopping list. Roast lamb, of course, but what to serve with it? And the dessert?

She collected some recipe books from the kitchen and sat down with pen and paper, making notes as she leafed through them. It was beginning to get dark and after a while she reached up to switch on the lamp. When she'd finished this list of ingredients she'd draw the curtains.

She had stood up to do so when the front doorbell chimed, loud in the silence, and she froze, glancing at the clock on the mantel-piece. Eight fifteen. Who could be calling at this time?

She hesitated. *Why* hadn't she drawn the curtains earlier? Whoever was at the door had only to glance to his or her left to see her illuminated in the lamplight. She straightened her shoulders. This was ridiculous. It was early evening in a respectable neighbourhood; what on earth was the matter with her? Before any doubts could return, she walked quickly into the hall and opened the door, totally unprepared to see Luke on the step.

Her eyes went quickly to the road behind him, but under the light of the street lamp it was deserted. 'What are you doing here? I explained why—'

'We can't leave it like this,' he said quickly. 'At least hear me out!'

'There's no point; I shan't change my mind, so please go before anyone sees you!'

'They won't see me if you let me in!'

'Certainly not! Suppose—' She broke off with a gasp as he gently pushed her aside and came into the hall, leaning against the door to close it.

'Luke, no! You can't just barge in like that!'

'Looks as though I already have! Now, if you'll just calm down we can talk this through sensibly—'

'We've already talked it through!' she cried, angry now at his persistence and trying to steer him to the door. 'There's no more to say!'

He shook her off, becoming angry in his turn. 'I said *calm down*! Stop making such a fuss, for God's sake!'

Aware their voices had risen, she glanced anxiously up the stairs and for a heart-stopping moment thought she caught a flash of white. But no, she must have imagined it. Nonetheless raised voices in the hall might wake the children and she reluctantly let him into the sitting room.

'Now listen to me,' he began quickly, 'this morning was a disaster in more ways than one – I know that. You were right, we should never have gone there – it put both of us on the wrong foot, compounded by your friend seeing us. But we can put it behind us; she's promised to keep quiet, and next time we won't take any risks with the venue.'

Sarah's breathing quickened. 'I keep telling you there won't *be* a "next time"! It should never have started in the first place – we both know that – but it did and for a while it was great. But it was only sex, wasn't it? It's not going to leave either of us broken-hearted!'

This was proving harder than expected and his breathing also accelerated. 'It might only have been sex, Sarah, but it was unbelievable and it's certainly not over for me! You might be able to turn your feelings off like a tap, but I can't!'

She lifted both hands helplessly, palms up. 'Luke, I'm sorry if you're hurt, but this wasn't what we agreed to. "No strings", you said. So . . .'

He caught hold of her arms, his fingers digging into her flesh. 'If you don't feel as I do, why did you let me think you did?'

'It was *sex*, Luke, not love! What I *felt* was purely physical! Please let go, you're hurting me!'

'So you were just playing me all along!' His tone had changed and she felt a prickle of unease. 'Did it give you a feeling of power, making me want you so much? Or was it just a way of getting back at Lily?'

'Of course not!' she denied swiftly. 'Oh look, please don't spoil what we had!'

But he was not to be deflected and gave her a little shake. 'Did it amuse you,' he said in her ear, 'seeing me so desperate? Pity you couldn't boast about it to your friends!' Abruptly he dropped her arms and as his hands moved to her throat hers flew up to intercept them.

'God, if I'd known how shallow you are I'd never have allowed myself to get into this state! You're just a cheap little tease!'

'Luke' – she choked, her fingers frantically clawing at his hands – 'please—'

It was good to see her pleading, good to know that at last he had the upper hand. His grip tightened, the rage misty red in front of his eyes. Then, to his surprise, she stopped struggling, went limp. He loosened his hold and watched, disbelievingly, as she slid to the floor and lay unmoving.

'Sarah?' he said uncertainly, and gently nudged her with his foot. 'Come on, get up! I promise not to do that again.'

She didn't move, and a pulse started beating high in his throat. 'Sarah?'

Almost fearfully he bent down. Her head was turned to the side and her open eyes bulged. God, no! *No!*

He dropped to his knees beside her just as a beam of light momentarily flooded the room, and he realized to his horror that a car had turned into the drive. Charles was home!

Swiftly he rose and, bent below the window level, hurried out of the room and down the hall to the dark kitchen, taking up a position behind the door. Oh God, God, God! What had he done? Surely she couldn't be *dead*?

Above the rushing of his blood and the clattering of his heart he heard the front door open and close. Charles mustn't find him here! Once he'd gone into the sitting room he'd be so centred on Sarah that Luke could slip out unnoticed, but it would be wise to be prepared in case things went wrong. He looked quickly round the room and, as his eyes grew accustomed to the dim light, saw the knife board by the sink. Stepping forward, he withdrew a small blade.

Then came Charles's anguished cry. 'Sarah? My God, darling, what's happened? Sarah!'

Seizing his chance, Luke moved quickly back down the hall, but the fates were against him. A floorboard creaked, and Charles, who'd stumbled to his feet to fumble for his phone, looked up and saw him.

For a moment, stressed as he was, the sight of Luke in his house didn't strike him as odd. 'Have you phoned for an ambulance? What happened, do you know? Did you see her fall?'

Then Luke, frozen into immobility, saw a frown begin to form and, without thought, stepped forward and struck the knife forcefully into his chest. Charles's look of surprise as he fell would be a lasting memory, but now an all-consuming need for self-preservation took over.

He looked quickly round the room, aware from countless television dramas that there must be no trace left of his DNA. What had he touched since arriving this evening? Not the door nor any piece of furniture, only Sarah herself – and the knife.

He took out his handkerchief to delete any evidence, then paused, realizing it too would bear his DNA. What to use? Almost stumbling in his haste he returned to the kitchen, illuminated by the hall light Charles had switched on as he came in, and looked feverishly around. Hanging by the sink was a crumpled tea towel and, using his handkerchief as double protection, he grabbed it and hurried back to the sitting room.

Think! he ordered himself. Follow the sequence of events: first Sarah, then Charles. Steeling himself, he crouched beside her, carefully avoiding her staring eyes, and rubbed the damp cloth over her arms and neck and under the lifeless nails that had so recently clawed at him, before turning to Charles sprawled beside her. Despite the gushing blood the knife was still in his chest and, biting his lip, Luke again used the cloth to lift the dead man's hand and close it round the handle, watching as, having left its prints, it fell back to the floor. Then he rose unsteadily to his feet, aware of a pressing need to vomit but determinedly suppressing it.

Before replacing the cloth in the kitchen he used it one last time to open the front door, moments later having to risk a corner of his handkerchief to close it behind him. Another three minutes and he'd rounded the bend where he'd left his car and was driving away, white-faced in anguish not for Sarah, who had bewitched him, but for Charles, who'd been his friend.

He'd withstood the vomiting, but now a merciless shivering took hold of him, rattling his teeth and causing the car to swerve as his hands juddered on the steering wheel. And through it all, calling on every ounce of willpower, he held his mind suspended, blotting out both past and future.

The lights of an off-licence caught his eye and he pulled in to buy a bottle each of whisky and vodka before driving the final mile home and turning into his drive, mildly surprised to find the outdoor light on as, in another life, he'd left it.

The house felt cold; with Lily away the temperature was set lower and, still shaking uncontrollably, Luke turned up the thermostat before carrying the two bottles through to the kitchen and setting them on the table. He decided to have a hot shower while the radiators warmed up, then he'd settle by the gas fire with the first of the bottles.

Upstairs he undressed slowly, his stiff fingers fumbling with buckles and buttons, and carefully hung his clothes over a chair. Then, taking a thick dressing gown off the back of the door, he went to the en suite and stood for an unmeasured length of time under a stream of scalding water that stung his flesh, turning it scarlet. And still, with increasing difficulty, he held his mind suspended. Finally, having rubbed himself dry and enveloped himself in the warm robe, he emerged on to the landing, already anticipating the promised anaesthetic of the whisky bottle.

But as he turned towards the stairs the half-shut door of the guest room caught his eye and, despite himself, he pushed it open. The light of a street lamp shone through the uncurtained windows illuminating the bed, its sheets still rumpled from his time there – was it really only this morning? – with Sarah.

And without warning all his self-imposed defences collapsed and he gave a groan, his hands over his ears as though to shut out the sounds and sights that assaulted him. Stumbling forwards he launched himself on the bed, burying his face in the pillows that still held the memory of her scent. Sarah! God in heaven, what had he done? What had he *done*? But at least, he defended himself, it hadn't been deliberate. Whereas Charles . . .

He shook his head to dispel the image. He couldn't just leave them there! Why hadn't he phoned the police? He could say he'd called at the house and seen them through the window! No need to give a name. But he must use a call box, and one not too near his home.

About to swing his legs to the floor prior to getting dressed again he stopped. What good would that do? It wasn't as though they could be saved by medical intervention. They were *dead*!

No, surely that wasn't possible! Gingerly he lay back on the pillows, staring up at the ceiling across which the headlamps of passing cars threw fleeting shadows. And as though to punish him for his temporary censorship, memories came flooding back – memories of the early days when he first came to Sherborne and, watching a local rugby match, got talking to Charles. It was Charles who'd nominated him for the golf club, who introduced him to his own crowd of friends and even invited him to his wedding. Charles, whom, less than two hours ago, he had stabbed through the heart.

Though he turned his head from side to side to dispel the memories they continued relentlessly in an unstoppable stream. Sarah, shy and radiant with Charles's ring on her finger, and her bridesmaid Lily, blonde and cool, who had caught his attention and whom he'd married within the year. Then the years of close friendship – theatre outings, picnics, holidays abroad, and all the while Sarah no more to him than the wife of his friend.

So to the estrangement, which both he and Charles had tried

unsuccessfully to end, and the years apart until the fateful night of the golf club dinner.

Luke groaned again, clutching his hair. Why, why, why had he allowed that sudden, unexpected attraction to develop? And it was surely malign fate that threw them together again so soon afterwards. He remembered Sarah in his arms on the dance floor, the feelings she aroused in him. Fool! Criminal fool!

He sat up suddenly, no longer able to bear this room where he'd so recently made love to her. Tomorrow he'd strip the bed and wash the sheets, praying he could also wash away the memories they evoked. In the meantime, the bottle of whisky awaited him and he stumbled in his haste to get to it. Perhaps, if he emptied it, he'd be able to sleep tonight.

TWELVE

Present day

As arranged, Abby phoned her uncle on the Sunday evening. 'Abby!' he greeted her. 'Good to hear from you! How are things?'

'OK really, but there's something we're rather worried about, and we wondered if we could . . . talk it over with you?'

'Too bad you didn't phone yesterday; I was in St Cat's returning your grandmother.'

'I know. Sorry.'

'Well, I'm not sure when I can get over again. I've a busy week ahead.' He paused. 'Can't you just tell me now?'

Although he couldn't see her, Abby shook her head. 'It's not something we can discuss on the phone, and Mia needs to be there too.'

Theo sighed. Teenage girls! Something and nothing, no doubt. 'Is it urgent?'

She hesitated. 'Not urgent, perhaps, but it could be important.'

'Concerning what?'

'Mummy and Daddy.'

Theo frowned. This certainly wasn't what he'd expected. 'What about them?'

'The night they . . . died.'

He straightened, staring at the phone in his hand. 'What about it?'

'We think we might have remembered something.'

God, he knew something like this would happen! He'd tried his hardest to persuade his parents to arrange counselling for the children, but his mother in particular was adamant that they were too young and should be allowed to forget it. He couldn't even blame that bloody journalist, since to the best of his knowledge her digging hadn't reached the national press.

'Theo?'

'Yes, I . . . heard you.' He paused. 'What's brought this on, after all this time? Have you read or heard something about it?'

'No, it's been there all the time but we've only just realized we were both experiencing it.'

'And whatever "it" is could be important?'

'Yes.'

Damn it, he'd have to see them, probably before next weekend. They were obviously upset, and the sooner he could put their minds at rest the better. He checked quickly through his diary.

'I can't manage it before Wednesday, Abby, and it would have to be evening. Would that be OK?'

'Oh yes – thanks! That would be great!' Relief rang in her voice. 'Mia suggests we use her flat. She'll get rid of her flatmates for the evening and cook us something.'

'Very well, I should be able to get there by about seven. Try not to worry in the meantime. See you then.'

'Thanks so much, Theo,' she said.

The following day Maddy decided to follow up the holiday let, in the hope that although the estate agent who'd handled the house had closed, its records might have been passed to one of the others. Sarah's appearance in Swanage could be significant and this was Maddy's last chance of utilizing the information Alice Grogan had unwillingly provided.

It was a grey, drizzly day, hardly ideal for visiting the seaside, and the drive down was more of an endurance test than a pleasure. She parked on the front, pulled up the hood of her cagoule and, gritting her teeth, set off to walk to the house on which she'd placed so much hope. Though it looked as dreary as all the others in the slanting rain, it appeared well maintained, its paint new, its garden trim. It also looked empty.

More in hope than expectation Maddy walked up the path and rang the bell, hearing it echo inside. After waiting a minute she rang once more for luck before turning and retracing her steps. Nor was there any sign of life at its neighbours, hardly surprising at this time of year. All three houses seemed to huddle together for comfort on this November day.

Leaving the car where she'd parked it, Maddy trudged to the town centre and began her round of estate agents. The first four brought her no luck and, disheartened, she allowed herself a coffee break in a warm, steamed-up café to review her prospects. Admittedly they were not promising, but she was determined to complete her task, and if the remainder proved equally negative she could at least abandon Swanage in the knowledge that she'd done her best.

From those remaining on her list, she tracked down the agency that now handled the house, but they'd no knowledge of its history before they took it on. However, the last firm listed did offer a nugget of information. Her ploy of deliberately approaching the oldest-looking negotiator was rewarded when it transpired that he'd previously worked at the firm who'd had the house on their books in the early 2000s. But there, unfortunately, Maddy's luck ran out; he'd no recent information to impart.

'I must put you straight on one point, though,' he added as, disappointed, she turned to leave. 'In those days it wasn't a let; the house was privately owned by a couple from Sherborne who often came down for weekends.'

'Can you remember their name?' Maddy asked eagerly, but the man shook his head. 'Afraid not. I didn't deal with them personally. Nice couple,' he added reflectively, which wasn't much help.

Maddy pondered that point as she returned to the car. Sarah, married and with children, wouldn't have been free to escape alone for weekends, so either she and Charles were the couple in question, or her unknown escort was married with an unsuspecting wife.

*   *   *

James put the last piece of corrected homework on top of the pile and stretched for a minute before getting to his feet and wandering into the kitchenette, where he took a beer from the fridge. The remains of his supper – a gravy-smeared plate – was still on the tray, and with a grimace of distaste he took it to the sink, holding it under the tap before giving it a cursory wipe with a dish mop.

There wasn't anything that interested him on the telly – he'd checked – so nothing to tempt him away from his easel. He'd made some rough sketches while home for half term and it was time he made a start on completing them, particularly as he was hoping to frame one for his mother's Christmas present.

Accordingly he took his portfolio out of the cupboard and, extracting several sketches, sat down to study them. Some were of the family home drawn from various angles; and, as he'd admitted to Julia, three or four featured his favourite subject – brooding skies above the cliffs and storm-tossed seas. Nothing particularly new or inspiring here.

James put them to one side and extracted some more sheets, topmost among them one of his father sitting reading, unaware he was the focus of his son's artwork.

James smiled to himself and then, as he studied the sketch more closely, frowned. It hadn't struck him before, but the old man – addressed as such by his sons since he was in his forties – was indeed looking older. He was in his sixties now, and still, to the best of James's knowledge, hale and hearty. But there were lines his quick pencil had caught that hadn't, surely, been there before, folds of skin hanging a little loosely where all had been firm.

He felt the cold breath of time on the back of his neck. Home was home, unchanging though he himself had moved on, through school, university, a couple of teaching posts and more than a couple of girlfriends. And home necessarily included his mother and father, who weren't expected to change either.

He'd have a word with his brothers at the weekend; they both still lived in the south-west so saw their parents more regularly. He'd been on the point of choosing that sketch for his mother's present, but perhaps not. Perhaps she too would notice new lines, though since she saw her husband every day they mightn't strike her as unusual.

James sighed. He'd finish his father's portrait for his own satisfaction, but in the meantime he had still to choose one for his mother. Fortunately the next sketch provided the perfect solution. It depicted Jasper, the family dog, standing at the edge of the waves, his ears blown back by a strong onshore wind. Barking at the waves was one of his favourite pastimes, and James knew an illustration of this would delight her. He slid the discarded sketches back in the portfolio and moved, still a little reluctantly, to the easel.

The trouble with painting, though, as he'd found before, was that it left your mind free to wander, and his promptly returned to Julia. She was clearly unhappy, and since it had been the mention of her husband that brought on those tears, there was no prize for guessing the cause of them. Could he possibly be abusing her? It didn't bear thinking about, but if he was, how in heaven's name could James find out? And, having found out, do anything about it?

He thought back to those minutes in the supermarket car park. It had taken all his willpower not to kiss her when she lay sobbing in his arms. God, he should never have allowed himself to become so involved! Members of staff had always been taboo, married ones in particular, but Julia had been different from the start. Which didn't help either himself or her.

He wrenched his mind back to his easel, realizing that he'd painted the clouds too dark. A reflection of his mood, perhaps, he thought as he took steps to remedy it. Pity his own emotions couldn't be adjusted so easily.

Having finished her evening meal, Suzie had just settled down to her favourite soap when the doorbell rang. It was a wild night out there; rain lashed the windows behind the thick curtains and the wind roared in the chimney. Who'd be out in this weather?

If the bell didn't sound again, she decided, she'd ignore it. But it did ring, and going reluctantly to the door she called, 'Who is it?'

There was a pause. Then came a voice she knew. 'It's Terry, Suze.'

She stiffened, all the hurt and betrayal she'd felt at his desertion sluicing over her. 'And what do you want?' she demanded, trying to steady her voice.

'Just to speak to you. Please, Suze. It's bloody freezing out here!'

Against her will she slid back the bolt and opened the door. In the light from the hall he presented a pathetic figure dripping with rain, and to her consternation she saw he was wearing his backpack.

'Ten minutes, that's all,' she said firmly as he came inside.

'Cheers! You're a gem!'

She stalked ahead of him into the living room and switched off the TV, her heart beating fast. He dropped the backpack and went straight to the fire, holding out his hands as steam began to rise from his parka.

'What do you want, Terry?' she asked again.

He pulled back his hood, running a hand through his curly hair. 'Another chance. God knows I know I don't deserve one, but I'm desperate.' His eyes dropped away from hers. 'I lost my job and, crucially, I've nowhere to live.'

'Well, that didn't last long! Where have you been living up to now?'

'With the bloke that got me the job, on his sofa. But when he heard I'd chucked it in he threw me out.'

'And why did you chuck it in?'

He flushed. 'I had one too many over lunch. It didn't go down well, and I made things worse by answering back. So I got a bollocking, lost my temper and handed in my notice. And when I apologized and tried to take it back, they wouldn't play ball.' He hesitated, then added in part mitigation, 'I've managed to find another, but it's only bar work in the evenings.'

'So, thinking I'd be a soft touch, you came here.'

He bit his lip. 'If there's anything I can do to make amends . . .'

'Like what?' she challenged.

He lifted his shoulders and did not reply.

'Tell me one thing, Terry. When you left here, was there a girl involved?'

His startled glance was answer enough, before the flush that immediately followed it.

'Well, was there?'

'It was nothing,' he blustered, 'just a flash in the pan.'

'But worth deserting me for.'

He shook his head. 'I was a bloody fool, Suze. It wasn't—'

'How old was she?'

'What's that got to do with it?' he prevaricated.

'Just answer the question.'

His eyes fell. 'Twenty-two,' he mumbled sulkily.

Roughly half her age. It was as she'd suspected, but it smarted nonetheless.

'Look,' he broke out desperately, 'I admitted I've been a bloody fool and I'm not asking for forgiveness, just a bit of . . . charity. Give me a roof over my head and I'll do whatever you ask, help out in the shop, whatever.'

She thought things over for a moment, then drew a deep breath. 'These are my terms, Terry. Since I can hardly turn you out into the rain, you can have the use of the spare room for one week provided you concentrate on finding accommodation. After that, whether you've managed to or not, you'll have to make other arrangements. And since you're presumably earning something from the bar you're working at, you can pay for your board and keep. Finally you can bloody well give that girl the push, if you haven't already done so.'

'It's over,' he muttered.

No doubt she dropped him as soon as he lost his job. There was uncharitable satisfaction in that.

'Then you can take your things upstairs and make up the spare room bed. You know where everything is.'

'You're an angel, Suze!' he proclaimed, retrieving his backpack.

'I'm an idiot,' she corrected. 'You can thank your lucky stars it's such a bad night or you might have had a different reception. And if you haven't eaten, there are things in the freezer. Just don't expect me to wait on you.' And she returned to the TV.

Since Abby's phone call on Sunday his nieces had been on Theo's mind, arousing a somewhat belated sense of guilt. It struck him for the first time that he barely knew them, had, in fact, never spoken to them except in the presence of his mother. Surely he owed it to Sarah to have taken more interest, to have involved himself in their lives *in loco parentis*. Now, to heap burning coals on his head, it was to him they had turned for advice, and he resolved to make himself more available in future.

Unfortunately by the time he reached St Catherine's on Wednesday evening he had a raging headache. It had been coming on all day and he'd meant to take a couple of pills before setting out, but found he'd run out of them. There must be a pharmacy open after hours, he assured himself, and Boots in Linden Road seemed his best bet. What was more, there was street parking, if he was lucky enough to find a slot. And he was lucky, on both counts.

He hurried into the shop, selected his purchase and with an impatient look at his watch joined the queue at the checkout, aware he was running late. The man in front of him glanced round, and Theo gave a start.

'Hey, it's Luke, isn't it? Well I'll be damned! Guy mentioned seeing you in these parts, but I didn't realize you lived in St Cat's!'

Luke searched his face – the beard was unfamiliar – then unwelcome recognition dawned, and with it a chill. 'Theo!' he said slowly. 'Don't tell me we're neighbours? Odd we've never come across each other.'

'Oh, I don't live here, I'm just meeting the girls for a meal.'

'The girls?'

'My nieces, Abby and Mia.'

Luke stared at him. Then he said slowly, 'Charles and Sarah's children?'

'Well, yes, but they're not children now, they're attractive young women!'

Luke moistened his lips. 'And they live here?'

'They do, as does my mother. You didn't know? They moved here straight after the tragedy.' He sobered. 'You've probably heard the whole ghastly business is being dragged up again and, frankly, I'm worried about them. That's why I'm here, actually. They want to tell me about some recovered memories they're experiencing, which they think might be connected with the night in question.'

Luke was staring at him, his face oddly blank.

Theo jerked his head towards the counter. 'Your turn, I think. Good to have seen you, and my best to Lily.'

Luke paid for his purchase and left the shop without looking back, urgently needing to assess this unexpected development. No real need for alarm, he assured himself as he emerged on to the cold street. To his knowledge he'd never seen either of the children, nor they him – and, dammit, they'd been little more than babies at the time. There was no way they could recognize him.

Nonetheless it was unnerving to know they lived here, and the old lady too. He'd only met her once, back in Sherborne, and didn't flatter himself she'd remember him. Even if she did, it was of no consequence; he and Lily had been friends of her daughter.

He frowned as he hurried along the street, hands deep in his pockets. The shock of hearing the family'd been so close all this time had initially overridden what Theo was saying: something about the girls having memories about 'the night in question'. But God, that couldn't be possible, could it? They'd been sound asleep upstairs!

A shiver ran down his back. Though he wasn't superstitious, meeting both Guy and Theo, who knew him from those days, while that bloody woman was pursuing the story in the press, was surely a reason for disquiet. Better to keep his head down for a while.

Theo turned into the driveway of the handsome old house in Regent Road and parked in the slot earmarked for visitors. He'd been here only once before, when his mother wanted his opinion before buying the flat for Mia, and remembered being impressed by it.

He retrieved the bottle of wine from the rear seat and, skirting some flowerbeds – dormant at this time of year – made his way to the front door, where he scanned the row of bells and pressed the one labelled 'Fairfax'.

'Hello?' Abby's voice in his ear.

'It's me,' he said. There was a brief buzz, the door opened and he stepped into the large warm hallway. Abby was at the top of the flight of stairs.

'Thanks for coming,' she said, as he went up to join her and kissed her cheek. 'Come in and get warm. Can I offer you a drink? Mia's just seeing to the meal.'

He handed over the bottle, nodding at her acknowledgement. 'Thanks, but as I'm driving I'll just stick to wine with the meal. But I would like a glass of water, please; I've the hell of a head-ache and the sooner I take something the better.'

'Of course. Poor you!' She gestured towards an open doorway. 'Go in and I'll bring you one.'

The room was as handsome as he remembered, beautifully proportioned with a wide bay window, now screened by heavy velvet curtains. Young Mia had certainly fallen on her feet, he thought, remembering this had been the show flat and Cicely bought it complete with furniture and fittings. An electric fire was installed in the hearth, false logs blazing realistically and helping to augment the heat from the radiators, while the soft lighting came not from the central fitting but from several lamps dotted round the room. The total effect was oddly soothing.

He pressed two pills out of the blister pack as Abby came in with a glass of water.

'Thanks; these should do the trick.'

Mia had followed her, face flushed from cooking. 'Thanks so much for coming, Uncle,' she said. She'd not yet dropped the title as her sister had some time since, which made her seem younger and, in the circumstances, more vulnerable. 'We've been quite worried, and we didn't want to upset Gran.'

'Then let's hope I'll be able to set your minds at rest.' They moved to the fire and settled in the comfortable chairs grouped round it. 'So what's this all about?'

The girls exchanged glances. It seemed Abby had been designated spokesperson.

'For as long as we can remember,' she began, 'Mia and I have been having strange dreams or memories – we're not sure which – that upset us, without our knowing why. But we've only just discovered we've been having almost the *same* dreams – as each other, I mean. It really came to a head when Mia banged her head a few weeks ago and briefly knocked herself out.'

Theo raised an enquiring eyebrow at Mia.

'When I came round I was . . . telling Mummy to wake up.'

He caught his breath. 'Go on.'

'Well, in the dreams I gradually became aware of someone there. He was talking but I couldn't distinguish what he said.'

'You said "someone there",' Theo interrupted. 'Where, exactly?'

'I wasn't sure. But when I told Abby, she said she'd been dreaming the same thing for years, about a man – not Daddy – talking to someone who could have been Mummy. She thought she was in a cage watching through the bars, but we wondered if . . . if she was really looking between the bannisters.'

Theo reached for the glass of water and took a steadying sip. 'Let's get this straight. You're wondering if something woke you that night and you went out on to the landing?'

They both nodded, anxiously awaiting his reaction.

'And you saw your mother in the hall?'

They weren't so sure of that. 'I think so,' Abby said.

'With your father?'

That brought an immediate and definite response. 'No, it definitely wasn't Daddy.'

Theo's mind was spinning. Charles had been out that evening, Sarah would have been alone with the children. Was it conceivable someone had called and, if so, would that someone have been admitted? Fleetingly he thought of the mysterious escort mentioned in the press, whom he and his mother had firmly discounted.

Mia said, 'At first I couldn't make out what the man was saying, but lately I've been able to decipher a few odd words.'

'They were arguing,' Abby said. 'He had hold of her arm.'

Theo took a deep breath. 'Have you by any chance heard of a journalist called Madelaine Peel?'

Their blank expressions gave him his answer before they replied together. 'No, why?'

'She covers the Sherborne area,' he said slowly. 'You remember that's where we used to live? And in the last few weeks she's decided to look into your parents' deaths – God knows why.'

Two startled faces stared back at him.

'And,' he went on deliberately, 'she reckons she's discovered some information that might . . . throw a new light on things.'

They waited in silence for him to continue, and reluctantly he did so. 'For instance, she claims to have an eye witness who saw Sarah down on the coast with some man.'

'Some man?' Mia repeated drily.

Theo nodded. 'In other words, not Charles.'

'You mean she might have been having an affair, and Daddy found out?' Abby said.

He sighed. 'That's what she's implying, though it's all circumstantial. She's claiming it would provide a motive, which was never established.'

Feeling her way, Abby said slowly, 'But if someone – perhaps the same man – really did come to the house that night, *he* might have killed her!'

There was complete silence. Then Mia whispered, 'So who killed Daddy?'

Theo said gently, 'Perhaps that part of the theory still holds. If, for instance, he came home from his meeting and found her dead.'

'But he'd never have left us alone!' Abby cried. 'That's what no one seems to understand!'

Theo stared into the glass he was still holding. 'Have either of you mentioned this to anyone else?'

'We told Nina,' Mia said.

Nanny Nina. A name from the past. 'And what did she say?'

'That we should tell someone in authority. So we thought of you.'

He half-smiled. 'I'm not sure I deserve that description, but, as they say, I know someone who does.' He paused. 'When we lived in Sherborne I was very friendly with a boy who later went into the police force. He's a detective now, and still based there. I'll get on to him tomorrow, tell him everything you've said, perhaps see if he's interested in speaking to Madelaine Peel. Will you be happy to accept whatever he decides?'

The sisters hesitated, looking at each other. It was the best solution they could think of, so after a moment they both nodded.

'Fine.' Theo drew a deep breath. 'Now, I don't know about you, but I'm beginning to feel hungry!'

THIRTEEN

Theo's thoughts as he drove home were not good company. Could there really be anything significant in what the girls half-remembered, half-dreamt? Was it conceivable that there had been a third person in the house that night? And at what stage should he mention the possibility to his mother?

He remembered, with a tug of the heart, that the last time he'd seen Sarah, at the farewell lunch at their parents', she'd seemed subdued. He'd had the impression she was worried about something, but she'd shrugged off his enquiries and he'd let it drop. Thinking back, that must have been only a week or two before she was killed. Should he have pursued it further, and if he had, might it have saved her life?

He shied away from the unbearable guilt inherent in that question. He'd get nowhere by battering himself with *what ifs*. Better avoid second-guessing till he'd spoken to Mike.

As he drove into the courtyard – they'd long since replaced the five-barred gate with an electronic one – he saw that the bedroom light was on. Imogen wouldn't settle until he was back home.

He let himself into the house, poured a much-needed whisky and went to join her. She was sitting up in bed, a book in one hand and a pair of large tortoiseshell-framed glasses balanced on her nose.

'So how did it go?' she asked. And, sitting on the edge of the bed, he told her.

'My God!' she said softly, when he came to the end. 'Do you think there's anything in it?'

'God knows. But I'm going to get in touch with Mike Henderson and see what he makes of it.'

She nodded. 'Those poor kids, though. They must have been going through purgatory all these years.'

Theo shook his head. 'It's only recently they've begun to piece it together. Don't forget, until Mother came clean a couple of weeks ago they thought their parents had died in a car crash.'

'"Oh, what a tangled web we weave",' Imogen quoted.

'Tell me about it!' Theo said grimly.

'Well, finish your drink and come to bed. Things might look clearer in the morning.'

'I doubt it,' he said.

The Fairfax girls had also been on Nina's mind that week. Was it possible they really had seen or heard something the night their parents died? On her walks to and from school and in other spare moments she found herself thinking back to the early days she'd spent with the family, searching her memory for anything that might have a bearing on their present anxieties.

Mrs Fairfax had asked her to join them as soon as possible, so the children could get used to her before the next change in their young lives, the move to St Catherine's. And she recalled with a twist of the heart that during her first week, if she attempted to speak to them, they'd run to the housekeeper and hide their faces in her apron.

They'd been so young, Nina thought achingly, picturing them as they were then: Abby, her dark hair in what she called 'front bunches', and little Mia, wide eyes and blonde ponytail, trotting from room to room looking for her mother. She'd wake several times a night crying and refusing to be comforted, and it was over six weeks before she spoke again.

Abby, on the other hand, had screamed and shouted throughout her nightmares, thrashing about as Nina tried to hold her. God, what was it she kept shouting? Always the same thing, or versions of it, considered to be part of the nightmare and therefore discounted. Perhaps if she'd paid more attention she could have helped, prevented those dreams continuing down the years, yet with Mrs Fairfax so set against counselling, realistically there'd have been little she could do.

Meanwhile her daily routine continued. The girls had promised to tell her their uncle's response, but on the Thursday morning she realized it was five days since they'd spoken and she'd heard nothing. She resolved to call them if they'd not contacted her by nine o'clock that evening.

The bell sounded in the corridor for break. Nina pushed back her chair and stretched. It had been a quiet morning – no interruptions, so she'd been able to get on with her reports. Now, though, she was ready for a change of scene and decided to go to the staff room for coffee rather than having it in her room. But before she could make a move there was a tap on the door, which opened to admit Julia.

'Hello!' Nina exclaimed in surprise. 'I didn't realize you were back!'

'It's been a week since the op, and we thought it would be good for Jamie to have two days' school to break him in gently. Then next week he'll be back to normal.'

'How is he?'

'Oh, fine. Wanting to play football, if you please!'

She looked pale, Nina thought, and there were dark circles under her eyes. 'And how about you? You look a bit peaky, if I may say so!'

'Just tired. I was wondering if I could cadge a cup of coffee? I'm not up to socializing in the staff room.'

'Of course,' Nina replied, discarding her plan.

'You're an angel!' Julia sank into a chair and closed her eyes. 'I feel as if I could sleep for a week!'

'Well, you don't need to worry about Jamie, by the sound of

it,' Nina commented, spooning coffee into the cafetière. 'Anything else on your mind?'

'Oh, just the usual.'

'Which is?'

Julia opened her eyes and straightened. 'Ignore me! I'm fine, really. How are things with you?'

Nina poured the boiling water into the jug. 'Fine too,' she replied, taking milk from the miniature fridge. Her worries were not for sharing and in any case Julia was too wrapped up in her own concerns to be really interested.

'You survived the week without Richard, then?' she asked, setting two mugs on the desk.

Julia flashed her a glance. 'I did.'

'It must have been worrying for him, being so far away.'

'Not that you'd notice,' she replied evenly. 'Would you believe he didn't phone once to ask how Jamie was?'

So that was at the root of it. 'Well, he knew he was in good hands,' Nina said peaceably.

'Do you and Rob ever row?'

The sudden change of subject took Nina by surprise. 'We certainly argue from time to time,' she replied guardedly. 'What married couple doesn't?'

'What about?'

'Oh, nothing serious. What to have for supper, which programme to watch on TV.' She paused, glancing at her friend as she pushed down the plunger on the cafetière. 'Is everything OK, Jules?' she asked quietly.

'Not really.' Julia sighed. 'Richard and I are continually rubbing each other up the wrong way, and the boys are starting to notice.'

'Bad patches are an occupational hazard. You just work your way through them.'

Julia took a sip of too-hot coffee and winced. 'I know people talk about him,' she said in a tight little voice. 'They think he's arrogant and aloof, mainly because he doesn't come to parents' evenings or sports days.'

'Oh, I'm sure—'

She shook her head. 'But he does love the boys, you know. Especially Adam.'

Nina waited, and after a minute Julia sighed. 'He's always losing patience with Jamie – thinks he should stand on his own feet and blames me for what he calls "babying" him.'

She met Nina's eyes pleadingly. 'But he's a sensitive child; he needs treating gently, not being shouted at all the time! It doesn't help that Richard's often tired these days, especially after these trips. They seem to take a lot out of him and he's not getting any younger, though he won't admit it.'

'How old is he?'

'Forty-seven.'

Nina smiled. 'While quite a lot older than you, that's not exactly ancient!'

Reluctantly Julia returned her smile.

'Do I gather most of your arguments are about Jamie, then?'

'Most of them, yes, but I don't know – we're not the same with each other as we once were. Sometimes I get the brunt of his temper, and I don't help by snapping back. I suppose his being away when Jamie was ill, then not seeming interested in how he was, has brought it all to a head.' She paused. 'Especially when other people have been more understanding.'

Nina raised an eyebrow. 'Other people?'

Julia flushed. 'Well, you, for example.'

Nina was pretty sure it hadn't been herself Julia was thinking of. Was it possible she'd met someone, perhaps younger than her husband? If so, it could be dangerous; in her disenchanted state she was vulnerable.

'Why don't you talk it over with him, tell him you feel you're not as close as you were and aren't happy about it? He might have work problems and not realize he's bringing them home with him.'

Julia shrugged and continued to drink her coffee.

'When was the last time you felt really close?' Nina pursued.

'Well, we've made love occasionally, but even that isn't what it was.' She thought back. 'I suppose the last really good time was on our wedding anniversary last month, and even then he had to spoil it by criticizing Jamie.'

Nina studied her with concern. Personally she'd always thought Richard Coulson a cold fish, but she could see he was also attractive. Not a good combination.

'Well, any time you need a shoulder to cry on!' she said.

*   *   *

As it happened, Abby forestalled her that evening by a couple of hours.

'I was just about to call you!' Nina said.

'Yes, sorry, but we didn't manage to see Theo until last night. He came round for supper.'

So that explained it! 'And what was his opinion?'

'He knows someone in the Sherborne police and he's going to have a word with him.'

Nina caught her breath. 'So he thinks there's something in it?'

'Enough to pass on, anyway. And he told us something else which is rather odd: for some reason a journalist in Sherborne is looking into events leading up to what happened, and she's found someone who saw Mummy with a man down on the coast.'

'Hold on a minute! Why on earth is a journalist suddenly interested in the case?'

'I've no idea!'

'And someone saw your mother with a man? When?'

'Again, I don't know. It's all rather weird though, isn't it, coming to light just now? As if . . . as if everything's starting to . . . come to a head.'

Nina repressed a superstitious shiver. 'No doubt this policeman will be seeing her, then.' She paused. 'Do you think perhaps your grandmother should be told about this?'

'We can leave that to Theo,' Abby said thankfully.

Friday morning, and Mia, arriving at Maybury Books, came to a dead halt, staring down the length of the shop to the little room at the back, where a familiar figure was sitting.

Suzie emerged from one of the alcoves, a pile of books in her hand. 'Don't ask!' she said.

'But – are you back together?'

'Not in the way you mean; I'm giving him a roof over his head while he finds somewhere to live. Don't worry, he's not a permanent fixture and he won't be throwing his weight around as he did before.' She smiled slightly. 'This is a chastened version!'

To Mia, though, Terry was an unwelcome reminder of her fall and the complications that had arisen from it and were continuing to arise. She walked slowly down the shop, unbuttoning her coat on the way, and he looked up as she approached.

'Hi!' he said, with a tentative smile.

'Hello.' She hung her coat on the peg and unwound her scarf.
'Everything OK?'

He expected only a token reply, Mia reminded herself, but how
to answer? She solved the problem by simply nodding, and as an
afterthought added, 'And you?'

He gave her a curious look. 'I will be,' he said.

Suzie joined them, hoping her presence would dispel any
awkwardness. 'Just time for a quick coffee before we open,' she
said. 'Will you see to it, Terry?'

'Of course.' He pushed back his chair and went to fill the kettle.

'You'll be coming in tomorrow, won't you?' she went on.
'That'll work well, because Mia switched her free Saturday from
last week.'

Terry glanced at her. 'Going somewhere special?'

'We'd hoped to go to the theatre last week, but when Lola
phoned they were fully booked. Luckily they had seats for
tomorrow.'

'What's the play?' Suzie asked, taking a mug from Terry, and
was gratified that the ensuing discussion completed the restoration
of the status quo.

Unlike Mia's friends, in whom, despite her request for their
absence on Wednesday evening, she still hadn't confided, Abby's
flatmate Stephanie was fully aware of the situation and increasingly concerned about her. They were having supper in their little
flat above the dental surgery, the gas fire doing sterling service
against the wind and rain playing havoc outside.

'So your uncle's going to look into it?' she recapped, spearing
a potato.

'Well, he's passing it all on to his police friend. I suppose he'll
at least be able to check on what the journalist's dug up. After all
this time I'm not too hopeful.'

'It's so tantalizing that you can't remember any more of those
dreams – if they are dreams, and not buried memories.'

Abby shivered. 'As I said, bits keep coming back. It's like
watching a photograph develop. Or a jigsaw, perhaps, gradually
being filled in: Mia has some of the pieces and I have others, and
we must fit them together to make a complete picture.'

Steph put down her fork and pushed her plate away. Outside,
the rain lashed at the window.

'Let's try something,' she suggested. 'Just relax and try to clear your mind.'

Abby said sceptically, 'You're not going to start swinging something in front of me, are you?'

Steph laughed. 'No, but it's along those lines. Close your eyes and try to think yourself back to that evening.'

'Oh, come on!' Abby protested.

'Seriously, just give it a try. Go on, close your eyes.'

With a shrug, Abby did so.

'Now,' Steph spoke slowly and quietly, 'you can feel the carpet under your bare feet and the shiny bars of the bannisters between your hands. Your face is pressed close to them, because you want to know what woke you. Take long, slow breaths and keep your eyes shut.'

Abby stirred uneasily. 'I don't think I like this.'

'There are two people in the hall below. Describe them.'

At first she thought Abby wasn't going to reply, but after a minute she said slowly, 'I'm pretty sure one of them is my mother, but she's blurry round the edges.'

'And the other?'

'A tall man, who has hold of her arm.'

'And they're speaking?'

Abby nodded.

'What are they saying?'

'I don't know. At least . . .'

'Yes?'

'They've both raised their voices. He's telling her to calm down but I can't make out the rest.'

Steph was holding her breath. 'And what does she say?'

Another long silence. Abby's eyes were still closed and she was frowning. 'I can't decipher it but she's very angry.'

Steph tried to conceal her disappointment. 'And then?'

'That's all.' Abby opened her eyes and blinked. She gave a little shiver. 'That was weird. It seemed more real than before.'

'Then we should try it again tomorrow. With luck, the repetition will stimulate your memory.'

'I'm not promising anything!' Abby said. 'Now, let's get the table cleared; it's nearly time for *Death in Paradise*.'

* * *

Later that evening, Abby phoned Mia and reported the experiment. 'The point is, Mi, I'm almost sure he said something about calming down, and—'

'What *exactly* did he say?' Mia interrupted.

Abby thought for a minute. 'Not sure about exactly, but something like "Calm down! Don't make such a fuss!"'

She waited for her sister to make a comment, and when she didn't, prompted, 'Why did you want the exact words?'

'Because,' Mia said expressionlessly, 'that's what he said in my dream last night. I was going to call you.'

Abby drew in her breath. 'Did you hear anything else?' she asked almost fearfully.

'No, I couldn't see or hear them any more. Abby, what's happening to us?'

'Well, I suppose it could be telepathy, both of us "dreaming" the same thing, but I think it's more likely that whatever was blocking our memory is starting to shift.'

'You mean it really did happen?'

'I don't know, Mi, but it's the first time I've been able to "remember", if that's what it was, while I'm awake, and I'm frightened about what might happen next.'

Theo had arranged to meet his police contact for a pub lunch in Sherborne on the Saturday and as he drove down he was trying to think of the best way to present the facts, such as they were, in order to engage Mike's cooperation.

He saw him as soon as he entered the pub, a tall, lanky figure with a shock of fair hair and shrewd grey eyes who, catching sight of him, came quickly across with hand outstretched.

'Theo! It's been a long time! Nearly didn't recognize you behind that beard!'

'Well, you at least haven't changed! Good to see you, Mike!'

They ordered pints and carried them across to a vacant table.

'You know,' Mike began soberly, 'it struck me after you called that I haven't seen you since your sister's death. It happened soon after you moved, didn't it?'

'It did, yes. Brilliant timing.'

'My sincere condolences, even if they're more than a tad late.' He took a draught of beer. 'I presume you've come about that pesky business in the local rag? I'm surprised you heard of it, up in Somerset, but no doubt you still have friends in this area.'

'It was Guy Burnside who alerted me; he'd been down here seeing his folks. However . . .' Theo in his turn took a drink, '. . . that's only partially why I'm here. Hell of a coincidence, actually, but it's to do with my nieces. They're in their late teens now, and it's transpired that they've been having what they call dreams but what sound to me more like flashbacks. The point is,' he added awkwardly, 'they were told their parents died in a car crash, so they didn't at first realize the possible significance.'

Mike frowned. 'What "possible significance" would that be?'

Theo looked down at his glass, turning it slowly between his fingers. 'During these episodes they seem to be looking through bannisters at figures in the hall of their home, a man and a woman. They think the woman might be Sarah but are adamant the man's not Charles.'

Mike stirred uncomfortably. 'Where were they when their parents died?'

'Asleep in bed. Or so everyone believed.'

'And you said this was a dream, right?'

Theo looked up, meeting his eyes. 'I'm damned if I know, to be honest. It's slightly unnerving that they're both "dreaming" the same thing.'

'The inference being,' Mike said slowly, holding his gaze, 'that their father wasn't the guilty party. I think most kids could go along with that.'

'Wishful thinking, you mean? Possibly, but for the record I for one could never get my head round it. They always seemed a devoted couple.'

'So what price this possible lover down in Swanage?'

'It seems almost equally unbelievable.'

'I checked the records, of course, when all this started in the press, and a woman did come forward to say she'd seen them together, though she later refused to confirm it. But she knew both Sarah and her husband, at least by sight, and was positive the guy wasn't Charles.'

'As were the girls.'

Mike looked at him quickly. 'You're telling me this was the same guy?'

'I'm not telling you anything, Mike,' Theo said heavily, 'other than what my nieces are dreaming.'

Mike stared at him for a moment. 'I think it's time we ate,' he said.

There was a welcome break while they ordered and then ate their steak pies and chips, carefully keeping up an inconsequential exchange as they did so. But as soon as the last chip was eaten it was back to business, and Mike leaned back in his chair.

'So what exactly do you want me to do?'

Theo made a gesture of protest. 'I can hardly—'

'Come off it!' Mike broke in. 'Why else did you come here today?'

Theo held his eyes for a moment, then grinned shamefacedly. 'Well . . .'

'So come on. Give!'

'OK. I'd be very grateful if you would interview this journalist and find out exactly what she knows – or thinks she does. Who lived in this holiday home at the time, whether anyone else saw this couple. Give me a break, Mike, you know far better than I do what you should be asking.'

Mike raised an eyebrow. 'Should?'

'Could,' Theo amended hastily.

Mike thought for a minute. 'Well, obviously I can't do anything official at this stage, but there are a few people who owe me favours I could call in. Put out some feelers and keep you posted. How's that?'

'More than I have the right to expect,' Theo said sincerely. 'I'm really grateful, Mike.'

'What are pals for?' asked DI Henderson rhetorically, finishing his pint.

It had been a pleasant day. They'd gone into Bristol early and looked round the shops, buying a few small Christmas presents before an early lunch, and the play, the main reason for the outing, had proved to be the perfect choice. The cast included names familiar from television; the plot was light-hearted; and Mia, determinedly concentrating on the here and now, had enjoyed herself.

It was dark when they emerged from the theatre, and considerably colder. As they queued for the bus to take them to the station a biting wind whistled down the street, and they pulled their scarves more tightly round their necks, thankful when it lumbered into sight. They'd intended rounding off the outing with a pub meal, but as they emerged from its warmth they agreed that once they reached their flat they'd be reluctant to go out again, and decided to opt for a takeaway instead.

The train was crowded, mainly with Christmas shoppers whose carrier bags and parcels took up as much room as they did. The girls were unable to sit together, but the carriage emptied considerably at St Cat's and once on the platform they moved in a steady stream towards the exit.

Somewhere behind them a child cried out suddenly, gabbling about leaving something on the train. Then a man's voice rose above it.

'I said calm down! Stop making such a fuss!'

Mia froze, coming to a sudden halt, and the woman behind bumped into her. She stumbled and would have fallen had Tamsin not caught hold of her arm. 'Mia! Are you OK? You've gone white!'

Barely aware of putting one foot in front of another, Mia let her friends lead her out of the concourse and across the road to the bus stop where, luckily, a bus stood waiting. Tamsin pushed her into a seat and sat down beside her, while Lola slid into the seat in front of them and swivelled round.

'Mia, what is it? Are you hurt?'

She blindly shook her head, but the rest of her body also started shaking and the girls exchanged worried glances, praying she wouldn't collapse, lose consciousness as she had in the bookshop. But she'd not banged her head this time, so what had caused this reaction was a mystery; she'd been fine on the train.

To their relief the bus reached their stop without further incident and Tamsin had her key out before her feet touched the pavement. Minutes later they were in the safe warmth of their flat, helping Mia up the stairs and into the sitting room, where Lola immediately lit the gas fire.

'Get a glass of water!' she instructed over her shoulder, and Tamsin hurried to fetch one. Mia huddled in the chair nearest the fire, holding her hands out, her eyes frightened and her face still alabaster pale. Lola sank on to the rug at her feet and grasped her hands. 'What happened, honey? What frightened you?'

Gradually Mia's eyes focused on her face. 'It wasn't only the same words,' she said. '*It was the same voice!*'

FOURTEEN

Maddy leaned back in her chair. 'So that's the story of my trip to Swanage,' she finished. 'Not sure it was worth the petrol!'

'Well,' Steve replied philosophically, 'on the grounds of leaving no stone unturned, it's another lead you can eliminate.'

Maddy toyed with her glass. 'Bloody annoying, though; the info from Mrs Grogan looked so promising, but we seem to have come to a dead end.' She paused. 'There's something else I wanted to run by you, though; I had a rather odd phone call last week and I'm still not sure what to make of it.'

'Spill!'

The Clarion told me some guy had called them wanting to speak to me and when they said I wasn't available he asked for my phone number.'

The Clarion was the local paper running her piece.

'Uh-huh!'

'Of course they didn't give it, but he insisted on leaving his and asked them to pass it on. Said he wanted to meet me because he'd important information on the Drummond story.' She hesitated. 'He wouldn't leave his name.'

Steve snorted. 'Which is dodgy for a start!'

'Still, I couldn't afford to ignore any lead so I duly called him, said I'd be grateful for any info and so on. But he insisted he couldn't say anything over the phone and wanted to arrange to meet me.'

'God, Maddy, don't tell me you fell for that!'

She flashed him a scornful glance. 'I wasn't born yesterday, Steve. What made it even more dodgy was he still wouldn't give me his name.'

'So what happened?'

'Nothing. I rang off, and since I'd used the paper's phone he still hadn't got my number.'

'Thank God for that!'

'But the point is, he seemed to know something. He said he lived here at the time and actually knew the family.'

'A come-on if ever I heard one! Ignore it.'

'Suppose he's genuine, though?'

'Then he can go to the police,' Steve said firmly.

Maddy hesitated. 'If we arranged to meet somewhere very public . . .'

'*No*, Maddy! It has to be a new line in chat-ups – either that or something more sinister.'

'But in public?'

'Still no!'

'Suppose he knows the name of the man from Swanage? It could be just the lead I need!'

'Then you'll have to survive without it! Better that than ending up somewhere with your throat cut!'

'Oh, for heaven's sake, Steve!'

'I'm serious. Don't even *consider* meeting him.' He studied her stubborn face. 'Promise me!'

'Look—'

'*Promise me*, cross your heart and hope to die!'

A reluctant smile tugged at her mouth. 'As an alternative to having my throat cut?' And as he seemed to be waiting, she added, 'Oh, all right, I promise!'

'Good girl! On the strength of that I'll buy you another pint!'

'*What* was the same voice, Mia?' Lola asked softly.

Mia took a sip of water from the glass Tamsin handed her, and shivered.

'Just now,' she said. 'At the station. He must have been somewhere behind us.'

The girls exchanged worried glances. 'Who must?'

Mia frowned slightly. 'The man from the dream.' She gave herself a little shake. 'Of course, I'd forgotten. You don't know, do you?'

'Suppose you tell us,' Lola suggested.

And at last Mia did, starting with the true version of her parents' deaths that she'd learned so recently herself, then, ignoring their gasps of horror, going on to describe the recurring dreams of the shadowy figure in the hall that were gaining more clarity, and how Abby was having virtually the same dream. And finally she explained the significance of those crucial words, *I said calm down . . .*

'My *God*, Mia!' Tamsin exclaimed. 'You mean this has been on your mind for years? Why didn't you tell us? We might have been able to help!'

'I don't see how.'

'Actually,' Lola said tentatively, 'there's nothing unusual about the words. At the station, I mean. People say that all the time.'

'But it was his voice!' Mia insisted. 'I recognized it at once. I must warn Abby.'

'You really think it was this man who killed your mum?' Tamsin asked, trying to make sense of the strange account.

Mia nodded.

'Well, shouldn't you go to the police or something?'

'We told my uncle, when he came round on Wednesday. He knows someone in the police.' She took another sip of water. 'I suppose I'll have to tell him this too, but he'll think I'm just imagining things.'

'At least he'll pass it on,' Lola said.

Since his meeting with Guy Burnside, events Luke had long thought safely buried in the past had been re-emerging, causing him increasing unease. What the devil had motivated some tin-pot journalist to drag it all up again?

His first thought had been to confront her, find out exactly what she knew, and if necessary . . . but there his imagination skidded to a halt. In any case she'd refused to meet him – which, he supposed, was only to be expected. And after more careful consideration, he accepted that if anything unexpected *should* happen to Madelaine Peel, it would add fuel to her story rather than obliterate it, with possibly drastic results.

Then, as if all that wasn't enough, he'd bumped into Sarah's brother, of all people, and learned that his nieces not only lived locally but were allegedly dreaming about their parents' deaths – though *what* they were dreaming he couldn't imagine.

While still convinced nothing could link him to the murders, he could do without these reminders. Over the years he'd almost succeeded in convincing himself he'd had nothing to do with them, and the nightmares he'd suffered for years had gradually ceased. Now, suddenly, they were in the forefront of his mind again.

The sites he'd somewhat feverishly consulted had revealed no one called Drummond living in St Cat's, and he'd been forced to conclude the girls must have changed their name. The obvious choice would, he assumed, be that of their grandparents, but though he must once have known Theo's surname, he couldn't now recall it. Finally, when the need to know overcame logic, he phoned Lily.

'Hello, Luke, this is a surprise! Is there more news on the building project? I haven't heard anything.'

'No, this is more by way of a social call.' He strove to lighten his tone. 'You'll never guess who I've just learned are living in St Catherine's – Sarah Drummond's mother and the two girls!'

'Good Lord! Talk about a small world! They must be grown up now.'

'Yes; trouble is I can't for the life of me remember the old lady's surname, which could be embarrassing if I happened to bump into her.' Lily wouldn't remember he'd barely known the woman. 'Can you help me out?'

'Fairfax,' Lily replied promptly. 'I remember her quite well. A pussy-cat with claws she kept sheathed in public!'

He gave a hollow laugh. 'Does that count as character assassination?'

'Probably! Well, if you do see her give her my best. Must dash, someone's waiting for me. Let me know when we need to meet again.' And she was gone.

Fairfax. Luke took a deep breath. Now at least he had something to go on.

Mike Henderson joined his colleagues at one of the long canteen tables and sat down with his plate. During a break in conversation, he asked casually, 'What do you make of this line they're running in the local rag about the Drummond case?'

Ricky Jones grunted. 'Always reckoned it would come back and bite us in the rear!'

Mike raised an eyebrow. 'Oh?'

'Well, we thought at the time there was more to it, didn't we, though we bust a gut trying to prove it.'

'Just didn't smell right,' agreed Fred Davidson, 'but SOCO turned the place inside out and there was no trace of a break-in or a third party.'

'Prints from the husband, then?'

Fred shook his head. 'Not even that – or at least, nothing they could use, just a few smudged traces from both of them. Mind you,' he added thoughtfully, 'they never got to the bottom of that bloke she was reportedly seen with. Witness chickened out and withdrew her statement, but if it was all innocent and above board why didn't he come forward?'

'Would you, if a bird you were seen with snuffed it?' Ricky asked, spearing a sausage.

It seemed wise to treat that as a rhetorical question.

'What's your interest, Mike?' Fred again.

'Theo Fairfax, the victim's brother, is an old buddy and he's asked me to look into it. Turns out the two kids who were supposedly asleep that night might have seen something; they've been having dreams about people in the house, hearing them talking and so on.'

'Get away!' Ricky laid down his fork.

'Sounds like overactive imagination to me,' Fred said dismissively.

'Whatever, I'm going to ask around unofficially. Theo gave me the name of a guy in St Cat's who was living here at the time. With luck he might remember something useful. Can't harm to have a word, anyway. Wish me luck!'

'You'll need it!' Ricky said glumly.

It was one of those rare days when Julia had a couple of hours to herself. The school day was finished, but Jamie had a rehearsal for the end-of-term concert and Adam was playing away at an under-tens rugby match. Richard, of course, wouldn't be home for three hours or more, and she was sitting in her car wondering listlessly how best to fill the time. She was even up to date with her marking, she thought with a wry smile.

All she was certain of was that she didn't want to return home, where she'd be prey to all the anxieties that had been building over the last weeks. Richard was becoming increasingly irascible, constantly criticizing both herself and the boys, and she was starting to dread the times they were thrown into each other's company.

She gave herself a mental shake; she couldn't go on sitting here indefinitely! Christmas shopping, then? But she hadn't her lists with her, and the thought of crowded stores and queues at the tills was daunting. Seize the chance of some fresh air and exercise? There was another hour or so of daylight and the park was lovely at this time of year.

She was weighing the odds when, as once before in different circumstances, there was a tap on the car window and she looked up to see James smiling at her. This time she wound it down.

'I'm just wondering how to fill a couple of free hours!' she told him.

'Then I've the perfect solution!' he said. 'Come back to the flat for a cup of tea! It's only along the road, and I've something to show you.'

It was a pivotal moment in their lives and they both knew it, but Julia barely hesitated. 'That sounds great!' she said.

Minutes later, as Nina waited to cross the road, she saw Julia's car approaching and was about to wave when she saw to her surprise that she was not alone. Seated next to her in the passenger seat was the new master, James Monroe.

James's flat, Julia found, was situated only a few hundred yards beyond the turning to Nina's house and formed part of a custom-built apartment block erected some ten years ago after the demolition of the original house.

He directed her into one of the parking slots labelled 'Visitors' and they went together into the foyer and took the lift to the first floor. 'It's pretty basic,' he warned her, turning the key in the lock and pushing open the door, 'but it suits me well enough, and of course the ten-minute walk to college is a bonus.'

He gestured her ahead of him and she walked down a short passage to a large airy room. The walls were the ubiquitous magnolia, but the carpet and curtains were blue and the two armchairs covered in oatmeal tweed, giving a pleasing effect. There was a small table, a corner cupboard with a television on it, a bookcase crammed mainly with paperbacks and, more unusually, an easel set up in front of the window. Dotted around were various personal items – a photograph of an elderly couple, a carriage clock and a fairground ornament of a donkey in a straw hat.

'A present from my nephew!' James said, intercepting her glance. 'Now, first things first: take your coat off and make yourself at home while I put the kettle on.'

He disappeared into the adjoining kitchenette and, having draped her coat over one of the chairs, Julia went to inspect the easel. The canvas depicted what he'd told her was his favourite subject, a storm-tossed seascape with gulls flying low over the waves and dark clouds massing overhead. It was certainly atmospheric and, as far as she could judge, competently painted, but not something she'd hang on her own wall.

Turning away she glanced through the window and saw that darkness had already fallen. She'd barely have had time for that walk after all.

James reappeared bearing a tray with two mugs and a plate of ginger biscuits.

'Humble fare!' he apologized. 'In the words of the old song, "If I Knew You Were Comin' I'd've Baked a Cake!" Appalling grammar, but there you go!'

Julia laughed, taking the chair he indicated. 'Ginger nuts are my favourites!'

'Adam's at a rugby match, I know,' James went on, sitting down and passing her the plate of biscuits, 'but what have you done with Jamie?'

'End-of-term concert. He's playing the recorder.'

'Ah!'

She glanced again at the window. 'Can the rugby continue once the light's gone?'

'The pitch will be floodlit,' James replied. 'What time do you have to meet him?'

'Five.'

He nodded. 'The coach is usually late – rush-hour traffic – but you have another hour or so.'

There was a brief silence and Julia's heart set up an anticipatory beat. 'You said you had something to show me,' she reminded him.

'Ah yes. I've painted a picture of the family pooch for Mum's Christmas present and would like your opinion of it.'

'I won't know if it's a good likeness!' she pointed out.

'Touché! But at least you can say if it looks lifelike rather than resembling a stuffed toy!'

He went to the cupboard and, taking out a portfolio, brought it to the table, extracted the first sheet and laid it in front of her.

'Meet Jasper,' he said.

She found herself looking at a vibrant portrait of a black poodle standing at the edge of the waves, its ears blown back by the wind and its mouth open in an excited bark. Every line was indicative of life, energy and anticipation.

'Oh, that's lovely, James!' she exclaimed involuntarily. 'I'm sure it must be just like him!'

'Well, thank you, ma'am!'

'Your mother will love it!'

'Now I just have to find a suitable frame.'

He was about to replace it in the portfolio when she said quickly, 'Can I see the other paintings?'

He hesitated. 'Most of them are only sketches, done quickly at the time to be worked on later. Or not, depending on whether I think they're worth keeping.'

'Even so?'

'All right, but don't say I didn't warn you!'

He took out the rest of the sheets and, still standing behind her, bent forward to lay them on the table one by one, explaining them as he went. Some were of the family home from various angles, a few more of the dog asleep by the fire and a couple of members of his family. 'That's Lucy, one of my sisters-in-law. She didn't know I was drawing her and wanted to destroy it, but I managed to persuade her to let me keep it.'

The sketch in question was of a young woman sitting on the floor, her feet tucked under her, absorbed in a magazine. Again, it seemed a moment frozen in time, just waiting for the hands of the clock to move forward for her to spring into action. Still life, Julia thought.

'She's very real!' she said.

He gave a short laugh. 'I wish all art critics were as complimentary as you!'

She turned to smile up at him and as if it were the most natural thing in the world he bent down and kissed her on the mouth. It was a deep and tender kiss, and for several long moments she lost herself in it. Then, as if by mutual consent, they moved apart.

James said quietly, 'I'm not going to apologize, because I've been wanting to do that for a long time.'

'James—'

'It's all right, I shan't try to make mad, passionate love to you, much as I'd like to; because even if you agreed, a hole-in-the-corner affair isn't what I want for us.'

'What do you want?' she asked, barely above a whisper.

'I think you know. To spend the rest of my life with you.'

Her eyes filled with tears and she looked away.

'Julia? I need to know if I'm right in hoping you want it too?'

After a moment she nodded and he reached for her hand and kissed it. 'Then I'm happy to wait for as long as it takes. There are the boys to consider as well as your marriage so we can't rush things. It'll work out in the end, I know it will.'

Reluctantly she withdrew her hand and stood up. 'And talking of the boys . . .'

'Yes. Time to come back to earth, unfortunately.'

He helped her on with her coat and together they went down in the lift and out to her car, where he kissed her again.

'I love you, Julia,' he said, marvelling that it was the first time he'd said those words to anyone.

She reached up and laid her hand briefly against his cheek. 'And I love you,' she said. Then she got in the car and, without looking back, drove to meet her son.

Although Mia had immediately told Abby about her experience at the station, she'd still not contacted Theo, and she'd seemed so traumatized her friends hadn't liked to push her. By the Wednesday evening, however, they'd decided to exert more pressure.

'If your uncle's asked the police to look into it, they'll need to know this,' they argued.

'He'll think I dreamt it or something,' she said again.

'It's what the police think that counts,' Lola said firmly. 'So go into your bedroom and call him now, while we finish getting the meal ready.'

She gave her a little push, and with a resigned sigh Mia picked up her phone and left the room.

In fact, she wasn't far out in her estimate of Theo's reaction. Though he listened to her account and made the appropriate responses, he was shaking his head when he rejoined Imogen in the sitting room.

'I hope I'm not leading Mike on a wild-goose chase,' he told her. 'Mia's dreams are beginning to impinge on real life.'

She looked up from her book. 'How so?'

'She's now saying she heard the bloke from her dream at St Cat's station on Saturday!'

'*What?*'

'Exactly! Simply because someone was telling a child to calm down, she's convinced herself it was the man she saw and heard in her dream. The sooner we can get them both to counselling the better!'

Imogen said slowly, 'It doesn't do just to dismiss it, though. The mind can play odd tricks, resurrecting buried memories when one least expects it.'

'Don't you start!' Theo scoffed. 'I mean, come on! How likely is it that the same man should have been in Sherborne at the time and turn up now in St Cat's?'

'Luke has!' said Imogen.

Theo, interrupted in mid-flow, stared at her. 'Well, yes, but—'

He broke off, remembering Luke's suddenly blank face at the pharmacy when he'd mentioned the press report and the girls living in St Cat's. It had been shock, no question of it, brought on, he'd assumed, by reawakened memories of their friendship. That must have been the cause, he insisted inwardly. Mustn't it?

'Good evening, Guy.'

'Hi, Theo! How are things? I gather we're due at your place for a meal at the end of the week?'

'Yes, but I wanted a private word before that. Are you free to talk?'

There was a surprised pause. Then, 'Yes, Anya's knee-deep in supper preparations. What's up? Sounds serious.'

'It might be, but it might also be totally paranoid.'

'Intriguing! Fire away.'

'Remember telling me you saw Luke at a petrol station somewhere?'

'Luke? Yes, why?'

'This is the paranoid part: how did he seem?'

'Seem?'

'Put another way, did you mention the press reports? You were on your way back from Sherborne, weren't you?'

'Yes,' Guy answered slowly. 'Could I just ask what this is all about?'

'I'll explain in a minute, but what did you talk about?'

'Well, I said it was a coincidence bumping into him because we'd just come from there, and I told him some journalist was dragging up the case again, saying Sarah had been seen with a man or something.'

Theo held his breath. 'And how did he react?'

Guy paused, thinking back. 'As a matter of fact it was rather odd. He – he suddenly lost his colour, went . . . still, somehow.'

Theo released his breath, but before he could comment Guy went on, 'Then I remembered how he and Lily had been on holiday with them and everything and apologized for bringing it all back. Incidentally, they divorced years ago; he probably has a new wife now.'

'Oh, right. And that was all?'

'Yes. He went in and paid for his petrol and we didn't speak again. Now what the hell is this all about?'

So Theo explained that Luke had a similar reaction when he'd met him and mentioned that the girls now lived in St Cat's, which he hadn't seemed to know, and that they'd been having dreams about the night their parents died – which led to another, longer explanation. And he ended with Mia's conviction that she'd heard the voice from her dreams at St Cat's railway station.

'Whereupon,' he ended heavily, 'I pooh-poohed the idea to Imo, saying how unlikely it was that a man who'd been in Sherborne all those years ago should now happen to turn up in St Cat's. And she pointed out that Luke had. And, frankly, the more I thought about it, the more it put the fear of God into me.'

'Ye gods!' said Guy Burnside.

Theo gave a short laugh. 'Are you going to call for the men in white coats?'

'It's the hell of a lot to take in.'

'I know. And I might have put two and two together and made nineteen.'

'Or you might have made four. This could be dangerous, Theo; you should go to the police.'

'I already have, but this last has only just materialized.'

'But in heaven's name, *Luke*?'

'I know; it seems beyond belief, doesn't it? Perhaps it is. Needless to say, this is all totally confidential.'

'Obviously. Well, good luck, and let me know how you get on.'

'Thanks, Guy.' He paused, and wryly aware of a descent into bathos, added, 'See you on Saturday.'

During their evening meal Theo returned to the subject with Imogen.

'I told him the girls live there,' he said. 'I could have unknowingly put them in danger!'

'Let's not get carried away,' Imogen advised. 'All this is wild supposition at the moment. You and Guy could have been right in your first impressions, that Luke's shock might have been caused by hearing names from the past that conjured up upsetting memories.'

Theo gave a short laugh. 'Ironically I'd suggested Mike might like to contact him, that he might be of help!'

'Well, he might! More than he expects, perhaps.'

'I think I'll have a word with him,' Theo said thoughtfully.

'Luke? Have you got his number?'

'Yes, I'd looked it up to pass on to Mike. If, "as a matter of courtesy"' – he made quote marks in the air – 'I tell him I've given his name to the police, who are following up the press story, it should warn him off, stop him going near the girls, shouldn't it?'

'I suppose so,' Imogen said doubtfully.

'Then that's what I'll do. Things are suddenly moving too fast, and I'm not going to get any sleep till I've satisfied myself on this. I'll call him this evening and see how he reacts.'

The phone rang as Julia was coming out of the kitchen, and she caught it up.

'Hello?'

'Hello, could I speak to Luke, please?'

She hesitated. 'I'm afraid you have the wrong number. There's no one called Luke here.'

'Oh, sorry! Force of habit! I meant—'

Julia gasped as Richard pushed her aside and snatched the phone from her. 'Hello?'

About to protest, she saw that all his attention was focused on the call. He gave a forced laugh. 'No, that's all right.'

Curious, she watched him as he listened intently to the caller. Finally he said, 'I see. Well, thank you for letting me know. Unfortunately, though, we weren't so friendly towards the end; the girls fell out and we'd drifted apart. Still, I'll . . . be pleased to give whatever help I can.'

He put the phone down and stood for a moment, his hand resting on it, head bent. Then he straightened and gave her a strained smile.

'Who's Luke?' she asked.

'My alter ego!' He sounded breathless. 'I don't know who started it, it was just a silly nickname based on my surname – Coulson, Cool Hand Luke. It stuck, and all my friends in Sherborne knew me as Luke.'

'And that was one of your Sherborne friends on the phone?'

He nodded absently.

'Why did he need your help?' Julia prompted.

'Questions, questions! What is this, the Spanish Inquisition?'

Before she could reply Adam came padding barefoot down the stairs.

'I want a drink of water,' he said, passing her on his way to the kitchen.

'Well, mind it *is* water and not Coke! You've brushed your teeth!'

And when she turned back with another question, Richard had gone into the sitting room and shut the door. Obviously the subject was closed.

FIFTEEN

'I don't suppose you know anyone called Fairfax?' Richard asked at breakfast the next morning.

'It's the name of the family Nina used to work for,' Julia replied absently, concentrating on getting Jamie to finish his cereal. 'The girls went to college but the younger one left at the end of last term.'

'Do you happen to know what they're doing now?'

'I think she said Mia works in a bookshop. Why?'

'Someone mentioned the name and I just wondered if you knew them.'

Normally Julia would have enquired further but she was barely paying attention. While outwardly dealing with family matters, inwardly she was revelling in the knowledge that James loved her and wanted to marry her.

'Hurry up, boys, it's time we were leaving. Adam, have you got your gym kit? If not, go and get it – and hurry or we'll be late for registration. Have a good day!' she added to Richard, as she always did, and propelled the boys out of the house and into the car, all thoughts of his odd query forgotten.

'You're very popular at the moment, Maddy!' said the operator. 'Someone else wanting to speak to you urgently!'

'Not the same guy?'

'No, a woman this time, and very insistent. In fact, she's holding on in case I can put you straight through. Do you want to take it?'

'Might as well. Not much else is happening.'

'OK, here you go then.'

A click, then an anxious voice: 'Is that Madelaine Peel?'

'It is, yes. Who am I speaking to?'

'My name's Gemma King.' A pause. 'I was a friend of Sarah Drummond.'

Maddy drew in her breath. 'Yes?'

'There's something I should tell you. In fact, I should probably have told someone years ago.'

Her voice was shaking and Maddy feared she might lose her nerve and end the call.

'I'm listening,' she said.

'The point is I saw her – on the day she died. With someone. I phoned to tease her about it but she was upset and swore me to secrecy. Then . . .'

She paused, struggling for control. 'Well, it was all so terrible and we were so shocked, and I was sure it was because Charles had found out. So I convinced myself it would only make her look bad if I said anything, that I owed it to her memory to keep her secret. Misguided sense of loyalty, I suppose. But now you're writing about it and it's all come back again and I just had to say something.'

'You're doing the right thing, Gemma,' Maddy said carefully. 'So who was she with and where did you see her?'

'As to who, I don't know; I'd never seen him before. But they were coming out of the gate of a house along the road.'

'In Swanage?' Maddy broke in.

'What? No, no, here in Sherborne.'

'But obviously not her own house?'

'No.'

Maddy held her breath, but when she didn't continue, prompted, 'So where was it?'

'In Maple Road.'

'Number?'

'I don't know. I'd been to the dentist and as I was coming out I saw them further down the street.' She gave an embarrassed half-laugh. 'I was so upset after Sarah's death that I changed my dentist. I've not been back there since.'

Maddy crossed her fingers. 'Would you come with me and show me?'

'Oh, I don't think I could! I can give you the dentist's number, but—'

'I still wouldn't have a clue which gate they came out of,' Maddy pointed out. 'Please, Gemma, you've been so brave coming forward – please help me pinpoint it. It could be crucial in identifying him.'

'But why is that important now? It can't help Sarah.'

'Suppose it wasn't Charles who killed her?'

Gemma gasped. 'You don't mean—?'

'It was always circumstantial. So – will you come and show me?'

'Well, I don't know.' She paused but Maddy didn't speak, and she added uncertainly, 'When were you thinking of?'

'As soon as possible. This afternoon?' Before she could change her mind.

'I suppose so,' Gemma said reluctantly.

'That's great! If you give me your address, I'll come and pick you up.'

'No, no, someone might see you.' She thought for a moment. 'I'll wait for you in Sainsbury's car park at two thirty. I'll be in a blue Honda Jazz and I'll park as near to the entrance as I can.'

'Thanks, Gemma. I'll be in a red Mazda. I look forward to seeing you then.'

Could this be the break she'd been waiting for? She'd soon know.

It was the quiet period after lunch, when most of the residents retired to their rooms and were generally considered to be incommunicado. If she'd no engagements Cicely adhered to the general practice, using the time to deal with correspondence and make any necessary phone calls.

It was therefore a surprise when there was a tap on her door and, despite her somewhat impatient summons, no one attempted to come in. With a sigh she went to open it, her surprise deepening to find Mrs Nash outside, clearly in a state of some agitation.

'Oh Mrs Fairfax, I'm so sorry to interrupt you, but this really can't wait! I feel so dreadfully guilty, but I assure you I knew nothing about it!'

'Whatever's the matter, Mrs Nash? Come in and sit down.' Cicely led her to one of the easy chairs. 'Can I get you a glass of water?'

'No, no thank you. Oh dear, I really don't know how to tell you this!'

Cicely said calmly, 'Well, assuming that no one has died, whatever it is can't be that bad!'

To her further surprise, this created more agitation. 'But that's the point, you see! Somebody *did* die! That's what makes it so unforgivable!'

Cicely frowned. 'Now you really are worrying me.'

'It's Madelaine, you see. Her latest story that she was so excited about! I'd no idea what she was looking into – how could I have? But that doesn't make it any easier now!'

'Mrs Nash, I really must insist you pull yourself together and tell me, first what's wrong, and second what it has to do with me.'

Her visitor drew a deep breath and launched into a rapid explanation as though afraid that, if she slowed down, she might not be able to finish it.

'She was here for lunch, you see – Madelaine, that is – and she saw you across the room and thought she'd seen you before. And later she remembered where and when, and because there seemed to be some loose ends she decided to look into it, and discovered things that hadn't come to light before, and—' She interrupted herself. 'I should perhaps explain that Madelaine lives in Sherborne.'

Cicely stiffened, light finally dawning. 'Am I to understand it's your niece who is digging into my family tragedy?'

Mrs Nash's eyes filled with tears and she literally wrung her hands. 'She didn't mean any harm – in fact, she thought that if she could throw any new light on it, it might make things easier for you.'

'By printing some rubbish about my daughter having an affair?'

'I understand how you feel about that, but it seems it could be the key to the whole affair. Oh!' Her hand went to her mouth, realizing she'd repeated the offensive word. 'Anyway, she asked me to tell you she's sorry if she's caused you distress, but now that the police have started to ask questions—'

'The police?' Cicely interrupted sharply.

'So I believe. And she wanted you to know she won't be writing any more in the meantime.'

There was a moment or two of silence, then Mrs Nash rose to her feet. 'Well, I won't disturb you any longer, but I hope you'll accept my very sincere apologies on Madelaine's behalf.'

Cicily said abruptly, 'Would you like a cup of tea? I think I could do with one.'

'Oh, I . . . Well, that's very kind of you.'

Cicely rose and went to fill her kettle. 'You mustn't think I hold you in any way to blame,' she added, her back to her visitor, 'and I appreciate it must have been difficult for you to tell me what you have, so I'm grateful for that. Now, if you don't mind, we'll consider the matter closed.'

'With pleasure!' said Hester Nash with profound relief.

Maddy was parked outside Sainsbury's with ten minutes to spare, her heart beating high in her throat. Suppose Gemma's nerve failed her? Suppose, despite everything, they missed each other and she gave up and went home? If today's meeting didn't materialize, Maddy doubted she'd have the courage to fix another appointment.

Greatly to her relief, however, the looked-for blue Honda drew into a slot just along from her and a tall, dark woman in her forties got out. Maddy scrambled to join her.

'Gemma? Thank you so much for coming!' She held out her hand, which was taken.

'Madelaine.' The woman was regarding her with a mixture of relief and apprehension.

'It's Maddy. Would you prefer to go in my car?'

'Yes, please.'

Maple Road was a residential area of fairly substantial houses built between the wars that had become the favoured location of the medical profession, and most bore silver plaques listing the doctors, dentists or consultants who worked there.

The drive across town had been largely silent, but as they reached their destination Gemma moistened her lips.

'My former dentist is at number twenty-four, halfway down on the right.'

'And where was Sarah?'

Gemma nodded further ahead. 'On the left, several houses down.'

Parking meters were in operation, but their luck was in. As they approached, a woman came down one of the paths, got into a car and drove off, and Maddy seamlessly slid into the space. Gemma waited while she put money in the meter and they started to walk along the road.

'Suppose she was just visiting *her* dentist, and the man happened to leave at the same time?' Maddy suggested as the unwelcome thought suddenly occurred.

Gemma shook her head. 'In that case she'd have said so when I phoned. She more or less admitted an affair, but said it was over.'

'Since when? That afternoon?'

'I did wonder. Perhaps they'd just broken it off.'

'What were they doing, exactly, when you saw them?'

'Coming out of the gate and getting into a car parked a couple of doors further along.'

'Not in the driveway of the house,' Maddy mused. 'Which either means it wasn't his house, or he didn't want his car to be seen in the drive.'

They'd now arrived at the gate in question and come to a halt. There was no plaque beside the door, so it was a private house.

'Number forty-seven,' Gemma said. 'Can we go now?'

Maddy studied the house. 'I want to try something,' she said. 'If you don't want to be involved you can start walking back to the car.'

Gemma looked at her wide-eyed. 'What are you going to do?'

'Ring the bell and find out who lives here now.'

'Maddy, you can't!'

'Watch me!' Maddy pushed open the gate and started to walk up the path, aware that Gemma had hastily set off down the road.

Her ring was answered by a pleasant-faced woman in her sixties.

'Oh, hello!' Maddy said. 'I wonder if I could have a word with Mrs Frances?'

The woman shook her head. 'Afraid you've got the wrong house, love. There's no Mrs Frances here.'

'Oh, I'm sorry. I was sure she said number forty-seven.'

'Well, I can assure you we've lived here for ten years! Perhaps you want Maple Drive?'

Maddy pursed her lips thoughtfully. 'I wonder, did you by any chance buy the house from people called Frances?'

The woman began to look impatient. 'No, we didn't. And as I said, it was ten years ago anyway.'

So no alternative vendor was offered; pity.

'Yes, of course,' Maddy said hastily. 'I'm sorry to have troubled you.' And, her mission accomplished, she meekly walked back down the path.

She caught up with Gemma just before she reached the car. 'They've been there ten years,' she said, using the key fob, 'and she didn't say who they bought it from. But even if she had it wouldn't have meant anything, because we don't know the man's name. And he mightn't have lived there anyway!'

'So this was all a waste of time!' Gemma said bitterly.

'No, indeed it wasn't!' Maddy eased out of the parking slot. 'We have Sarah being seen with a man on the day she died, and the address where they met. I think I'd better pass it on to the police, since they're now showing an interest. They can search the deeds or something for previous owners and see if any names are significant.'

'Well, for God's sake don't mention mine!' said Gemma King.

'I wish that guy would make up his mind,' Terry remarked. 'He's been staring at the window display for the last five minutes.'

Suzie glanced at the window and her heart gave a little jerk. Dreamboat was back! Could he be interested after all?

'He was in a week or two ago,' she said – casually, she hoped – 'buying a Michael Haywood; I told him there's a new one out this month.'

'So if he knows what he wants, what's keeping him?'

It was nearly closing time; could Richard Coulson be waiting to help her wash up again? Wishful thinking, no doubt, but perhaps if Mia and Terry could make themselves scarce . . .

'There's no need for you to stay, Mia,' she said. 'You look a little peaky and there's not much cashing up to do.'

Mia, who'd been suffering period pains, felt a wave of relief. 'Are you sure?'

'Yes, go home and relax. You've had a busy day.'

'OK, thanks.'

And, having collected her coat and bag, she left the shop with a grateful 'See you tomorrow!'

Now, how could she dispatch Terry? His week with her was almost up but the fact hadn't been referred to, and to be honest she'd quite enjoyed having him back. He'd been careful to make himself useful and it had been good to have company in the evenings.

She was wondering if she could send him on some errand when he took matters into his own hands.

'There's something I have to do,' he said suddenly. 'Shan't be long!'

And before she could question him, he'd hurried out of the shop. Coast clear! But when Suzie glanced back at the window Richard Coulson was no longer there.

'Theo?'

'Mother! I was about to call you!'

'Really? What about?'

'Things have been moving rather fast on that newspaper story.'

'So I gather,' Cicely remarked drily.

'Oh?'

'Apparently the journalist causing all the trouble is the niece of one of the residents.'

Theo gave a low whistle. 'That's quite a coincidence!'

'Not really; she recognized me when she came for lunch, and decided to refresh her memory.'

'Actually, Mother, she might have done us a favour. As I say, things have been gathering momentum.'

'Which is why I'm phoning. Mrs Nash says the police are now involved. Can that possibly be true?'

'In the person of Mike Henderson, yes. You might remember him? I'm afraid there's rather a lot you don't know, which is why I haven't called earlier; I was hoping to come over and tell you in person.'

'That sounds ominous!'

Theo took a deep breath and embarked on the story of his nieces' dreams over the years and the voice Mia insisted she'd recognized at the weekend.

As he feared she was deeply shocked, blaming herself again for not having arranged counselling.

'I can't believe they've been going through that and not told me!' she said.

'They thought they were just dreams. It was only recently they discovered they were sharing what seemed to be buried memories, and as they didn't want to upset you they came to me.'

'I deserve to have been upset!' Cicely said bitterly. 'But if Mia thinks she heard him here in St Catherine's – could she be in danger?'

'I honestly can't see how; he won't *know* she heard him on either occasion – if, in fact, she did.' He hesitated, but was reluctant to mention Luke in case he was on the wrong track. 'Anyway, Mike's hoping to come up in the next day or two, and when I've seen him I'll let you know what he thinks.' Theo paused. 'In the meantime, it might be better if you didn't mention the dreams to the girls; they're in a rather fragile state at the moment.'

'And I've done enough damage already!'

'That's not what I meant!' he protested.

Suzie glanced at her watch with mounting impatience. It was now forty minutes since Terry had left so precipitately; she'd done the cash, locked up and wanted to get home. If he wasn't here in five minutes, she promised herself, she'd leave without him and he could find his own way back. Her mood wasn't improved by the fact that she was still castigating herself for indulging in such whims of fancy about Richard Coulson, though what the hell he *was* doing gazing in the window she couldn't imagine.

She was about to find out. She'd actually picked up her bag prior to departure when there was a tap on the door and she unlocked it to admit Terry. Before she'd a chance to say anything he burst out, 'Honestly, that really is the pits! That guy was *following* Mia! And he's old enough to be her father, the creep!'

Suzie gazed at him, aware of a creeping coldness. 'What guy?'

'The one that was looking in the window. It must have been Mia he was watching. I happened to notice that when she left he fell into step behind her. I thought he'd just decided to go home, but then she stopped suddenly to speak to Lizzie outside the boutique and he also stopped and gazed into the window alongside him. And when she went on, he started walking again. So I decided to go after them myself and see what happened.'

Suzie was leaning against the counter for support. 'And what did happen?'

'Well, he kept at a discreet distance behind her and I did the same behind him. Because she'd left a few minutes early Linden Park was still open and she cut through. It was pretty dark in there and I was afraid he might try something so I moved in a bit closer, but he didn't.

'Mia lives in one of those big houses opposite, did you know? Anyway, she went in, and after waiting a minute or two her stalker finally walked away – down the road, since they'd locked the gates behind us. Anyway, she's safe home, which was all I was worried about.'

Suzie cleared her throat. 'What do you think he wanted?'

Terry snorted. 'The usual, probably. Scumbag! Anyway, if it's OK with you I'll see her home for the next few nights, to make sure she's OK.' He gave a shamefaced grin. 'I've always felt I owed her since I knocked her off that ladder!'

'Good idea,' Suzie said. 'And now let's go home ourselves.'

It was later that evening that Mike Henderson phoned.

'I've had a word with my boss,' he said, 'and got the all clear to come up and make some enquiries. I'll be bringing my partner with me – she's a female officer, incidentally, which might be an advantage when interviewing the girls.'

'That's great, Mike,' Theo said. 'Thanks so much.'

'In the meantime we've done a fair bit of digging, looked up the records and so on and I've familiarized myself with the details. We've also checked the electoral roll and PNC for the suspect you named and I contacted Somerset for any local knowledge, though as far as they're aware the bloke appears to be kosher. And I had a word with the journalist Madelaine Peel, who started the ball rolling. She looked into the sighting in Swanage and was able to pinpoint the house, but the estate agent who'd handled it had closed down. She did learn, though, that it was owned at the time by a couple from Sherborne, but there the trail went cold.'

'A married couple? I'm probably barking up the wrong tree,' Theo said, 'in which case you'll be charging me with wasting police time!'

'Don't worry, it's only a ten-year sentence!'

'Seriously, Mike, I could be slandering the guy big time!'

'Possibly not, as it happens; Peel called in today with new information. I don't want to raise your hopes, but it looks as though things might be starting to come together.'

'God, that would be beyond wonderful!'

'Yeah. Anyway, we'll be up there tomorrow, so any chance of meeting for a pie and a pint? I need all you can give me on this character.'

'I'll be glad to meet you, but I'm not sure what more I can say.'

'Everything you can remember. I'll also need contact numbers for your nieces; we're hoping to see them when they finish work.'

'Of course.'

When the arrangements had been made and the call ended Theo felt a surge of excitement. He reflected on all the vague suspicions that had arisen in the last week or two: Luke's reaction on hearing of the press story, which both he and Guy had noticed; the dreams the girls shared; the mythical figure allegedly seen with Sarah, whom the family had categorically discounted; the voice overheard at the station; not to mention this new development Mike had mentioned. Was it even remotely possible that they were merging together to point an unmistakable finger at Luke Coulson?

Nina said, 'I'm worried about Julia.'

Rob smiled. 'Well, you're always worrying about someone! What's she done?'

'I'm not sure. That's what's worrying me.'

'Oh, come on! If you want my advice, you'll have to stop talking in riddles!'

'Sorry. It's just that I saw her driving along College Road with James Monroe.'

'And who, pray, is James Monroe, apart from not being her husband?'

'One of the masters – started this term.'

'He's not wasted any time, then!'

Nina said crossly, 'I don't know why I bother telling you things!'

'Sweetheart, you *haven't* told me anything! Or nothing important, anyway. So you saw a man in Julia's car. Why should that worry you? She was probably giving him a lift.'

'For one thing, he's young and good-looking and she's

vulnerable at the moment. She's looked really run down these last few weeks.'

'Well, she's been worrying about the boy, hasn't she?'

'Oh, he's fine – back at his desk now. No, my guess is it's to do with her husband; last time we spoke she said he was getting more irritable, always snapping at her and the boys.'

Rob shook his head. 'If it's marital problems, I advise you to keep well clear. It's nothing to do with you, and if you interfere it could do more harm than good.'

'I'm not proposing to *interfere*,' Nina said indignantly, 'but Julia's my friend and, as I say, she's vulnerable. And if anyone else saw her with James rumours could start, which would put both their careers at risk.'

'Then it's to be hoped no one did; but seriously, love, take a step back. Just let her know you'll be there for her if she needs your help.' He put an arm round her. 'OK?'

Nina sighed. 'I suppose so,' she said.

Mia said, 'But I don't understand! Who is he?'

'His name's Richard Coulson. Do you know him?'

She shook her head, and Suzie saw to her dismay that she looked really frightened.

'Look, we're probably overreacting,' she cut in hastily. 'After all, he's a customer and he seemed . . . very charming and pleasant.' She bit her lip. 'Perhaps Terry jumped to the wrong conclusion.'

Mia shook her head. 'I don't think he did.'

'So you *do* know him?' Terry demanded.

'Not personally, but things have been happening and – I might as well tell you, the police are coming round this evening to talk to me and Abby.'

'The *police*? What about, for God's sake?'

'Something that happened when we were little.'

They stared at her blankly but she shook her head, unwilling to go into details.

After a minute Suzie said, 'Even if it's nothing to do with that, will you tell them about Richard Coulson?'

'Oh yes,' Mia said, 'I'll tell them.'

At least there were perks for the long hours he put in at work, Theo reflected, and, of course, for his senior position. Though he seldom took advantage of them, it meant he could if necessary block out portions of his diary for personal engagements – and it had never been more necessary than now.

He drove under the archway to the car park behind the Fox and Grapes, where he'd arranged to meet Mike and his partner and, with a feeling of sick anticipation, went in to meet them.

Knowing its popularity he'd taken the precaution of booking a table in what he judged to be the quieter area and, as he'd intended, was the first to arrive. The pub was already filling up with business people, being in a commercial area of the town, and rather than seating himself Theo remained standing to enable him to see the door over the heads of the clientele.

And there they were. He raised a hand. Mike nodded and they came over to join him. His colleague, introduced as DS Jackie Holmes, was small and neat with naturally curly hair, intelligent brown eyes and, Theo couldn't help noticing, a rather large bust.

They shook hands and, drinks obtained and food ordered, settled down to their discussion.

'So,' Mike began, 'I'd like you to go back to the first time you ever heard of Richard Coulson.'

'Well, that's a difficult one because I always knew him as Luke.'

Mike frowned. 'Why was that?'

'A nickname based on Coulson, I was told. Cool Hand Luke. Silly, but it stuck and no one used his real name. As to when I met him, it would have been through Lily, his first wife. She and my sister were at uni together and remained close friends. She was one of Sarah's bridesmaids when she married Charles.'

'Was "Luke" at the wedding?'

'Yes, that's where he met Lily. It was apparently a *coup de foundre* and they were married within the year. The two couples were very close for years, going on holiday together and so on.'

Mike was silent, mulling over the information as he stared into his tankard. It was Jackie who spoke first.

'Was there ever any suggestion of attraction rather than friendship between them?'

'Good God, I don't think so!'

Mike asked, 'Were they still close at the time of the deaths?'

'No, they began to grow apart around the time Sarah and Charles started a family. I never knew why, but I suppose they were no longer so free to go out together.'

'But no friction that you know of?'

'Not that I know of, but as I warned you, I barely knew them.' He hesitated. 'You said there'd been a development with the journalist?'

Jackie glanced quickly at Mike, who looked a little embarrassed.

'Sorry, I shouldn't have let that slip; I was rather cackhandedly trying to stop you blaming yourself for speculating. There *has* been a development, yes, and it's fairly significant, but I can't say any more at the moment.'

Their order number was called and Theo, feeling somewhat frustrated, went to the bar to collect it.

When he returned the conversation seamlessly switched to the girls. Mike wanted to confirm how old they'd been at the time, how they'd reacted, and Theo had to admit that though they'd been traumatized they'd not been offered any counselling.

Jackie said tentatively, 'I'm not quite clear what caused that trauma; weren't they told their parents had been killed in a car crash?'

'That's right.'

'Which naturally would have been a shock, but they were very young and children are known to be resilient. I'd have expected them to absorb it without any psychological damage.' She paused. 'Did no one ever suspect they might have seen something?'

'No,' Theo said baldly, and with hindsight wondered why the hell not.

'They were adopted by your parents, I take it?'

'That's right, and the family moved here to give them a fresh start. Imo and I were already living near Bath, so more or less on hand.'

'So when did these dreams start?' Mike asked.

'The first I knew of it was ten days ago, but they can fill you in better on that.'

Mike took a drink of beer. 'And after the initial trauma did they show any continuing signs of withdrawal or mental disturbance? Hysterical outbursts or anything like that?'

'Certainly not to my knowledge,' Theo said a little stiffly. 'They had as happy and normal a childhood as was possible in the circumstances.'

Mike glanced at him. 'I'm not criticizing your family, Theo, just trying to estimate when these dreams might have started.'

'I know, sorry. To be frank, the lack of counselling has always been an issue.'

'It might have helped, certainly.'

'But then,' Theo pointed out, chancing his arm, 'we wouldn't have had what might turn out to be a valuable lead as to what actually happened!'

Mike grinned, looking suddenly younger. 'Touché!' he said.

There was little more to be said on the subject, and soon afterwards they left to go their separate ways, Mike promising to keep Theo in the loop as far as possible.

By twenty past five there'd been no customers in the shop for at least ten minutes and both Mia and Terry were getting restive.

Suzie came to a decision, and to their surprise went to the door, turned the notice to 'Closed' and pulled down the blind.

'Give me a hand cashing up, Mia,' she said, 'then we'll all leave together and I'll drop you off on our way home. No point Terry trailing all that way and back again, and it'll take longer now because the park will be closed.'

They both looked relieved, and ten minutes later the plan was put into action. Terry kept a sharp eye open throughout the drive, but there was no sign of Coulson. Perhaps having found out where Mia lived he was content to wait for a while. The worrying thing was why he'd needed to know in the first place.

SIXTEEN

As the car drove off Mia heard her name called and saw Abby approaching.

'Who was that dropping you off?' she asked as she reached her.

'Suzie and Terry,' Mia replied.

'The Creep? He's on the scene again?'

'To be fair, Abs, he's been a star this week. He . . . walked me home last night.'

'Don't tell me he fancies you!' Abby mocked. 'Handbags at dawn with Suzie!'

They went inside and had started up the stairs before Mia said flatly, 'Someone had been following me.'

Abby came to a halt and stared at her. 'What do you mean, following you?'

'From the shop all the way back here. Terry noticed and tagged on behind till I was safely inside.'

'But who was it?' Abby was totally bewildered.

'Someone called Richard Coulson, one of the customers. Heaven knows why.'

'Perhaps *he* fancies you,' Abby said, but she was no longer joking.

There was half an hour before the police were expected and they tidied the room in readiness.

'Do we offer them coffee or something, like they do on the telly?' Mia wondered.

'We'll play it by ear,' Abby said. 'I just hope they won't think we're wasting their time.'

'Well, it was Uncle Theo who arranged it so they can blame him! All we have to do is answer their questions; it shouldn't take long.'

'As a matter of interest, what have you done with your flatmates?'

Mia smiled. 'They're getting used to this! They're meeting the gang for fish and chips and the cinema.'

'Talking of fish and chips . . .'

'I've ordered a takeaway for seven thirty. The police should have finished by then, but if they haven't it can go in the oven.'

The intercom buzzed and they both jumped. It was Abby who answered it.

'DI Henderson and DS Holmes, Dorset Police,' said the disembodied voice. 'I believe you're expecting us?'

She pressed the buzzer. 'Yes, please come up.'

It wasn't as nerve-wracking as they'd feared. Once settled in the sitting room the detectives dispensed with their titles and became Mike and Jackie, and the inspector chatted for a few minutes about Theo and their time as boys in Sherborne before progressing smoothly to his worries about what they'd been experiencing.

'So I'd like you tell me in your own words when this all started and exactly what form the dreams took.'

The girls began, striving to be as accurate as they could and occasionally prompting each other ('You told me . . .' and 'Didn't you say . . .?').

The dreams tallied to a surprising extent and Mike suspected that since the sisters had begun comparing notes in the last week or two they might subconsciously have overlapped with each other. Nonetheless, they made disturbing hearing. Abby then went on to describe the 'experiments' she'd tried with Stephanie and the further memories they'd evoked.

'Thank you,' Mike said, when they came to an uncertain halt. 'That gives us a much clearer picture. Now Mia, this incident at the station: could you tell us exactly what happened? You'd been to Bristol, you said?'

'Yes, to the theatre.'

'What train did you catch home?'

She thought for a minute. 'It would have been the five fifty-five. We had to hurry to catch it.'

Mike glanced at Jackie to confirm she was taking notes. 'And the journey takes how long?'

'Fifteen minutes.'

'So you'd have been leaving the station at about six ten, give or take a few minutes?'

'I suppose so, yes.'

'Did a lot of people get off there?'

'Yes, it was quite a crush leaving the platform.'

'And what exactly did you hear?'

She tensed and Abby, seated next to her, took her hand.

'Somewhere behind us a little boy started shouting and a man's voice replied . . .'

She closed her eyes briefly. 'A man's voice replied, "I said calm down! Stop making such a fuss!" Which was almost exactly what he'd said in my dream!'

'Can you be sure,' Jackie probed gently, 'that it really was the same voice? You could only just make it out in your dream, and it was a pretty everyday remark.'

'I'm sure,' Mia said quietly.

Abby said, 'Tell them what you just told me.'

Mia flushed. 'I don't see how it ties in, but someone followed me home the other evening.'

Mike frowned. 'Was any approach made?'

She shook her head. 'I didn't know anything about it. Someone from the shop saw him and followed along behind.'

'So it could have been coincidence?'

'I don't think so; it seems the man had been looking in the window for some time, and as soon as I left he started after me. Terry says he tracked me all the way home until I turned in at the gate. Then he walked away.'

'And you've no idea who this could have been?'

'Oh yes,' Mia said, to his surprise. 'I don't know him, but he's one of our customers. His name is Richard Coulson.'

There was a moment of total silence. Then Mike said quietly, 'We'll look into it.'

After a moment he continued, 'About these so-called experiments, Abby. I'd advise you not to repeat them – they could be dangerous. It's safer to leave anything in the realms of hypnotism to the experts.'

She nodded and, signalling to Jackie, Mike got to his feet. 'Thank you both for being so frank with us. It's been very helpful.'

'Do you think we really did see something,' Abby asked anxiously as they moved towards the stairs, 'or is it all in our imaginations?'

'At this stage it's hard to say, but our Sherborne enquiries are ongoing and with this additional input we might have a clearer idea of what we're looking for. In the meantime, Mia, please make sure you don't go out alone until we've had a word with this Richard Coulson.'

As the front door closed behind them, Mike gave a low whistle. 'I can tell you it took all my willpower not to ask if she'd heard Coulson speak!'

'Presumably not, as she said she didn't know him.'

He opened the car door and she got in.

'Not often we get a prize like that handed to us on a plate!' he added, as he slid in beside her. 'OK, let's call it a day, but we'll be back in the morning for a word with Mr Coulson.'

It was their Saturday coffee morning, and Henry settled happily into his usual chair.

'So,' Rose began, handing him his cup and saucer – Minton

today – 'what's been happening in that exciting metropolis you inhabit?'

Henry took a sip of coffee. 'You may mock, but a couple of unexpected things did occur this week. First I came upon Mrs Nash in tears in the television lounge. No one goes there in the mornings, but I'd left my book the previous evening and went to collect it.'

'Oh dear! Did you discover what was wrong?'

'Not really. She was most embarrassed and tried to make light of it, but I gathered it was to do with her niece.'

'The journalist? I hope nothing's happened to her!'

'Probably nothing too serious, but you remember her saying people might resent her looking into their affairs? I imagine it's along those lines.'

'Well, it goes with the job, I suppose,' Rose rejoined, losing interest.

'And the second unusual thing,' Henry continued, unperturbed, 'is that later, during the quiet time after lunch, I saw her go into Mrs Fairfax's room.'

Rose's eyes widened. 'The holy of holies? That can't have anything to do with the journalist, surely?'

'It does make one wonder,' Henry said.

Richard stood at the window staring out at the winter garden. Sodden leaves littered the grass and the branches of the evergreens drooped unhappily. A lone blackbird was digging for worms on the lawn.

The bleakness of the scene mirrored his thoughts. Theo Fairfax's comment about his nieces had set alarm bells jangling, though he'd repeatedly assured himself there was no need. Even if there were a grain of truth about these dreams, there was no way to link them to him. It was most likely, though, that they were simply the overheated imaginings of teenage girls.

On reflection, it had been a rash decision to seek one of them out, though for some unspecified reason he felt better knowing where she worked and lived, and since she'd had no inkling he was following her, no harm was done.

Saturday morning sounds drifted to him from various parts of the house: Julia was vacuuming the hall, and loud electronic noises from upstairs indicated that the boys were in their rooms as usual.

He should have chivvied them outside to get some fresh air, but for the moment couldn't be bothered.

Normally at this time on a Saturday he'd be out on the golf course, but he hadn't had a game booked and felt no inclination to go along on spec. Still, he couldn't hang around the house all morning. Perhaps after all he'd take the boys for a walk, work off some of their surplus energy and at the same time shake himself out of this lethargy.

The doorbell rang and the vacuum's whine subsided. A late postal delivery, no doubt. He was preparing to go up to the boys when Julia appeared in the doorway, a bewildered expression on her face.

'Richard, there are two police officers to see you. They say they're from Dorset.'

He'd heard of hearts dropping like a stone but thought it hyperbole. He'd been wrong.

'I've shown them into the dining room,' she added uncertainly.

He moistened suddenly dry lips. 'Right. Thank you.'

Like an automaton he walked out of the room, circumnavigated the vacuum cleaner and entered the dining room, closing the door behind him. The room felt chill since the radiator was switched off during the day, but it was no match for the coldness inside him.

A man and a woman. Without knowing why, he was mildly surprised.

'Can I help you?' he said.

The man came forward and held out his hand. 'Mr Richard Coulson? DI Henderson and DS Holmes, Dorset Police. We're making enquiries about an incident in Sherborne fifteen years ago and contacting people who lived there at that time.'

He paused, but Richard made no comment.

'We have reason to believe you were the owner of a property there at the time, namely number forty-seven Maple Road. Is that correct?'

Richard swallowed past the lump in his throat. 'Yes.'

'We also believe you knew, or had some connection with, Charles and Sarah Drummond?'

This simply could not be happening. 'What of it?'

'Could you confirm that, please, sir?'

'All right, yes, I knew the Drummonds. At one time my former wife and I were friendly with them.'

'At one time?'

'Unfortunately there was some cooling off between the girls and we drifted apart.'

'Were you still in contact at the time of their deaths?'

Richard thought rapidly. Was there any evidence of the two occasions on which they'd met publicly? He noticed uneasily that the woman had seated herself at the table and was taking notes.

'Not voluntarily, but it happened that we attended a couple of the same public events shortly before their deaths.'

'Was there any hostility on those occasions?'

Richard forced a smile. 'Daggers drawn, you mean? No, of course not. We all behaved in a perfectly civilized manner.'

'Odd you should mention daggers, sir,' observed the DI, and Richard could have bitten his tongue out. But before he could make some extenuating comment, Henderson had moved to another, totally unexpected, subject.

'Could you tell me, sir, how you spent last Saturday, the sixth of November?'

Richard stared at him blankly. 'What?'

'Last Saturday, sir. Where were you?'

'What the hell has it to do with you?' he asked slowly.

'Just answer the question, please, sir.'

'Well, if it's any business of yours, I took my sons to an exhibition in Bristol.'

'Which was?'

'"We the Curious", at the science centre.' He added with heavy sarcasm, 'I probably still have the ticket stubs, if you'd like to see them.'

'You drove there?'

'No, we went in by train.' A weight had shifted with the change of subject.

'And what time did you return?'

'God, what is this? The centre closed at five but the boys were hungry, so we went for a hamburger.'

Henderson waited patiently.

'Which meant that we missed the five twenty-six and caught the fifty-five.' He paused. 'I'm afraid I can't tell you which carriage we were in!'

'And your sons were with you, you say?'

'Of course. That was the object of the exercise.'

'Did anything upset them on the way home?'

'*Upset?* Oh! Is this to do with Jamie leaving his mobile on the train? I wouldn't have thought it was a police matter! It was handed in at the next station.'

Henderson neither confirmed nor contradicted the assumption. He nodded to his sergeant, who put away her notebook and rose to her feet.

'Thank you, sir. We'd be grateful if you would come to the police station tomorrow morning at ten thirty to sign a statement.'

Richard stared at him. 'A *statement*? You can't be serious!'

'Very, sir. Thank you for your time. We'll see you in the morning.'

Like hell you will! Richard thought, as he saw them out.

'So you'll caution him when he comes in?' Jackie asked as they got into their car.

'Definitely, and in all probability charge him. We have more on him than he knows but I wanted to keep some things back in case he took fright. However, it looks as if Mia Fairfax's evidence is confirmed – he was at the station at the crucial time and no doubt did make the comment she overheard and apparently recognized, not to mention his following her home. And as if that wasn't enough, this witness who came forward pinpointed the house where she'd seen Sarah Drummond on the day she died, and it was owned by Coulson. Who else could the man with her have been?'

'It still doesn't prove he killed her!'

'Give me time!' Henderson replied.

'James?'

'Hello, darling! This is a pleasant surprise!' Then, more cautiously, 'Is everything all right?'

'No, I don't think it is!' Julia glanced towards the house, just visible through the tangle of bushes at the end of the garden. She was supposedly sweeping up leaves but had slipped her mobile into her pocket.

'What's happened?' James asked sharply.

'Two police officers from Dorset came to speak to Richard this morning, and he's been behaving very strangely ever since. He won't tell me what it was about.'

'When you say strangely . . .?'

'He doesn't seem to hear when I speak to him and he keeps looking about him as though he's . . . taking stock of everything. Even the boys have noticed.'

'Why the Dorset police, for heaven's sake?'

'It's where he used to live.'

James frowned. 'I don't like the sound of that.'

'You think he might have robbed a bank?' Julia asked with a little forced laugh.

'Is there any excuse you can make to come and meet me?'

'Not that I can think of. Anyway, what good would that do?'

'Then do you promise to call if things begin to . . . escalate in any way?'

'James, you're worrying me! I phoned for reassurance!'

'Sorry, darling, I'm going into protective mode! Try not to worry – it was probably a parking fine! Is that better?'

'Not very convincing!' she said.

Saturday continued to be out of kilter in the Coulson household and the boys were on edge, constantly looking to Julia for reassurance. After weeks of unrelenting criticism Richard barely spoke to them and they were obviously uneasy in his presence.

During supper, when they were in bed, Julia again tried to get through to him.

'Something's upsetting you,' she said anxiously. 'Won't you tell me what it is? Perhaps I can help.'

'Nothing's wrong, Julia, don't fuss,' he said. 'I have a lot on my mind, that's all.'

'To do with the police visit?' she asked, greatly daring.

'In part.'

'What did they want?'

'Oh, just a few questions about something that happened a long time ago.'

'When you lived in Sherborne?'

'Yes.'

'And were you able to help them?'

His mouth twisted in a smile. 'An interesting question!'

But he didn't answer it, and she didn't dare pursue it further.

*   *   *

She woke a couple of times in the night, to find his side of the bed empty. Once, she saw him outlined at the window, staring into the night. The second time he wasn't in the room and she was too sleepy – and too apprehensive – to go in search of him. When she woke finally at seven thirty he was beside her, lying on his back and staring at the ceiling.

It seemed Sunday would be as edgy as Saturday. Breakfast was eaten more or less in silence and the boys escaped as soon as they could to the blessed normality of their rooms. Julia uneasily peeled the vegetables for lunch. At one point she heard Richard go upstairs and speak to the boys. Then he came into the kitchen, picked up her mobile from the counter and slipped it into his pocket.

She stared at him, her uneasiness rapidly increasing. 'What are you doing?' she asked, realizing he must have confiscated the boys' as well.

'Just making sure there are no interruptions,' he said, and she watched in disbelief as he went first to the back door, then the front, locked them and slipped the keys in his pocket. And then the house phone rang.

'Don't answer it!' he said quickly.

God, how could she contact James?

After the set number of rings, the answerphone cut in. 'This is St Catherine's police station, with a call for Mr Richard Coulson. You were expected to report at ten thirty this morning to sign your witness statement. Please attend as soon as possible.'

Not a parking fine, then. 'Why didn't you go?' she asked, striving to steady her voice.

'I have nothing more to say to them,' he answered calmly.

'But they wanted you to sign something.'

'Not necessary.'

'Richard, please! You can't just ignore the police! They'll—'

He went to the phone and disconnected it. 'Julia, there are things I need to do and I can't have interruptions. I'm going to the study now to sort out some papers – please see that I'm not disturbed.' And he left the room, the house phone in his hand.

Fighting down a rising tide of panic she hurried from room to room, checking to see if any of the windows were negotiable. They weren't, and the patio door keys were, as she might have guessed, missing. To all intents and purposes, she and the boys were prisoners in the house.

God, what could she do? What was Richard going to do?

'Mummy?'

She spun round to see both her sons standing in the doorway. Before she could reply they ran to her, burying their faces against her.

'What's happening?' Adam's voice came muffled.

'Daddy's not feeling very well, darling,' she told him. 'He wants to be left alone so we mustn't disturb him.'

'He's taken our mobiles!'

'I know; he'll give them back to you soon.'

Jamie looked up and her heart lurched at his frightened eyes. 'Is the doctor coming?' he asked.

'Later, perhaps.' Please God, *someone* would come.

She took them into the sitting room and settled them in front of the television. 'Which video would you like?' she asked. 'We'll watch it together.'

They were still sitting there an hour later when the doorbell rang. Julia stood up. 'Stay where you are,' she told her sons, and went to answer it, shutting the sitting room door behind her. There was a window alongside the door, and she could see a police car at the gate.

'Hello?' she said tentatively.

'Dorset Police again, Mrs Coulson. We'd like a word with your husband.'

'I'm sorry, he's . . . busy at the moment.'

'Will you open the door, please?'

'I can't,' she said. Then, her voice breaking, 'He's locked us in!'

DI Henderson's face appeared at the window, concern written all over it. 'Please tell him we need to speak to him.'

'I don't think he'll come.'

'Are you telling me you and the boys can't leave the house?'

She nodded.

'Are they all right?'

'Yes, they're watching television.'

Henderson turned to someone out of her sight and held a muffled conversation. Then the other man hurried back down the path, got into the police car and started speaking on the phone.

'Where is your husband, Mrs Coulson?'

'In his study. He said he had some papers to sort out.'

'Will you please ask him to come and speak to us?'

'I don't think—'

'Just ask him, please.'

She turned away obediently and Henderson turned to Jackie Holmes. 'I don't like this at all. It looks as though we might have a full-blown hostage situation on our hands. I must say I didn't see this coming—'

He broke off as there was a frantic rattling at the lock and the front door was wrenched open to reveal Julia, wide-eyed and white-faced.

'Get a doctor!' she gasped. 'My husband's stabbed himself! Down the hall,' she added as Henderson pushed past her. 'I think he's still alive!'

'Call nine-nine-nine!' he shouted back over his shoulder, but Jackie already had her phone out and, having made the call and signalled to the policeman in the car, she took Julia's elbow.

'The boys are happy watching TV?'

Julia nodded, her eyes welling with tears of shock.

'Then we'll go to the kitchen and make a pot of tea. There's nothing you can do at the moment, but help is on its way. You've been under considerable strain and you need to wind down a little before you can be any good to your sons.'

And Julia, thankful to concede authority, complied.

Richard Coulson died in hospital a few hours later, but he left a full confession on his desk, outlining his doomed affair with Sarah and its tragic conclusion.

If it's any comfort to the family, the details of that night have haunted me all my life. Sarah's death was an appalling accident, but it's Charles's that has caused me the most pain. He was my friend, and not only did I kill him in a fit of blind panic, but the blame for Sarah's death has been laid at his door ever since.

Finally, I should like to apologize to both my wives, each of whom in her turn loved and supported me and neither of whom deserve the notoriety my death is bound to bring. I don't deserve their forgiveness but I hope they won't withhold it.

And his signature and the date.

It was ten days later and the family had gathered for a memorial lunch in the Royal George's private dining room. Theo was still concerned about his mother; she'd lost weight and lines had at last appeared on her smooth cheeks.

'I shall never forgive myself for the things I said about Charles,' she said again. 'I just wish George had lived long enough to learn the truth; he was always reluctant to believe the worst.'

She turned to her granddaughters. 'And of course you are the heroines of this saga. Foolishly we never imagined that you could have been aware of anything that happened that night. I trust that now it's all come to light there'll be no more dreams.'

'We're just so glad it wasn't Daddy,' Abby said.

'We mustn't forget Madelaine Peel,' Cicely continued. 'Without her digging we might not have got any further. I've invited her to lunch next week to thank her.' She smiled slightly. 'One good thing to come out of all this sadness is that I seem to have made a friend at the Rosemount! Mrs Nash and I have been spending time together and discovered we have quite a lot in common.'

'That's great, Cicely!' Imogen said. 'I know you were sorry Molly Barnes was no longer there.'

'Time for a toast!' Theo said, raising his glass. 'So let's drink to Sarah and Charles, much loved and much missed!'

'Sarah and Charles!'

'Mummy and Daddy!'

And as they clinked glasses the past settled back into its appointed place, leaving the future free of its shadows.